THE
HOLDER
OF THE
WORLD

THE
HOLDER
OF THE
WORLD

BHARATI
MUKHERJEE

HarperCollins*Publishers*Ltd

This Is a Borzoi Book
Published by Alfred A. Knopf

Copyright © 1993 by Bharati Mukherjee

All rights reserved under International and Pan-American
Copyright Conventions. Published in the United States
by Alfred A. Knopf, Inc., New York. Distributed by
Random House, Inc., New York.

Library of Congress Cataloging-in-Publication Data
Mukherjee, Bharati.
The holder of the world : a novel / by Bharati Mukherjee. — 1st ed.
p.   cm.
ISBN 0-394-58846-0
1. Americans—Travel—India—Fiction.
2. Puritans—New England—Fiction.
3. Women—New England—Fiction.
4. Women—India—Fiction.
I. Title.
PR9499.3.M77H65   1993
813'.54—dc20   93-22066   CIP

Manufactured in the United States of America
First Edition

To Anne Middleton,
and all travelers to uttermost shores

THE
HOLDER
OF THE
WORLD

Thou still unravish'd bride of quietness,
Thou foster-child of silence and slow time . . .

PART ONE

I LIVE in three time zones simultaneously, and I don't mean Eastern, Central and Pacific. I mean the past, the present and the future.

The television news is on, Venn's at his lab, and I'm reading *Auctions & Acquisitions*, one of the trade mags in my field. People and their property often get separated. Or people want to keep their assets hidden. Nothing is ever lost, but continents and centuries sometimes get in the way. Uniting people and possessions; it's like matching orphaned socks, through time.

According to *A & A*, a small museum between Salem and Marblehead has acquired a large gem. It isn't the gem that interests me. It's the inscription and the provenance. Anything having to do with Mughal India gets my attention. Anything about the Salem Bibi, Precious-as-Pearl, feeds me.

Eventually, Venn says, he'll be able to write a program to help me, but the technology is still a little crude. We've been together nearly three years, which shrinks to about three weeks if you deduct his lab time. He animates information. He's out there beyond virtual reality, re-creating the universe, one nanosecond, one minute at a time. He comes from India.

Right now, somewhere off Kendall Square in an old MIT office building, he's establishing a grid, a data base. The program is called X-2989, which translates to October 29, 1989, the day his team decided, arbitrarily, to research. By "research" they mean the mass ingestion of all the world's newspapers, weather patterns, telephone directories, satellite passes, every arrest, every television show, political debate, airline schedule . . . do you know how many checks were written that day, how many credit card purchases were made? Venn does. When the grid, the base, is complete, they will work on the interaction with a personality. Anyone. In five years, they'll be able to interpose me, or you, over the grid for upward of ten seconds. In the long run, the technology will enable any of us to insert ourselves anywhere and anytime on the time-space continuum for as long as the grid can hold.

It will look like a cheap set, he fears. He watches "Star Trek," both the old and new series, and remarks on the nakedness of the old sets, like studio sets of New York in 1940s movies. The past presents itself to us, always, somehow simplified. He wants to avoid that fatal unclutteredness, but knows he can't.

Finally, a use for sensory and informational overload.

Every time-traveler will create a different reality—just as we all do now. No two travelers will be able to retrieve the same reality, or even a fraction of the available realities. History's a big savings bank, says Venn, we can all make infinite reality withdrawals. But we'll be able to compare our disparate experience in the same reality, and won't that be fun? Jack and Jill's twenty-second visit to 3:00 p.m. on the twenty-ninth of October, 1989.

Every time-traveler will punch in the answers to a thousand personal questions—the team is working on the thousand most relevant facts, the thousand things that make me me, you you—to construct a kind of personality genome. Each of us has her own fingerprint, her DNA, but she has a thousand other unique identifiers as well. From that profile X-2989 will construct a version of you. By changing even one of the thousand answers, you can create a different personality and therefore elicit a different experience. Saying you're brown-eyed instead of blue will alter the withdrawal. Do blonds really have more fun? Stay tuned. Because of information overload, a five-minute American reality will be denser, more "lifelike," than five minutes in Africa. But the African reality may be more elemental, dreamlike, mythic.

With a thousand possible answers we can each create an infinity of possible characters. And so we contain a thousand variables, and history is a billion separate information bytes. Mathematically, the permutations do begin to resemble the randomness of life. Time will become as famous as place. There will be time-tourists sitting around saying, "Yeah, but have you ever been to April fourth? Man!"

My life has gotten just a little more complicated than my ability to describe it. That used to be the definition of madness, now it's just discontinuous overload.

My project is a little more complicated.

2

THE RUBY RESTS on a square of sun-faded green velvet under a dusty case in a maritime museum in an old fishing village many branches off a spur of the interstate between Peabody and Salem. Flies have perished inside the case. On a note card affixed to the glass by yellowed tape, in a slanted, spidery hand over the faded blue lines, an amateur curator has ballpointed the stone's length (4 cm) and weight (137 carats), its date and provenance (late 17c., Mughal). The pendant is of spinel ruby, unpolished and uncut, etched with names in an arabized script. A fanciful translation of the names is squeezed underneath:

> *Jehangir, The World-Seizer*
> *Shah Jahan, The World-Ruler*
> *Aurangzeb, The World-Taker*
> *Precious-as-Pearl, The World-Healer*

In adjoining cases are cups of translucent jade fitted with handles of silver and gold; bowls studded with garnets and sapphires, pearls and emeralds; jewel-encrusted thumb rings; jewel-studded headbands for harem women; armlets and anklets, necklaces and bangles for self-indulgent Mughal men; scimitars rust dappled with ancient blood, push-daggers with double blades and slip-on tiger claws of hollow-ground animal horns.

How they yearned for beauty, these nomads of central Asia perched on Delhi's throne, how endless the bounty must have seemed, a gravel of jewels to encrust every surface, gems to pave their clothes, their plates, their swords. Peacocks of display, helpless sybarites, consumed not with greed but its opposite: exhibition. And how bizarre to encounter it here, the spontaneous frenzy to display, not hoard, in this traditional capital of Puritan restraint. Spoils of the Fabled East hauled Salemward by pockmarked fortune builders. Trophies of garrisoned souls and bunkered hearts.

The Emperor and his courtiers pace the parapets above the harem, caged birds sing, and the soft-footed serving girl fol-

lows them at a measured distance, silently fanning with peacock feathers at the end of a long bamboo shaft. Below, a
hundred silk saris dry on the adobe walls. Lustrous-skinned
eunuchs set brass pitchers of scented water at the openings in
the zenana wall. Old women snatch them up, then bar the
venereal interior to the dust and heat. Above it all, the
Emperor—a stern old man, sharp featured in profile with a
long white beard—contemporary of the Sun King, of Peter
the Great and of Oliver Cromwell, splices the sunlight with
uncut gems. The world turns slowly now in a haze of blood,
then glitters in a sea of gold, then drowns in the lush green
that chokes his palace walks. He is the monarch of rains and
absurd fertility, bred with dust and barrenness in his veins,
this fervent child of a desert faith, believer in submission now
given infidel souls to enslave, unclean temples to scourge and
a garden of evil fecundity to rule. How useless it must have
seemed to those ambassadors of trade, those factors of the East
India Company, to lecture an exiled Uzbek on monochromatic
utility and the virtues of reticence.

The gaudiness of Allah, the porridge of Jehovah.

"C L O S I N G in fifteen minutes," barks the curator, a pink-
domed curiosity of a man with bushy white brows, a pink
scalp and billowy earmuffs of white hair. His name is Satterfield; the captions are in his hand.

"Comes from the Old English. Slaughter Field," he offers,
uninvited. Perhaps he sees me as a searcher-after-origins,
though nothing in my manner or dress should reveal it. High
Yuppie, Venn would say: toned body, sensible clothes, cor-
dovan briefcase, all the outward manifestations of stability,
confidence and breeding.

"Masters," I say. "Beigh Masters." I give him my card—

estates planning, assets research. No one ever asks what it means: they assume I'm a lawyer or with the IRS. Back on the scepter'd isle, three hundred years ago, we were Musters, or musterers. A clever vowel change, in any event. "Looks like 'Bee,' sounds like 'Bay-a,' " I say.

According to a brass plate in the foyer of this old clapboard house, now museum, on an outcropping of cod-, lobster- and scallop-rich granite where a feeble estuary meets the sea, from this house a certain William Maverick once guided sloops of plundering privateers. Each conqueror museums his victim, terms him decadent, celebrates his own austere fortitude and claims it, and his God, as the keys to victory. William Maverick credited his own hard-knuckled tolerance of cold and pain and hunger to a Protestant God, and credited Him for guiding his hand over the sun-softened Catholics. It pleased him to know that "shark-supp'd Spaniards would have an eternity to offer their novenas."

It is perhaps not too great an adjustment to imagine pirates sailing from comfortable homes like this after laying in a supply of winter firewood for the wife and family, and chopping it, then some fish and salt pork, molasses and tea, before raising a crew and setting out to plunder the Spanish Main. We're like a reverse of Australia: Puritans to pirates in two generations. Our criminal class grew out of good religious native soil.

The first Masters to scorn the straitened stability of his lot was one Charles Jonathan Samuel Muster, born in Morpeth, Northumberland. In 1632, a youth of seventeen, C.J.S. Muster stowed away to Salem in a ship heavy with cows, horses, goats, glass and iron. What extraordinary vision he must have had, to know so young that his future lay beyond the waters, outside the protections of all but the rudest constabulary, at the mercy of heathen Indians and the popish French. By 1640 he was himself the proprietor of a three-hundred-acre tract that he then leased to an in-law recently arrived, and then he returned to Salem and the life of sea trade, Jamaica to Halifax. Curiosity or romance has compelled us to slash, burn, move on, ever since.

Twelve years ago I did a research project which led to an undergraduate thesis on the Musters/Masters of Massachusetts for Asa Brownledge's American Puritans seminar at Yale; everything I know of my family comes from that time when I steeped myself in land transfers, sea logs and records of hogsheads of molasses and rum. And that seminar set in motion a hunger for connectedness, a belief that with sufficient passion and intelligence we can deconstruct the barriers of time and geography. Maybe that led, circuitously, to Venn. And to the Salem Bibi and the tangled lines of India and New England.

THE YEAR that young Charles Muster secreted himself among the livestock aboard the *Gabriel*, a noblewoman in India died in childbirth. It was her fourteenth confinement, and she was the Emperor's favorite wife. The Emperor went into white-gowned mourning while supervising the erection of a suitable monument. So while the Taj Mahal was slowly rising in a cleared forest on the banks of the Yamuna, young Muster was clearing the forest on the banks of the Quabaug and erecting a split-log cabin adjacent to a hog pen and tethered milch cow. Three years later, barely twenty, he abandoned the country and built the first of many houses on an overlook commanding a view of the sea and the spreading rooftops of Salem. For the rest of his life he scuttled between civilized Salem and the buckskinned fringes of the known world, out beyond Worcester, then Springfield, then Barrington, gathering his tenants' tithes of corn and beans, salted meat and barrels of ale, selling what he couldn't consume and buying more tracts of uncleared forest with the profit, settling them with frugal, land-hungry arrivals from Northumberland, while running his own sea trade in rum and molasses, dabbling in slaves, sugar and tobacco, in cotton and spices, construction and pike building. He was a New World emperor. Even today, five townships carry his name.

In this Museum of Maritime Trade, the curator's note cards celebrate only Puritan pragmatism. There is no order, no hierarchy of intrinsic value or aesthetic worth; it's a fly's-eye view of Puritan history. More display cases are devoted to nails, flintlock muskets, bullet molds, kettles, skillets, kitchen pots and pothooks, bellows and tongs than to carved-ivory powder primer flasks and nephrite jade winecups. The crude and blackened objects glower as reproaches to Mughal opulence, glow as tributes to Puritan practicality. As in the kingdom of tropical birds, the Mughal men were flashy with decoration, slow moving in their cosmetic masculinity. What must these worlds have thought, colliding with each other? How mutually staggered they must have been; one wonders which side first thought the other one mad.

About children reared in our latchkey culture, I have little doubt. I've heard their teachers on guided tours, listened to the whispered titters of Cub Scouts and Brownies: *We beat those Asians because our pots are heavy and black and our pothooks contain no jewels. No paintings, no inlays of rubies and pearls. Our men wore animal skins or jerkins of crude muslin and our women's virtue was guarded by bonnets and capes and full skirts. Those Indian guys wore earrings and dresses and necklaces. When they ran out of space*

*on their bodies they punched holes in their wives' noses to hang more
gold and pearl chains. Then they bored holes in their wives' ears to
show off more junk, they crammed gold bracelets all the way up to
their elbows so their arms were too heavy to lift, and they slipped new
rings on their toes and thumbs so they could barely walk or make a
fist.*

No wonder!

I move from unfurbished room to room, slaloming between
us and *them*, imagining *our* wonder and *their* dread, now as a
freebooter from colonial Rehoboth or Marblehead, and now as
a Hindu king or Mughal emperor watching the dawn of a
dreadful future through the bloody prism of a single perfect
ruby, through an earring or a jewel from the heavy necklace.

The curator returns to an empty darkened room where he
can watch me, while lifting the covers off two large, wooden
crates. The tea-chest wood is nearly antique in itself, except
for the crude, Magic Markered notation: "Salem Bibi's Stuffs."
The Salem Bibi—meaning "the white wife from Salem"—
Precious-as-Pearl! I have come to this obscure, user-hostile
museum to track her down.

The opened crates overflow with clothing, none of it from
the Bibi's time. It's like a Goodwill pickup. Satterfield paws
through the upper layers, lets them spill around the crates,
unsorted, still in tangles. Only the moths will know this
history.

More layers; the crates are like archaeology pits. I want to
stop and examine, but the decades are peeling by too quickly.
Not all that survives has value or meaning; believing that it
does screens out real value, real meaning. Now we're getting
down to better "stuffs," fragments of cotton carpets and silk
hangings, brocade sashes and exotic leggings.

I think we're about to hit pay dirt. An old rug. Satterfield looks up. "Closing time," he says. Museum hours: Closed weekends, Monday and Friday and Wednesday afternoon. Open Tuesday afternoon and Thursday morning.

"I've come a long way to see this," I say. "Won't you let me stay?"

My eyes are more often called steely or forthright than pleading, but to Satterfield they convey, this day at least, the proper respect and sincerity. I get down on my knees, and help lift.

"Wherever did you get this?"

"A donation," he says. "People in these parts, they have a lot of heirlooms. A lot of seafaring families, grandfathers' chests and things."

"You mean someone had all this in his attic?"

"Friends of the museum."

"Looks Indian," I say. "Indian-Indian, not wah-wah Indian." I hate to play stupid for anyone, but I don't want him to suspect me. Traces of the Salem Bibi pop up from time to time in inaccessible and improbable little museums just like this one. They get auctioned and sold to anonymous buyers. I believe I know her identity, and the anonymous donor.

Mr. Satterfield settles on one knee and lifts out the frayed wool rug with a hunting motif—old, very old—and carefully unfolds it. Inside, there is a stack of small paintings; he lifts one, then two, and finally five crudely framed miniatures from the folds of the carpet. Then he smooths the carpet out.

"Pretty good shape for the age it's in."

I get down on my knees, smoothing the carpet in the manner of a guest who, with indifference but a show of interest, might pat a host's expansive hunting dog. "Well, aren't those very interesting paintings," I say. "Don't you think?" My voice has caught a high note; I want to cough or clear my throat, but it would seem almost disrespectful.

"We don't keep pictures here. This is a museum of maritime trade."

There is surely one moment in every life when hope surprises us like grace, and when love, or at least its promise, landscapes the jungle into Eden. The paintings, five in all, are small, the largest the size of a man's face, the smallest no larger than a fist. They make me, who grew up in an atomized decade, feel connected to still-to-be-detected galaxies.

The corners are browned by seawater or monsoon stains. White ants have eaten through the courtiers' sycophantic faces and lovers' tangled legs, through muezzin-sounding minarets and lotus blooms clutched by eager visitors from pale-skinned continents oceans away. But the Mughal painters still startle with the brightness of their colors and the forcefulness of their feelings. Their world is confident, its paints are jewels, it too displays all it knows.

Here, the Salem Bibi, a yellow-haired woman in diaphanous skirt and veil, posed on a stone parapet instructing a parrot to sing, fulfills her visions in the lost, potent language of miniature painting. She is always recognizable for the necklace of bone. Later, when the Indian imagination took her over, the bone became skulls.

"I need to pack these up," says Mr. Satterfield.

Here Precious-as-Pearl zigzags on elephantback, by masoola boat, in palanquins—the vast and vibrant empire held in place by an austere Muslim as Europeans and Hindus eat away the edges.

In the first of the series, she stands ankle-deep in a cove, a gold-haired, pale-bodied child-woman against a backdrop of

New England evoked with wild, sensual color. The cove is overhung with cold-weather, color-changing maples and oaks, whose leaves shimmer in a monsoon's juicy green luxuriance. At the water's edge, a circle of Indians in bright feathered headdresses roast fish on an open fire. More braves stand in shallow water, spears aloft, as grotesque red salmon climb the underside of giant breakers. Their wolf-dogs howl, neck hairs rising, as children toss stones in play from the shingled beach. Around her submerged high-arched instep, jellyfish, dark as desire, swirl and smudge the cove's glassy waves. Crouched behind her, in the tiny triangle of gravelly shore visible between her muscled legs, black-robed women with haggard faces tug loose edible tufts of samphire and sea grasses. I was right—they were fascinated by us. The artist cannot contain the wonders, fish and bird life bursts over the border.

"Really. It's getting very late." He begins to turn the miniatures over and folds the ancient carpet over them.

"Where will you be selling them?" I ask, but he shrugs.

"That's up to the owner, isn't it?"

In a maritime trade museum in Massachusetts, I am witnessing the Old World's first vision of the New, of its natives, of its ferocious, improbable shapes, of its monstrous women, that only the Salem Bibi could have described or posed for. Her hips are thrust forward, muscles readied to wade into deeper, indigo water. But her arms are clasped high above her head, her chest is taut with audacious yearnings. Her neck, sinewy as a crane's, strains skyward. And across that sky, which is marigold yellow with a summer afternoon's light, her restlessness shapes itself into a rose-legged, scarlet-crested crane and takes flight.

The bird woos with hoarse-throated screeches, then passes

out of sight. The painting could be covered by the palm of my hand.

I lift the final one. I want to memorize every stroke.

In the largest of the series—its catalog name is *The Apocalypse*, but I call it *The Unravish'd Bride*—beautiful Salem Bibi stands on the cannon-breached rampart of a Hindu fort. Under a sky on fire, villages smolder on purple hillocks. Banners of green crescent moons flutter from a thousand tents beyond the forest, where tethered horses graze among the bloated carcasses of fallen mounts. Leopards and tigers prowl the outer ring of high grass; the scene is rich in crow-and-buzzard, hyena-and-jackal, in every way the opposite of fertile Marblehead. In a forest of blackened tree stumps just inside the fort's broken walls, hyenas lope off with severed human limbs; jackals chew through caparisoned carcasses of horses; a buzzard hops on a child's headless corpse.

Salem Bibi's lover, once a sprightly guerrilla warrior, now slumps against a charred tree trunk. He grasps a nephrite jade dagger hilt carved in the shape of a ram's head and, with his last blood-clotted breath, pledges revenge. His tiny, tensed knuckles glint and wink, like fireflies, against the darkness of his singed flesh. The poisoned tip of an arrow protrudes through the quilted thinness of his battle vest. An eye, gouged loose by an enemy dagger, pendulums against his famine-hollowed cheek, a glistening pink brushstroke of a sinew still connecting it to the socket through which the smoky orange sky shows itself. The lover's one stationary eye fixes its opaque, worshipful gaze on the likeness of the Salem Bibi painted on the lover's right thumbnail.

Near Salem Bibi's dying lover, under a multirooted banyan tree smeared with oils and ashes holy to Hindus, the upper body of a lotus-seated yogi slain in midmeditation holds itself serenely erect. An infant, chubby and naked, crawls from blood-splattered shield to shield inventing happy games. A thief crouches behind a pretty purple boulder and eyes the necklets of pearls, rubies, diamonds, on courtier-warriors' stilled chests. Broods of long-haired monkeys with black, judgmental faces ring the heaps of dead and dying.

In the clean, green distance beyond the conflagration's range, on a wide road that twists away from ruined forts and smoking villages, a gloomy, insomniac conqueror on a sobereyed elephant leads his procession of triumph-aroused horsemen, foot soldiers, archers, gunners, lance bearers, spies, scouts, mullahs, clowns, poets, painters, bookkeepers, booty haulers, eunuchs, courtesans, singers, dancers, jugglers, wrestlers, cooks, palanquin bearers, tent pitchers, storytellers, to the next gory and glorious field of slaughter. Their eyes form a perfect, glitter-pointed triangle: Salem Bibi's, her Hindu lover's, the Mughal conqueror's.

On the low-parapeted roof of the fort, Salem Bibi chants stubborn and curative myths to survive by. Her braceleted hands hold aloft a huge, heavy orb of unalloyed gold and a clear, multifaceted diamond through which a refracted lion and a lamb frolic in a grove of gold grass as supple as silk. At her henna-decorated, high-arched feet, a bird cage lies on its side, its microscopic door recently ripped off its hinges. The newly exposed hinge glows against the cage's duller metal, a speck of gold-leaf paint.

"Thank you, Mr. Satterfield."

It is a feast of the eyes, and I must steady myself, take a breath, palms outstretched on the museum's floor. You can study it for a lifetime and find something new each time you look. It's like an Indian dessert, things fried that shouldn't be, hot that should be cold, sweet that should be tart. And an art that knows no limit, no perspective and vanishing point, no limit to extravagance, or to detail, that temperamentally cannot exclude, a miniature art forever expanding.

Go, Salem Bibi whispers, her kohl-limned sapphire eyes cleaving a low-hanging sky. *Fly as long and as hard as you can, my co-dreamer! Scout a fresh site on another hill. Found with me a city where lions lie with lambs, where pity quickens knowledge, where desire dissipates despair!*

T H E R E   A R E no accidents. My Yale thesis on the Puritans did lead to graduate school, but it also took me here. My life with Venn Iyer, father of fractals and designer of inner space, is no accident.

I drove out to this museum to track down for a client what he claims is the most perfect diamond in the world. The diamond has a name: the Emperor's Tear. For eleven years, I have been tracking the Salem Bibi, a woman from Salem who ended up in the Emperor's court. I know her as well as any scholar has known her subject; I know her like a doctor and a lawyer, like a mother and a daughter. With every new thing I've learned, I've come imperceptibly closer to the Emperor's Tear. In that final Götterdämmerung painting, she is holding it: I have seen the Emperor's Tear atop its golden orb. Three hundred years ago, it existed in her hands; I know where she came from and where she went. I couldn't care less about the Emperor's Tear, by now. I care only about the Salem Bibi.

I should have let the keyboard do the tracking, but, like shamans and psychics, I've learned to go with hunches as well as data bases. The easiest way for a white-collar felon to make a stone vanish for a while is to loan it to a small, grateful museum under a plausible alias. And if the museum, finding itself too cluttered already, and out of its curatorial depths, were to sell it in some obscure auction in Europe or Canada, and the owner just happened to show up and buy it, he'd have title, free and clear, wouldn't he?

What I hadn't figured on was the secret life of a Puritan woman whom an emperor honored as Precious-as-Pearl, the Healer of the World.

3

SHE WAS Hannah Easton, only surviving child of Edward and Rebecca Easton, née Rebecca Walker of Brookfield, in the Massachusetts Bay Colony. Brookfield, today, lies about mid-way between Worcester and Springfield in the foothills of central Massachusetts, east of the gentle floodplain of the Connecticut River. In Hannah's time it was Indian country: smack in the middle of Nipmuc land with Mohican and Narragansett to the south, Pennacook and Abnaki on the north all the way to New France.

The dates are not important. I'll summarize them later.

All of Massachusetts must have been an extended family. A cousin shipped out, an in-law followed, an uncle got news of free land, a chance for rebeginning . . . like villages in

Poland and Italy and Ireland emptying for America two centuries later.

Case in point: my family.

Rebecca Easton née Walker's grandmother was a cousin
of Charles Jonathan Samuel Muster's father; her family had
been legitimate passengers on the *Gabriel* (two years later to
sink off Pemaquid, Maine) that Charles had stowed away on.
Vaguely, then, I'm part of this story, the Salem Bibi is part
of the tissue of my life. Walkers appear on the ship's records,
but Charles Muster never did. They'd probably settled in Boston, or even Rhode Island. Perhaps primogeniture did him
out of land or inheritance, but by 1653 Elias Walker, his wife
and infant daughter, Rebecca, arrived in Brookfield and leased,
from their distant relatives the Masters (the three sons of
Charles Jonathan Samuel Muster), three hundred acres of prime
Quabaug River bluff and bottomland. By all accounts, Elias
Walker was a frugal farmer and stockman; by 1665, he had
purchased his land outright. My direct Masters ancestors pock-
eted the cash and further dissipated their father's wealth.

At that time, Brookfield was a hesitant hilltop Puritan
outpost deep inside Nipmuc country. Elias Walker held the
usual attitudes of his time, and ours, toward the Indians: they
are children; they are trusting; they are proud and generous.
Even capable of nobility. But at heart they are savages: bestial,
unspeakably cruel. He counseled, and cultivated, the path of
mutual avoidance. Eight years later, the Walkers gained a
neighbor, a sickly looking but resourceful recent arrival by the
name of Edward Easton, who purchased with his English savings a brown ribbon of a field, a rickety shed, a cabin with
privy and two barns.

The stage was set: older bachelor farmer with education

and some money. The robust farmer's daughter next door was only eight years old when first glimpsed, but no one was going anywhere. By the time she was fifteen, in 1668, Rebecca Walker was married to Edward Easton.

By seventeen, she'd had two pregnancies. The second, a daughter named Hannah, survived. In the remotest of ways, Hannah Easton is a relative of mine. Hannah Easton would walk the parapets of a Mughal fort, would hold the world's most perfect diamond in her hands.

This was country for those raw and strong enough to hack prosperity out of wild, volatile land. And this was country for the middle-aged and bitter, discontented city dwellers and immigrants to start over in the wilderness, where the Prince of the Air was said to reign. Edward Easton was forty-three (already living on borrowed time, statistically speaking) the year that Hannah was born.

> 1632 *Charles Jonathan Samuel Muster arrives in Massachusetts.*
> 1653 *Elias Walker and family arrive in Brookfield. Birth of Rebecca Walker.*
> 1661 *Arrival of Edward Easton.*
> 1668 *Marriage of Rebecca and Edward.*
> 1670 *Birth of Hannah Easton.*

Of Edward Easton's life before the winter of 1661, when he showed up in Boston, little is known. He sailed out of the Downs soon after Charles II, the Stuart restored to the English throne, had Oliver Cromwell's embalmed body dug from its secret grave and decapitated, and the head stuck on a pole in Westminster Hall. They sent potent messages in those days;

Edward, a Roundhead sympathizer, must have caught the first packet boat to the colonies.

In the Old World, Edward Easton had been an East India Company man with a sedentary occupation, a doughy-skinned, soft-bellied, fact-fevered scribe hunched over ledgerbooks, letters and memoranda in the Company's Leadenhall Street offices in London. Back in my junior year abroad, in London, I checked the Company's books and papers stored in the India Office in Whitehall. Edward Easton's entries stand out because of the singular primness and angularity of his handwriting.

I knew my own family's names and fragments of rumored history, of course. When I got to England, I went straight to the shipping records, the baptismal records, the recordings of deeds. Seeing the names of relatives, reading of their deaths and births and marriages all placed me within a context that I found somehow thrilling, as though nothing in the universe is ever lost, no gesture is futile. I've since then doubted the significance of many of those innocent discoveries, but seeing those "Salem Bibi's Stuffs" boxes on the floor of the maritime museum, those Mughal paintings, brought the importance of those feelings back.

A twenty-year-old girl, really, contemplating her place in the universe and the ways of the world had appropriated an ancestor, a man who had gone before her, and though he was writing of strangers, she cherished his observations like an intimate letter from home:

> *A petty ruler on the Coromandel Coast of India is given the gifts of armour, a wool coat and a spying glass.*
> *A ship on its way to Masulipatnam is stocked with 1420 hogs and 250 oxen.*

The mother of a factor who died on board a Company vessel sailing home from Fort St. George is denied the diamonds she claims he was bringing back for her.

A cabin-boy is whipped and his lacerations brined for having stolen a vial of musk.

Did the cabin boy live to be a sea captain? Did the petty ruler wear his bribe to his next battle and did the armor save his skin? Was Edward Easton's mind so demented with details that he fled to the wilderness? Or did he merely look up and out the grimy window, see the forest of mastheads and yardarms on the river and the white Crosses of St. George fluttering like birds on the Company's pennants and finally walk away from his old self? As his wife and his daughter would do, again and again.

Edward Easton arrived in Boston with sufficient skills and savings to make him desirable as a son-in-law to any Boston patriarch with too many daughters, but within weeks he bought himself a horse and cantered westward. Was it disgust with the old life, or was he enticed by a new, wholly imagined one that drove him away from safe and stable port towns like Boston and Salem? Did the Puritans, with their gloomy quest for godliness, hold for him more terror—as, later, they would for Hannah—than the presumed Satan who reigned over Pennacook, Abnaki and Nipmuc?

What is known is that he headed for the outer rings of settlements, stopping over first in Billerica, then in Chelmsford, then in Lancaster—where he was invited to sup at the home of John White, the wealthy landholder, and offered a modest bookkeeping job by White's son-in-law, the Reverend Joseph Rowlandson, Lancaster's first minister—then in Worcester, and finally either running out of energy or finding in Brookfield the dreamscape for starting over.

For this accidental frontiersman, the 1660s was a decade of self-transformation. Like an alchemist who turns dross into gold, he hardened his slack and bookish body into the wiriness of a tiller, transformed the forest into farmland, and disenchantment into desire. And when desire grew carnal and kept him awake all the summer nights of 1668, he married, after perfunctory courtship, the Walkers' bonny lass, strong and handsome, even comely, he wrote in that angular hand, with domestic skills and teachable aptitudes worthy of a freeborn woman of this new land.

He felt he might give her twenty years of husbandly service, begetting upon her a brood of worthy offspring. Already, he was cultivating a second career as village selectman.

I gasped the moment I opened Brookfield town registries and saw the same angular hand I'd known from Leadenhall. I thought then, with all the melodrama of undergraduate training, of Keats's odes, or of his "On First Looking into Chapman's Homer," for here I was, perhaps the only scholar in the world who had traced the work of an obscure clerk from London to Massachusetts. I could sense all the movements in his life, his determination to remake his life before it was too late, to go west to the colony instead of east, where surely his East India clerkship could have led him. I felt the same psychic bond with Edward Easton that Keats did with the revelers on the Grecian urn. He became a footnote in my thesis, but an assurance to me that my research in that era was somehow blessed. Of all the billions of births, the fires and floodings that separate me and my time from Easton and his, that the mundane work of this lone man should be preserved struck me as nothing less than miraculous and conferred on me a kind of wonderstruck confidence.

For most English colonists and certainly for Indian sachems, however, the 1660s was a win-or-die decade. So while Edward Easton was cutting trees down to stumps, raking his field, sowing his wife's fertile womb, prizing rocks from the ground and hauling them to build a wall, burying his firstborn, trading wool stockings and blankets for herbs with the Nipmuc, the Wampanoag chief, Metacomet (whom the colonists renamed Philip), was suing and skirmishing to oust alien usurpers, and the French *habitants* were selling flintlocks to Ninigret, sachem of the Narragansett, in hopes of stirring up anti-English riots.

In 1671, on September 29, the day that Hannah turned a year old and first toddled far enough away by herself to have to be brought back by a solicitous Nipmuc, and the day that, in a cold drafty hall in distant Plymouth, the colonial government curtailed the sovereign powers of the Wampanoag and humiliated the proud King Philip by imposing a fine of one hundred pounds for violating their laws, Edward Easton, while in his outdoor privy savoring the poetic paradox in an imported, treasured copy of *Paradise Lost* and the physical paradox of constipation's painful pleasures, died of a bee sting.

OF HER MOTHER, the twenty-two-year-old widow whom Hannah lost when the Nipmuc laid siege to Brookfield in the scorched month of August 1675, she had one long, disturbing memory.

Rebecca Easton loved to sing. She sang psalms by the light of a fish-oil lamp, always to the same five or six tunes. And though she could neither read the words to the psalms nor the notes to the tunes that Edward, perhaps in a rare desperately nostalgic moment, had scribbled on the back cover of the Psalter, she taught the child to sing antiphonally with her.

Hannah's memory is of one such psalm-singing night, their last one. Rebecca by the window, her neck long and arched, her throat throbbing with song. A voice so strong and sweet that it softens the sternest spiritual phrases into voluptuous pleas. The greasy, pale light of the lamp; the acute smell of the lamp oil. Rebecca singing each line by herself first, then nodding to encourage Hannah; Hannah repeating the line in a quavery, unformed voice. But, Hannah remembers, and this can never be separated from the angelic choir pouring from her mother's breast, there are faces at the window.

Of course, the memory coalesces several frames into a single emblematic moment. The child sees; the mother does not. The strangers are listening, tomahawks held high, about to smash the window and door, but they are stilled in midflight. The Indians know these songs, especially the women who sit in the rear of the church, walking in and out during the sermons but rising with the congregation to sing. Her memory is a window, letting in the fecundity of an unfenced world.

She has also what she calls sightings, rather than memories, of that early childhood on the farm. Rebecca and some Indian helpers must farm alone; Rebecca is a widow. A Nipmuc woman teaching her to clean and dress deerskin. A boy-child promising to grow for her the plumpest squashes and pumpkins, the crispest beans, the brightest corn. A Nipmuc man hunting wild turkeys and pigeons, and she bouncing along behind Rebecca. A season of drought. The same Nipmuc man, Rebecca and Hannah—a frontier family—scraping the last ladlefuls of stewed-together berries and bird eggs and ground nuts from a huge, carbon-encrusted pot. Her mother smiling as the Nipmuc presses a steaming gourd of coarse, spicy potage to Hannah's lips. She remembers her face against the soft deerskin of his jerkin.

King Philip changed Hannah's life as completely and as forcefully as King Charles II of England had changed her father's.

All through June and July of 1675, paranoia traveled up and down the Bay Path. Philip was arming his warriors for an all-out war! Wampanoag were breaking into and entering colonists' houses in Swansea and raiding farms abandoned on the thin, frayed neck of peninsular land. Isolated farmers were gathered up and garrisoned, losing their crops and cattle to the marauders. Messengers from Governor Winslow of Plymouth fanned their frenzy. Philip's men were looting and burning Middleborough, Dartmouth, Plymouth. The heathens were axing, scalping, abducting the decent Christian men and women and children of Mendon.

Hannah dreamed of Philip pressing his war-roused face at the window. Why not? Stray troopers coming through spoke of Philip as though he were an omnipresent phantom. One moment he was staking out pease fields, next moment he was fortifying snake-crowded swamps. And the next, he was impaling scalped heads and slashing the bulging sacs of milch cows.

Then, on the night of the second of August, Philip's War came to the Easton hearth in the person of Rebecca's Nipmuc lover. If he had intended the marking as disguise, it didn't work. Hannah knew him as her inadmissible father, the only man she'd ever seen her mother with. The child raised her hand. The mother stopped singing, and slowly turned around.

This is the night Hannah has willed herself not to remember. What happened survives only as Rebecca's neighbors' gossip, embellished with the speculations of scholars. The lover, now painted and feathered as befits a warrior, comes to woo her one last time. And Rebecca surprises him. Reading Hannah's eyes, she stands and slowly turns, facing the window without surprise or terror. She stands on a reed rug by the window, the very window where Hannah remembers her having led women and children through psalms, and peels her white, radiant body out of the Puritan widow's somber bodice and skirt as a viper sheds skin before wriggling into the brush. Her body is thick, strong, the flesh streaked and bruised, trussed with undergarments.

The Nipmuc enters the cabin, suddenly immense in his full battle regalia. He cradles the whimpering Easton hound under one arm.

Rebecca scoops Hannah out of her bed, clasps her and weeps as though the child were dead. The Nipmuc jerks his arm, the hound lurches, and a spume of blood leaps from his arms across the table. He swabs Rebecca's old garments in the blood, smears them with his feet over the floor, stabs holes in the cloth as they darken with blood, then hands her something new and Indian and clean to wear.

Outside, a Nipmuc woman who had taught her to sew deerskin into breeches, takes the child. Hannah watches the cabin grow small, and a fireball erupt from the spilled fish-oil lamp, as Rebecca and the Nipmuc take off for the river, and the woman, running hard and low to the ground, cuts into the woods, along the path to the Fitch farm half a mile away. She does not cry, and the vow she makes, bobbing in the arms of the nameless woman she has known all her life, to remain silent about this night, to sustain her mother in the ultimate lie, the ultimate unnatural crime of Puritan life, she will keep for sixty years.

Hannah's subsequent years can be read as a sermon on any topic, as proof of any interpretation. But she wills the memory of this night away; she will orphan herself to that memory, deny its existence, for that is the way her mother has planned it. She alone knows the nature of her mother's disappearance; she must carry the denial of this memory—a lump tenfold heavier than the memory itself—the rest of her life, chastising the lump inside her that is Rebecca with self-doubt and self-hate. Had she been perceived the daughter of a fornicator, not the offspring of an upright widow, no family would have taken her in. It is necessary not only to retain the memory of her beloved, absent mother, but to deny its final blinding, lustful image. To preserve above all the orphan's tragic tale above the wicked woman's demonic possession.

Has any child been so burdened? She has witnessed the Fall, not Adam's Fall, Rebecca's Fall. Her mother's Fall, infinitely more sinful than the Fall of a man. She is the witness not merely of the occasion of sin, but of the birth of sin itself.

And I who have studied Hannah's life nearly as closely as I have studied my own would say that Hannah Easton, whatever the name she carried in Massachusetts, in England, in India or even into history to this very day, loved her mother more profoundly than any daughter has ever loved a mother.

I feel for Hannah as the Nipmuc woman carries her off and drops her noiselessly on a pioneer family's doorstep, deflecting forever the natural course and location of her girlhood. And I envy Rebecca as she, impulsively, carelessly, leaps behind her lover, who is already on his horse, and vanishes into the wilderness. She has escaped her prison, against prevailing odds that would have branded her. Her lover might have come to the window that night to kill them both. Instead, he became the first man to read the scene between them as something sacred; in the fish-oil glow, to hear the music.

4

LIKE REBECCA, I have a lover. One who would seem alien to my family. A lover scornful of our habits of self-effacement and reasonableness, of our naive or desperate clinging to an imagined continuity. Venn was born in India and came over as a baby. His family are all successful; there was never question of anything different. He grew up in a world so secure I can't imagine it, where for us security is another kind of trap, something to be discarded as dramatically as Rebecca stepped out of dog-blooded widow's weeds into a life of sin and servitude.

Long ago, there was Andrew, self-described untouchable from a Boston Brahmin family who'd leased a summer home next to ours on Martha's Vineyard. He took me behind the sea-grape arbor, or perhaps I led him there from curiosity and boredom (he was my first), and later that day dolphins threw themselves on the beach and a crowd gathered to watch their threshing and not ours. I remember thinking, stretched nude on a dune above a squad of lifeguards and helicopter cameramen, I hope dolphins won't always be sacrificed to a fifteen-year-old's virginity.

Then came Blake, whose refrain to professors in my freshman year was always: "Can someone tell me why I should be learning stuff that's already in a book?" It was a revelation to me that mutants had been born in my decade and raised in my country with such a pure belief in the perfectibility of knowledge retrieval. Instead of memorizing the stuff, we should be inputting it. We paid huge sums to world-famous experts who sat in their offices and read all day—and in a lifetime they probably covered 5 percent of the written record in their field. The goal of every freshman should be to replicate the data base of the most learned professors in the world. Then they could start using it in their sophomore year.

Chase, a brief flirtation from a summer archaeology dig in Harvard Yard, with a knack for finding fragments: pottery, spectacle cases, clay pipes, bent spoons, Spanish coins. The secret, he said, was an ability *not* to separate the valuable artifacts from the centuries of landfill—anyone could do that, he said—but to merge them, to see continuities between sand and gravel and copper coins or fired-clay powder. He's the first of my friends to win a genius grant.

Devon, who got me through the first lonely months in London by taking me everywhere by bus and tube and walking, pointing out buildings, revealing how sheer love of a city, sheer awareness of one's setting, was an adequate replacement for food and warmth, until the day he disappeared and the police found sticks of dynamite and blasting caps in my closet, wrapped in my sweaters. His love of London was a targeting mission.

Gavin and Giles, who seem to be as interchangeable as

their names: each had a mum, and a red-faced da in a tight buttoned sweater, both aspired to emigration, New Zealand or the Yukon. They were pure air-and-water fetishists—they *monitored* things—rainfall and temperatures, pollution and pulse rates—and I dallied with them both on the same days, for I had become insatiable not for sex but for presences that were not immediately dismissible or transparently ridiculous. Their temperaments were sweet, what the French call *douce*, meaning mild, even gentle, as well as sweet. I thought of them as dolphins and wanted to protect them like endangered species. I had begun to despair that I'd taken a sip of some secret potion that would leave me forever scornful and impatient, which led, upon my return to Yale for my senior year, to a serious contemplation and the fear on the part of my parents that I might not marry soon, or at all.

I had slipped off the continental shelf of shallow, undergraduate affairs into the dark, cold, maritime trenches.

Love's old sweet story, fate supplies a mate, the melody lingers on, et cetera, et cetera, for then came the older men, the professors and the bosses and men with complicated lives and fatal flaws, addictions, recoveries, encumbrances, married men, older men, brilliant but unstable men, attractive but self-engrossed. My twenties passed in grad school and in travel and in short-term grants and short-term affairs that took me wherever I wanted to go. Past success became my credentials, and I picked up other men—Other men—meaning the natives of other countries whose immediate attractiveness I could judge, but nothing else about them; the codes were different. I forgave selfishness, petulance, unfaithfulness I would have despised in Americans; I fell for charm and sophistication and tolerated laziness that would have seemed insincere or egregious in the men I grew up with. My college friends and other colleagues had, by then, gone through much the same types and numbers and their first marriages; at least, I told myself, I didn't have a child. Then at thirty I asked myself why I didn't have a child. But by then, pills offered no protection, we were in the sargasso of disease. And so one night with my AIDS-free certificate in my handbag, I went to a lecture at Harvard Business School on assets recovery, and to a bar afterward, where I met Venn.

The man I was looking for by then would go to evening lectures in fields far outside his own. He would not be American. I'd always pictured him Chinese or perhaps Latin American, a scientist, one of those poetry-writing physicists or musical chemists who went to foreign films for recreation. I just didn't think he'd be from India, and three inches shorter than I.

I asked him what he did. "A kind of data processor," he said. "And you?"

Very few men in my recent past had deflected questions back to me. After ten years of bobbing in the tangle and clutter of semiserious relationships, the most attractive trait I could imagine in a man was a modest interest in other people, notably me, and a perceptible lack of self-involvement.

"What's a data processor doing at MIT?" I asked.

"I'm more an inputter than a processor," he said.

"Still—" I pursued.

"It's a special kind of data and a special kind of input."

"Try me."

"Four dimensional, digital."

"You've lost me."

"Tell me about asset retrieval," he said. "That's a little like what I do. That's why I went to the lecture."

I thought that night I had found the world's most modest man. He would not talk about his research; he belittled its potential, even as my own jaw dropped. He could stimulate sense responses—smell, touch, sound—in any subject properly equipped and programmed. But that didn't excite him. People will always respond to stimuli, but so will pond scum; the interesting problem was constructing an interactive model of historical or imaginative reality. Historical reality to begin with, since there was a data trail, indisputable facts to program in.

Not time-travel, he said. Time-retrieval, to put it in my terms.

5

ON SATURDAY, Hannah was moved again.

Nothing mattered. Not the slow, clumsy tenderness of the arthritic couple, Robert and Susannah Fitch, whose lives she had burst into Friday night. Not the screaming and cursing of their grown son, Thomas, who had ridden out with a parley party very early in the morning of that same Friday and whom Captain Ephraim Curtis rescued from a Nipmuc ambush in a defile and brought back, grievously bleeding. Thomas Fitch would never walk again.

The people of Brookfield couldn't believe the betrayal. The Nipmuc were good children of God, loyal to the King. They feared Wampanoag just like everyone else. The families of

Brookfield, or Quabaug, as they preferred to call it, all had friends among the Nipmuc, their wandering animals were often returned by Indians, and no white man, encountering an Indian in his fields, or by the river, ever raised his rifle or felt afraid. This whole dispute was unimaginable.

"French," said some.

Hannah kept her feelings—what must it have been but the world's harvest of sorrow and confusion, to be later winnowed into rancor and gratitude?—to herself. Shock disguised itself as serenity. She had not spoken, but she was, briefly, the center of everyone's concern. The little innocent, torn by a savage from her mother's cold breast, cruelly dumped by a guilty heathen, doubtless thinking it would gain him some credit in the afterlife, on a neighbor's doorstep.

"Only, we're not papists," cried Henry Young. "God has taken his measure. He who would slay the mother and spare the child is crueler than any brute animal."

When flaming arrows came through the roof of the house, she helped carry out canisters of precious salt, sugar and oil, and prayed with her new parents for divine Providence, then hurried with them behind Thomas's litter to a large, garrisoned house on the hill.

The two long days and longer nights of Brookfield's siege she bore as though the heat of eighty bodies huddled too close, the stench of their fear, the war whoops and burning roofs and musket fire were ordinary excesses of summer weather. Henry Young, rallying the defenders, paid with his life for drawing too close to a window.

Lucas Thorpe, a tall, yellow-haired boy who'd survived the same ambush that nearly killed Thomas Fitch and distinguished himself by his enthusiasm for vengeance, volunteered to run to Marlborough for reinforcements. Everyone feared their vaunted friendship with the Nipmuc would be believed, and the columns of relief would bypass Brookfield unless word of their distress got out. During a respite in the fighting, Lucas slipped out the back of the house. She watched, almost praying for the same sudden fate that had befallen Henry Young, as the boy grew small in the brush. And then, before he reached the woods, a dozen tall Nipmuc braves stood, and the colonists watched the boy turning and twisting, shouting but sending no message as the clubs fell upon his head and shoulders. He collapsed, and one brave dipped down with him, out of sight. When he next stood, he held the yellow patch in his hand, and now they could all hear the shouts, even over Goodwife Thorpe's screaming, and then the braves decapitated the corpse and passed the head among them, throwing it as a sport more than a trophy.

The only man truly to serve as her father was somewhere out there in the dark, pumping arrows into the garrison, or perhaps kicking a boy's head in an open field in full view of the house. She knew that her mother might be with him or might be inside one of the tents the colonists had boasted of going out to give a taste of eternal hellfire, the moment their liberators came.

The secret dynamic of Puritanism had at last taken flesh. *Now we know*, just when we had begun to doubt it and to sink to their level of easy virtue and soft surrender to effortless productivity, and to believe—blasphemy of blasphemies— that their life had something to teach us, some tenet of inborn nobility: they really *are* devils, the woods really *are* evil, *it's true, it's true*, God *is* testing us, demanding the sacrifice of our women and children, the slaughter of our livestock, the taking and defilement of possessions, our honor, our scalps! Gloried be His name! The biblically learned among them preached, "This place is Ziklag! Deliver us from Amalekites!" And King Philip might well have responded, "Taste my steel, Ananias!" Women sweated through childbirth. Children played war games under sturdy tables and rickety chairs. Goodwives and their modest daughters bled and bandaged the mangled bodies of amateur soldiers.

Ephraim Curtis, the practiced woodsman, crawled and ran thirty hellish miles—the first American Olympian—to get troops and supplies from Marlborough. This was life without God's protection, the life Brookfield had begun to take for granted. Nipmuc constructed a rolling fire spreader, a travois of barrels and shafts and wheels, and rolled the huge, blazing weapon right up to the house. Suddenly, histories tell us, a freak rainstorm rose up and put out the fires. God tests us a bit at times, but He listens; His children, seeing in the rain providential purpose, prayed for strength to survive His blank indifference. Major Simon Willard, riding at the head of his force of healthy troopers, arrived in partial fulfillment of colonists' prayers. The Major and his men checked the encampment's badly burned fortifications, salvaged what could be reused from vandalized houses and barns, then advised abandonment and relocation.

A continent of opportunity is a continent of cruelty. They had known that when they came; they hardened themselves to the message so long as they stayed in sight of Boston Harbor and the waters that separated them from the shamefulness of English history—but they'd forgotten. Now God had rededicated them, praise His name. Devastation exfoliates providential efficacy. Suffering is good, though sometimes

confusing. Brookfielders—no more this Quabaug nonsense—
scattered to sturdier Puritan garrisons.

Robert and Susannah Fitch settled in a modest, two-storied
house on Herbert Street in Salem, bringing with them Hannah,
the somber orphan, the living reproach to any forgiveness, any
mission to the savages, and Thomas, their newly crippled,
aborigiphobic son.

6

SALEM FORCED on the farming Fitches professions
suitable to a port town. The wharves were raucous with sailors,
settlers, whores and drunks. The world's races were repre-
sented, and a mini-congerie of languages. Spanish and French
coins were in circulation; it mattered little which regal head
graced the ducat. The finished products of the civilized world
were being unloaded in Salem, while holds were stuffed with
barbarian ballast, lumber and hides and salted foodstuffs for
the journey home. Easy livings could be made for the tough
and the imaginative. A successful merchant or barrister or
doctor had to live the role, had to command respect of common
men and foreigners, or else he invited gossip, envy and chal-
lenges to his authority. In any event, it was still a fragile
outpost rooted in free will and high sentence; no wonder its
self-proclaimed virtues decayed to conspiracy and gossip among
the backward elements.

As the rich got richer they grew cosmopolitan, at least by colonial standards, and slightly ashamed of their Nonconformist, fanatical origins. It was no longer possible for the virtuous to look about them at their fellow Bay Colony citizens and recognize, let alone assert, as their fathers and grandfathers had, their commonality. The wealthy sought instead to perpetuate their good fortune through their sons' education at Harvard and their daughters' distinguished marriages. London styles in dress and barbering led the Bay Colony by no more than three sailings: description, orders, delivery with local tailors to confection milady's silks, velvet for milord, wigs and lace for both.

But for the dispossessed from the country, for the veterans of Indian raids, demented survivors of scalpings, and for the families who'd never climbed even the first plateau of New World riches that had been promised them, the townsfolk's backsliding to worldliness and ostentation seemed little better than Catholicism of the English or Roman variety. Purity was no longer valued as the end of human effort, or the goal of social structure. The familiar stocks and pillory and lash post no longer aroused the same dread and inner accounting. As offenses to common morality grew less punishable, the gibbet took on greater natural force. According to Thomas Fitch, the true and faithful, though still numerically preponderant, were losing control by the month of the Holy Covenant that had bound their colony in the New World to Almighty God. Losing *by the day* to the carriage owners, the stone-fronted-house builders, the rising aristocracy who doubted a young man's loss of both legs to King Philip was the result of a blood encounter with the archfiend Prince of Darkness.

Fitch, out one day on an errand, had watched an old man

ridiculed for wearing a wide-brimmed bonnet on a humid summer's day, and young Latin School buffoons tossing stones at it, until he turned, doffed his hat, and revealed the hairless, fleshless bony carapace of a fellow survivor of King Philip's raids, a man who had survived the partial ripping of his crowning glory, and the Latinist cowards had fled his addled curses. The sight of some grimy, disreputable fellow with one of several possible letters of the sinner's alphabet—Adulterer, Blasphemer, Thief, Incest breeder—branded to his forehead, or an Indian patch sewn to a woman's sleeve for miscegenation, no longer excited the intended pity or fear; evidence of outrageous sin sometimes earned the wretch a farthing and a snicker. From his chair behind the upper window, Thomas would watch the boats unloading, calling out to his father the multiple offenses of unregulated greed, the blocks of marble for stone facades, the fine-grained imported hardwoods for palatial fireplaces—imagine, importing wood to the colonies!—the bales of Scottish wool.

Their world was ripping apart, thieves and cutthroats walking the street in open defiance of common decency; crafty, devious merchants without a ha'penny of godfear piling up ducats and doubloons and pleading too great a poverty to contribute to the Sunday offering.

ROBERT AND THOMAS took up cabinetmaking; Susannah and Hannah, sewing.

Hannah discovered in herself an obsessive love of needlework, which was, she suspected, an overflow of a nascent fascination with—or failing for—finer things. A stray sunbeam on her workbasket, kindling the weakest combustion of colors among twisted skeins of colored thread, could raise indecent palpitations in her heart. Temptation dogged the sensuous Hannah everywhere: in rich clients' halls as she delivered her handiwork of velvet gowns and quilted underskirts, coats flirty with ladders of bowknots and lingerie undersleeves, and caps of sheerest white muslin; at the baker's as she passed by shelves of German fried and sugared breads; at the wharf, as sweaty laborers wheeled and rolled cargoes smelling of figs and raisins and spices she couldn't name and hadn't yet tasted.

Her embroidery gave away the conflict she tried so hard to deny or suppress. She knew she must deny all she'd seen the night of her mother's disappearance and all she felt, for she, worthless sinner and daughter of Satan's lover, had been taken in and raised by decent souls. Instead, her needle spoke; it celebrated the trees, flowers, birds, fish of her infant days. Nostalgia, all the more forceful because it was unacknowledged, was augmented with fancy. Flora and fauna grew wild on fecund and voluptuous terrain.

Even at twelve, Hannah Easton's work was known, and families that would not have admitted her stepparents to their parlors insisted on showing her inside, offering her cakes and tiny tokens of additional payment. She would accept no extra money or sweets. She wanted only additional threads, sheer spools of color that the wealthy hoarded and were happy to share.

Susannah praised her needlework skill, but feared the wantonness of spirit it betrayed. She had the girl work exclusively on bonnets and farthingales. Hannah sewed assiduously in dim light from whale oil. Too assiduously, Susannah feared. Even diligence should not be indulged, lest it lead to pride of excess.

"The race is not to the swift, nor the battle to the strong," she admonished.

"Ecclesiastes, nine-eleven," said Hannah, not looking up.

She tried to correct the deformation of love. She brought *The Bay Psalm Book* to Thomas where he sat by the window in a mobile chair he had ingeniously constructed and had him locate a verse her needle could commemorate. Thomas could read and write as Susannah could not, and it was to Thomas that Hannah's education was wholly entrusted.

Thomas chose the most popular:

Aske thou of me, and I will give the Heathen for thy lot; and of the earth thou shalt possess the utmost coasts abroad.

He whomped *The Bay Psalm Book* shut so hard that a tong fell off its hook by the fireplace. Was Thomas, too, troubled by the ambiguities of providential messages? Did he, legless woodworker, feel bitter that "utmost coasts" were no longer possible for him to possess?

An uneasy memory stalled Hannah's hand as she reached for threads from the workbasket. Another window. Another psalm-sayer. Rebecca sang with sweet confidence.

Hannah sang from the compulsion of memory.

Desire of me, and I shall give thee the heathen for thine inheritance; and the utmost parts of the earth for thy possession.

Rebecca had sung from Psalms 2:8; Thomas recited from *The Bay Psalm Book* of 1640. *Aske thou of me. Desire of me.* Ask or desire—what's the difference, anyway? Except. Except that "ask" suggests aggression and self-righteousness. It seems like a clash of the sexes, a triumph of pioneer virility.

. . . heathen for thine inheritance. Heathen for thy lot.

Did Philip's Wampanoag warriors and Rebecca's Nipmuc lover suffer as they went from being "inheritance" to "lot" in Puritan vocabulary?

The verse emblazoned itself in colors so tropical that the threads Hannah used had to have been brought over from a mysterious place with a musical name: Bandar Abbas, Batavia, Bimlipatam. The result is, for me, one of the great colonial samplers (though she was not sewing it to prove her marriage-ability), far smaller than the usual quilt, not much larger than a bandanna.

On a field of light blue, Hannah created an "uttermost shore." A twelve-year-old Puritan orphan who had never been out of Massachusetts imagined an ocean, palm trees, thatched cottages, and black-skinned men casting nets and colorfully garbed bare-breasted women mending them; native barks and, on the horizon, high-masted schooners. Colonial gentlemen in breeches and ruffled lace, buckled hats and long black coats pacing the shore. In the distance, through bright-green foliage, a ghostly white building—it could even be the Taj Mahal— is rising.

"The Utmost Parts" (Anonymous, Salem c. 1680) sold to an anonymous buyer on the open market at Sotheby's (Tokyo), in 1983 for $6,000. Besides me, only one person in the world knows the names of both Anonymouses.

That little embroidery is the embodiment of desire. The full verse from Psalms is scrolled beneath the vision—for surely that is what it is: a pure vision. It is the first native American response to a world that could be African or Indian or anything not American. It employs the same economy, the same apparently naive sophistication as the Mughal paintings that would later feature her.

Thomas framed her handiwork in the finest cherrywood left over from a chest he had made for the fearsome old magistrate, the twisted John Hathorne (whose excesses in the witch trials would so torment his descendant, Nathaniel Hawthorne). He heaved himself as high as he could in his mobile chair and hammered the heavy object low into the wall behind her bed. The rainbow banner glowed, a genie's lamp, in a cold, narrow room. And at bedtimes when she knelt by it to pray, it shot the familiar virtues she prayed for—humility, gratitude, meekness—with a pagan iridescence.

I HAVE SEEN this handiwork and been bemused by its extravagance and ambiguity. It survives in the private collection of a Hollywood mogul, son of a Dachau survivor, the producer-director of five slug-and-chase movies, the kind that brings out popcorn munchers by the million to mall Cineplexes. In 1983 he flew me out to Bel Air for a proposition. He'd heard I knew Puritan art, that I was an asset hunter, and that I'd heard of the Emperor's Tear. He wanted me to work for him as his private art adviser. He has taste, and his taste is for colonial American.

Hannah's personal message has now become commodified; it is collectible art. Its current owner hangs it in a halogen-lit hallway in his Bel Air garrison. The high-tech hanging and lighting diminishes, I imagine, the original shock of the Salem Bibi's subtext. In Bel Air, the uttermost shore is a phone call away. All the same, in that overfurnished, overdecorated, over-surveillanced warehouse of museum-quality purchases, the Salem Bibi's covenant seems as ambiguous and as appropriate as ever. Bugs Kilken of Bel Air knows that his father—and, therefore, he—was spared. He believes in what Hannah would call grace; what he calls the luck of the draw.

For Bugs, who makes millions with schlock and for whom moviemaking is a kind of technological indulgence increasingly distant from art, true expression is found only in naive visions. He feels he should be simplifying his life. He's a vegetarian and doesn't drink; he admires the Shakers. He feels the world went wrong around 1700, and his art collection sets out to restore a little sanity.

Bugs's father survived Dachau because he could repair light bulbs. Simple as that; he'd been a poor boy in Poland who knew how to reconnect the filaments of blown light bulbs without breaking the glass or detaching the bottoms. The guards kept him alive. In their low cunning, they billed the authorities for new bulbs and kept the change. Kilken, Senior, came to L.A. after the war and started a lighting store. He remarried, and Bugs, and Bugs's studio, are the results. Bugs wants to make a movie about his father, about the petty and the grotesque maneuverings that killed millions and spared dozens, but he can't—he's locked into the industry. He can't downsize; he can't desert his fans and distributors. That day, he'd drunk Calistoga water and stared at Hannah's embroidery.

"It's a pretty little piece, isn't it?"

I said nothing.

"British. But from India. Bought it in an old estate sale in London," he told me. I couldn't tell if he was testing me or bragging. I knew that he'd bought it in Tokyo for six thousand dollars. I've since learned that's how he operates: buys cheap, donates it to a museum, repurchases to establish a public value.

"They embroidered like this in the American colonies," I ventured. "Never so beautifully, of course." Still testing me, he'd agreed. It could be American.

"Salem, perhaps," he'd said. "Could that be the Taj Mahal?"

"There's no record that anyone in America knew about the Taj Mahal," I'd said.

"I think it is the Taj. Whoever embroidered that was a very sophisticated person. There's so much we don't know about colonial America. A port city like Salem, or Boston— they were nerve centers of their time. Anything known in London would be known in Boston six weeks later."

But now I know: Hannah took that embroidery with her to England and then to India when she married. It *is* her sampler, and it probably stayed in Asia, perhaps in some maharaja's private collection, until Bugs Kilken redeemed it. That day, I'd pushed a little harder. "There was a piece like this that came up in a Sotheby's sale in Tokyo this year."

He smiled, a kind of guarded conspiracy. "Really? Not a crude copy, I hope."

And now, ten years later, Hannah has brought us together again. He's learned about Hannah. He knows I know about Hannah. He's discovered the Salem Bibi. He knows the fingers that did the embroidery have also touched the Emperor's Tear.

7

OVER THE YEARS Susannah Fitch passed on to Hannah all the conventional wisdom and housekeeping tips she

herself had needed to make for Robert an agreeable bride and
efficient helpmeet, and the one new skill—the sewing and
healing of scalped heads—that she had taught herself since
that frightful siege of Brookfield.

This was different from nursing. All frontier wives and
mothers know that knowledge of nursing is more valuable than
cooking and cleaning. There are always fights or accidents with
axes, drownings in streams with slippery banks, fevers that
maim the mind as well as limbs. One child in five might grow
up. But when King Philip's War heaped Indian rage quite
literally on colonists' heads, Susannah had the opportunity to
improve upon the scalp-healing technique of the very aged
Goodwife Brooks of Woburn.

Susannah adapted a technique she'd learned from a horse
doctor. When hunting and guard dogs got into fights with
raccoons, bears and wolverines, those that survived often required emergency surgery. And when the wounds were too
deep, or too broad, the doctor often snipped off pieces of skin
from smaller cuts and sewed them as bridges across the injury.
He considered regenerative processes limited to the lower animals, the way lizards and frogs grew back their lost limbs.
But Susannah experimented with the men of Brookfield and
found, more often than not, the bridge became permanent;
the bone was covered; the horrible puckering was reduced. She
found that perfectly good strips of skin could be cut from the
back of an unconscious man and sewn in bands across the scalp.
If he survived the scalping, he'd certainly live through the
harvesting from his back and ribs.

And Hannah, though squeamish at the sight of blood
drawn righteously through public whippings outside the meeting hall, took enthusiastically to assisting in Susannah's

sealings-up. Nursing, she still abhorred. Washing and bandaging wounds, cleaning up pus and vomit, all this she found too passive, too mundane. In rare moods, she remembered how much fun Rebecca had made their trips into the forest in order to pick herbs, scrape barks, squeeze or boil medicinal secretions of insects. But in the Fitch house, Rebecca's remedies would have been condemned as shameful witchery owing far too much to nighttime aboriginal conjurings (how would any decent white woman learn such things, test them, and trust them? And as always, Hannah had her terrible secret to bear).

Surgery, however, was respectable, especially when each success and each failure were ascribed to the glory or mysterious purposiveness of God. Hannah, cursed or blessed with too much intensity, improvised daring techniques on stray cats and slow squirrels, so that by the time she was fourteen she covertly but regularly practiced on small animals, first skinning their heads with speed and care as she had seen the Nipmuc women do, then stitching the flaps of skin to the raw, shiny flesh.

Her apprenticeship is chronicled obliquely. A 1685 diary entry of Providence Silsbee refers to a large and surprising plague of bald rodents in Salem. (Memories of this peculiar plague would figure later in witchcraft trials.) Silsbee had ascribed the damage to high-spirited boys, but he did remark on the brightly colored threads used to stitch the skin, the whimsical patterns that made squirrels at a distance look like recipients of gaily colored skullcaps.

Later she would make her way to a smaller subcontinent with a vaster wilderness and meet a fugitive Venetian surgeon or quack fleeing an emperor in a Capuchin's robes and learn from him one hundred and one ways to fix dented skulls and damaged souls. That Venetian, lacking a Puritan's humility but not a Puritan's familiarity with Scripture, would boast to her, *"I kill and make alive, I wound and I heal, neither is there any can deliver out of my hand."*

Hannah herself suffered a mysterious ailment in 1685. The ailment kept her in bed, a doleful insomniac, for six weeks. One moment, she was reciting a poem for company:

> *A tribe of female hands, but manly hearts*
> *Forsake at home their pastry-crust and tarts*
> *To knead the dirt, the samplers down they hurl,*
> *Their undulating silks they closely furl.*
> *The pickaxe one as a commandress holds,*
> *While t'other at her awkness gently scolds.*
> *One puffs and sweats . . .*

and the next she was sweating and writhing on the rug by the hearth.

Neighbors stopped by the Fitch house and made uplifting conversation. Others prayed and, remembering her doleful experience in the woods during King Philip's raid, began probing just below the threshold of consciousness. Of course their inquiries were always considerately phrased in proper Puritan language of bad influences, unchristian proclivities learned early and perhaps never expunged by the charities of Goodwife Fitch and her sober and righteous husband and suffering, unfortunate son.

For the Fitches, who viewed their foster daughter as especially talented and obedient, but of a secretive disposition whose origins could only be traced to the night in the woods when she saw her mother murdered before her eyes (and, worse, mysteriously disposed of so that not a trace remained), there was always the fear that the memory of that night would someday return. They feared for her sanity when they saw Indians on the streets of Salem, or scalped men, but she never revealed the slightest interest in any of the direct perpetrators or victims of that terrible night.

H E R   C L O S E S T   F R I E N D   was Hester Manning, daughter of the smith, whose house and forge on Herbert Street always gathered a crowd of Salem's least pious young men. Something about fire and hammers and horses, Hester said, brought out a male's recalcitrant streak. Or perhaps it was the presence of Hester herself, small and dimpled, with a saucy air that promised more favor than it ever delivered. Hester had lost an aunt when King Philip's warriors had massacred settlers in Lancaster in the winter of 1676, and she brought Hannah the book that she insisted everybody, *everybody*, was reading, even the fancy dressers on Chestnut Street, for whom Hannah would make breeches and farthingales as soon as she was well again. The book was *The Sovereignty and Goodness of God, together with the Faithfulness of His Promises Displayed; Being a Narrative of the Captivity and Restoration of Mrs. Mary Rowlandson. Commended by her to all that Desire to know the Lord's Doings to, and Dealings with Her. Especially to Her Dear Children and Relations.*

Hester had entrusted herself to marriage for deliverance. She had the sort of imagination that was all too compliant; she could see herself enacting nearly any situation a book, or an anecdote, even a whimsical suggestion, presented to her. This made her an ideal companion for Hannah, whose own sense of special mission in life was firmly set though rarely articulated. Anyone looking at these two fifteen-year-old maidens in the summer of 1685 would have thought them destined for opposite fates: Hannah to linger in Salem, Hester to reposition the stars.

Hannah must have shuddered or screamed when she heard the name Rowlandson. She must have wondered if this Rowlandson was not a relative of the minister Joseph Rowlandson, who hadn't succeeded in halting her father's mad ride to Brookfield and encampments beyond. I imagine her speculations. What if Edward Easton had stayed in Lancaster? Would Rebecca not have run off with her Indian? Would she and Rebecca have been taken prisoner like Mary Rowlandson, sold as slaves, moved from swamp to swamp, forced to beg for food scraps, even learn to savor the vile tastes of horse hooves and parched corn?

There were rumors, never put to rest, that not all white women abducted were enslaved or scalped or mercifully sacrificed to the heathen deities. This was Hester's special theory; she could fancy herself abducted by heathens. Of course it was the devil himself whispering into the pillow at night, and of course it was sinful even to mention it to one whose own mother—

Hannah raised her hand. She took no offense. In fact, truth be told, the wild improbability of Hester's fancy rendered its possible truth, even its attractiveness, totally credible. There were sightings, sworn by respectable witnesses, of fair-haired and light-skinned women, English gentlewomen, not barmaids or serving wenches, or the pope's own whores from the gutters of Paris, moving with bands of Indians on the outer fringes of civilization.

Hannah cringed from the memory of her own dread-filled hour. Over and over, Rebecca, with one saucy leap onto her lover's white horse, defected from Zion, defected from family love.

Pray, dear Hester, do go on.

Hester caught the flicker and felt encouraged to intone her favorite passage about a modest, decent woman's obscene afflictions. *"Now is the dreadful hour come . . . ,"* she started.

Did Hannah's rage target the Providence that had allowed a family to be broken up by death and desertion as well as by her mother? Or had the twin rage begun its process of coalescence, entwined in the dense embroidery of her life?

"Some in our house were fighting for their lives," Hester read on, her thin voice deepening with anticipation of violence, *"others wallowing in their blood, the house on fire over heads, and the bloody heathen ready to knock us on the head if we stirred out . . ."*

Hannah heard again the Nipmuc war cries and Thomas Fitch's screams. Flames singed the clean walls of the garrison on the hill. Bullets flew into the room, erratic as bats, and nested in infants' bowels and toddlers' kneecaps.

". . . Thus we were butchered by those merciless heathens, standing amazed, with the blood running down to our heels . . ."

Guard yourself against aliens, Hester's voice suggested. Hannah pulled her quilt tight over her head. The godless are invading the garden that the diligent have cleared from the forest primeval.

Hester put down her book. "Tell me what it was *really* like, Hannah. They say when you have these spells . . . you're remembering."

"They?"

"The boys at the forge. You're a great topic of speculation, Hannah Easton."

She had always thought of herself as one who watched,

who had the privilege of remaining outside family or society, by virtue of her loss and secret. She knew there had already been inquiries of possible marriage and that her foster father had politely intervened.

"Mrs. Rowlandson's account is such as the common press should wish of savages and gentlewomen alike," said Hannah. "Five years I dwelled in the forest and knew the forest and all its dwellers as a friend. And for perhaps a week, but especially for two days and nights, I knew it as a tempest. I count no man as my friend, nor as my enemy."

Then Rebecca stepped out of Hannah's memory, and spoke. Hannah was an infant again. And again Rebecca was initiating her daughter into a whispered, subversive alphabet. "*A* is for Act, my daughter!"

Hester heard Hannah babble deliriously from inside her quilted cave and fetched Susannah.

"*B* is for Boldness," Hannah pledged. "*C* is for Character. *D* is for Dissent, *E* is for Ecstasy, *F* is for Forage . . ."

And *I*, thought Hester, remembering the women who wore it emblazoned on their sleeves, is for Indian lover.

"*I* is for Independence," said Hannah.

The next morning Hannah came down as though she had been in bed only overnight and not a month and a half of nights. Her recovery was miraculous.

I do not choose the word carelessly. If God can speak through a bee sting, why cannot He speak through the ghost of life-loving Rebecca?

8

O F   T H E   next eight years in the Fitch household, only one
record exists. No, I take that back; an asset hunter knows not
to be arrogant, to keep pushing. You never know what might
be out there. From those eight years, I have found one relevant
exchange of letters. These are letters written not by her nor
to her, but about her.

The first is dated June 15, 1686. It is addressed to Robert
Fitch by William Pynchon, an innkeeper in Springfield, asking
on behalf of his son, Solomon, and in the formulaic phrases
of his time, leave for Solomon to court Hannah. His public
house, William regrets, has an uncertain immediate future.
But he promises to make over to Solomon five hundred pounds
by that September, and one thousand more the following
spring.

Solomon Pynchon must have carried that letter with him
to the Fitch house, for Robert Fitch's reply is dated June 16,
1686. I do not know when Solomon spied Hannah and thought
it worth his while to have his father negotiate for her hand.
He may have been living in Salem; he or his father may even
have had a cassock or buffcoat for a puff-sleeved linen shirt
sewn by her. Or he may have been passing through, scouting
a city and a profession, and found himself on an alert afternoon
stopping in on the aging-father and crippled-son cabinetmak-

ers. Hannah was fifteen, and by most accounts, pert and presentable, with the level gaze and open face of a country-raised child, despite the cramped and septic streets of Salem that had been her only society. The letter has survived in Pynchon family memorabilia, for the Pynchons are one of New England's upstanding families. I take no particular pride in having discovered it; it is reprinted in several anthologies. This modernized example comes from *Puritans Come A-Courting: Romantic Love in an Age of Severity* (University Presses of New England, 1972):

My dear Fitch:

    My son, Solomon Pynchon of this city, having attained the Age of three and twenty and completed the Apprenticeship suitable to his Calling and Competence in the Candling and Provisioning of Ships begs Leave to ask the Hand in Marriage of your fair Daughter, the esteemed Hannah Easton, beneficiary of your Christian Intervention at the Time of her ultimate Distress and Orphaning. The highest Praise of her sober craftsmanship and Diligence and Virtue have reached Our Ears, bespoken by those Patrons who wear and display with Pride its Evidence.

    I am not a Wealthy man but as a publican my Prospects rise with that of my City. The steady Progress of these past Years give no Evidence of soon abating. I am therefore Pledged to make over to my Son the Sum of Five Hundred (500) Pounds Upon Successful Completion of Marriage Agreements and binding over of Legal Documents, and a further one Thousand (1,000) to follow upon exchange of Marriage Vows. Such amount shall permit the Establishment in Boston of Solomon Pynchon Ships Candlers & Provisioners, which, through careful Nurturing and the Beneficent Protection of

*the One True and Almighty God, shall provide Comfort and
Security for the families and issue of this noble Union.*

That particular letter is well known and frequently an-
notated for the evidence of close attention paid to finances and
practicalities, and for the awkward display of passion in a
Puritan context. The evidence of a dialogue, a response, however, has never been presented. For three hundred years the
painfully earnest marriage proposal of the well-off Solomon
Pynchon to the anonymous seamstress of humble origins, Hannah Easton, has gone unanswered and unacted upon. (Hannah
apparently was known both by her birth name of Easton and
that of her adoptive parents, but scholars had never put the
two identities together.) For three hundred years, young Solomon has twisted in agony, a symbol of impotence and futility.
(See *Neyther Myles Standish nor Solomon Pynchon Bee: Marriage
Negotiation in Two New England Societies*, by my old Yale pro-
fessor Asa Brownledge.) Scholars have cited the letter as evidence of social mobility in Puritan New England; feminists
have seized upon its implied sexism. No one, however, identified Hannah Easton as Hannah Fitch aka Precious-as-Pearl
and the Salem Bibi. If Solomon Pynchon's marital overture
had been accepted, the history of the United States would have
been profoundly altered.

But there was a response.

"My dear Pynchon," writes Robert Fitch, revealing a tone
that seems slightly warmer, or at least indicative of earlier
contact,

*the Child to whom you refer and wish to welcome to your
Family if by her leave she be so willing, is not my rightful
Daughter, as might be ascertain'd at a glance, but is our*

Daughter none the less. Her father, an educated gentleman late of England, Cultivator and town Clerk, perish'd fifteen years ago most suddenly, still in the prime of his manhood, leaving the young wife and infant daughter without physical or pecuniary Protection in that most perilous and misbegotten of Townships, the Village of Brookfield. God's bountiful Mercy spared the Father and Husband the sight of slaughter and Abduction that Haunt the few Survivors even unto this Day.

The Child came into our family on the night of her mother's Abduction, and never in the intervening years has Word been rec'd of her Christian burial. The sauvages treat the body of their fallen with no more Courtesy than the carcass of a skinn'd bear, preferring their Dogs supp upon the remnants than they Bee commended to the Throne of God. I Believe the Ghost of the Girl's Mother still Dwells in the Heart and treads the Breast of our Daughter. She can never truly permit herself to Be Our Daughter.

It is the Ghost's teaching and there is nothing She has learned from my Goodwife or the Salem Congregation that causes her Fingers to be so infected, that so pollutes her Eye with infamous design, to make of the plain and simple Necessities that might cover the shame of Nakedness in Man and Woman a Proud and Unseemly Decorativeness, as Unneeded as Paints and feathers on a sauvage.

Allow me, my dear Pynchon, to spare your Son the Agonie we have known, and such can never be known by Those who have but Commercial Intercourse with Her; if the Angel of Death marks His Brides not with the Pain of physical Suffering, but is made known through Disruption of the Humours, Infections of the Very Soul, then we have been

Warned of His evil Intent to claim Her as His Bride, and
we shall Warn others in our Turn.

It is not from Scorn, but by Respect that we must now
Act and humbly decline the further Approach of your most
esteemed Son. Our Daughter rests comfortably as she is able
with us and we Guard her remaining Days. We do not seek
to more deeply Arouse yr. Son's Resolve through our contrary
Position, as is the Case with so many young Men these last
Days, but only to Spare him the Confusions and the Sadness
that caring for nervous Invalids must surely Impose.

We trust this Ardour shall pass in one so young and
Strong as your Son, and we have not intimated his Feelings
to our Daughter, lest it Disrupt her Balance further.

I want to think of Robert Fitch as a man ahead of his time,
or at the very least, a decent embodiment of the tolerant forces
in his age. He had suffered, yet survived; his type has endured
and is alive today, living by values they trust, disturbed and
finally confused by events larger than any system they can put
them into.

He could not understand Hannah. What she had witnessed, what she suppressed. It is just that Hannah is a person
undreamed of in Puritan society. Of course she must suffer
"spells" and be judged an invalid. Outside agencies—the
devil, the forest, the Indians—must be blamed. She is from
a different time, the first person, let alone the first woman,
to have had these thoughts, and this experience, to have been
formed in this particular crucible. Either she will take society
with her to a new level, or she will perish in the attempt.
Either people will follow, or they will kill her.

Looking at Hannah through the lens of history (I try to

tell Venn, who understands these things, who supports me as best he's able, who sees that the quest I'm on through history is also a kind of love song to him, his "inputting" and virtual reality, his own uncommunicable Indian childhood, the parts of him that I can't reach and the parts of me he's afraid to ask about) is like watching the birth of a nebula through the Hubble Space Telescope—a chance encounter that ties up a thousand loose ends, that confirms theories, upsets others.

Her life is at the crossroads of many worlds. If Thomas Pynchon, perhaps one of the descendants of her failed suitor, had not already written V., I would call her a V., a woman who was everywhere, the encoder of a secret history.

But no wedding came of the epistolary negotiation. If Hannah Easton or Hannah Fitch broke Solomon's heart, he did indeed get over it. Records show he fathered fifteen children by three wives, but that his Candlers & Provisioners burned down in 1703 and he never rebuilt or restored his fortune. He died a debtor and an alcoholic in 1713. And if Hannah ever learned of Solomon's interest, approved or despaired of Robert Fitch's extraordinary intervention, no record of her feelings exists.

"Incestuous, obviously," my cynical self, my well-trained feminist half, reading these notes, has told me. "The stepfather and stepbrother wanted her to themselves. They needed the money she brought in. She was an old maid of twenty, and we know she was a damned handsome woman. There must have been men beating down the door, and the old coot must have spread the rumors of her madness from Marblehead to Barnstable."

I am aware of multiple contingencies. It is the universe we inhabit. She might have been a prisoner; they might have been her tender guardians. The fact is, she stayed in Salem with the Fitches through the famous witch trials, in which she played a small role as counselor of women who fled marriages and husbands they no longer understood. Some of her customers who had patronized her with colored silks suddenly came to her on the street begging shelter. We know the Fitches feared their stepdaughter would be next, that she would personally intervene in some witch's trial, offering testimony that could only implicate her or her family, and that she could not depend upon her childhood woes as a reliable indulgence before a judge like John Hathorne or, worse, confess to having unnatural thoughts, impure impulses herself. They hid her wild embroidery; they barred entreaties; they monitored every visitor. Only the oldest friends, the Mannings, were allowed access.

Through the terrible winter of 1691, Hannah remained indoors, fed the news by her chair-bound brother, sung to and prayed over by her uncomprehending mother and father.

9

IN 1692 Hannah was twenty-one, still a maiden, and with slim expectations of being married—as we have seen. The barrenness of her future had to do with genealogy and poverty, and the hints of noncompliance, of contrary independence that her character had begun to reveal.

In the evenings she embroidered landscapes—frost stiffening blades of grass, pumpkins glowing like setting suns, butterflies dusting colors off their pastel wings against cassocks of black silk and breeches of black velvet. In fact, there was a wildness about Hannah. People sensed it. When she raced down Herbert Street, bolts of silk clutched against the dark wool of her bodice, they found themselves adding on her head an imaginary tiara of tightly furled red roses.

Hester Manning still had not married, which is not to say there had not been opportunities, entreaties and even the hint of a misalliance. Young men were now barred from the male camaraderie around the smithy's anvil. The raw communion of souls, the opportunity to view men, stand near them, even talk with them on the basis of some familiarity and power— she was, after all, daughter of the forge, occasional squeezer of the bellows, stoker of coal, forager among the clinkers with the long tongs—had been taken from her all because of the sudden appearance of Gabriel Legge.

He claimed to be the son of the owner of the *Swallow*, three hundred and twenty tons. He had come from London, but hailed from Ireland, to scout the colonies for investment, for new forms of imports and exports to the New World to mark its growing stature, its great wealth and taste for finer things. But the old Friends of the Forge, meeting now at a public house rather than the blacksmith's, guessed the scouting trip was for a wife, that his time limit was the three weeks it would take to load the *Swallow* with its cargo of hides and timber, and that his eyes had fallen on everyone's darling, Hester Manning.

Or rather, his eye had fallen. Gabriel Legge, though tall and dashing, had an eye patch. In a wild colony of scalped

heads, missing limbs, branded miscreants, maimed and dis-
eased survivors of fires and massacres, a one-eyed man—especially if the patch be black or red or green, sometimes silk,
sometimes velvet and even at times encrusted with fine
gemstones—is prince. And the stories he told! He made the
loss of an eye a stylish statement, pliable to all situations.

My eye! Oh, 'twas nothing, madam. A trifle.

Beware, my good fellow, or I'll take my vengeance here
and now!

Aye, there are savages abroad that make your heathen
Nipmuc and Narragansett the very lambs of God!

Tortured? Punished? Heroic? No one knew for sure. He
had a thousand stories of imprisonment by Turks; banishment
to forests; brigands, highwaymen, pirates.

N O O N E in Salem, admittedly, was a match for Gabriel
Legge. Many were stronger, of course, and as for the disposition
to place strength in the service of pugnaciousness, the young
men of Salem had few equals in the Bay Colony. But Gabriel
Legge had a quality—exercised a charm, some said, cast a
spell—over men and women alike. And there was always the
absence behind the patch, evidence that if charm and persua-
siveness failed him, he knew other, darker devices.

He painted great word pictures of a future Salem as great
as London, of wealth and grandeur, noble parks and public
buildings, and rows of opulent houses appointed with the finest
decorations of the Old World and the New. And Gabriel Legge
seemed to embody those qualities in his height and accent; he
was truly fit to rule, some said, like the worthy inheritor of
a bequest not yet given.

And the men wondered if Hester Manning would be fine

enough for Gabriel Legge? Hard to imagine the smith's daughter dressed as a lady, traveling from court to court, or even holding her own in Salem or Boston. She might have been too refined, too high and mighty, for the likes of local boys, but those very same boys began to see the awkwardness—the dullness—of Hester around Gabriel Legge. They noticed her trying all the harder to please, to be ladylike, however, and they felt a hint of Gabriel's disapproval, even in his kindly smiles toward her. He is the disconcerting agent of Providence in this history.

HANNAH WENT for long lonely walks each morning that May to flee the contrary love she detected in her two mothers' sharp-tongued injunctions. "Moderation!" Susannah Fitch cautioned, afraid not only of the mob psychosis of the street, but also of her daughter's destiny that was beginning to shape itself. But Rebecca, whose blood quickened her, and whose memory for its very remoteness knew no abatement, counseled confrontation. "Raze it, raze it, even to the foundation!" whispered her mother's ghost.

The ghost wore the outline of an Indian sewn on her sleeve. Indian lover.

On one such May morning, Hannah was skipping along a sheer, stony promontory near the new clapboard dwelling of Captain William Maverick, her footsteps as printless as an elf's, when she heard a man's throaty cry of grief. She loosened the knotted ribbons of her bonnet to see and hear better.

All around her was order, continuity, contentment. Winds scraped sibilant music off the moss. Hardy columbines pushed through the tiniest cracks in the rocks. Spring grass greened afresh between dried-out stalks of mullein. Dead, fallen-off branches ringed and enriched the roots of aged elms.

Who was crying out to her in so much anguish?

Winds lifted the bonnet, freeing her hair to curl around her face and surge around her shoulders in tense, electric waves. She lunged for her bonnet, but it whirled out of reach and spiraled down to the shore and finally snagged to rest on a clump of weeds. The bonnet was lost. All the same, she inched as close as she dared to where the promontory sheared away. She crept through a thicket of violets. Sorrowful voices floated up to her.

Three fishermen were beaching a small boat, men who pushed their prows through the horizon. Now the horizon had swallowed one of them. She recognized first of all Captain Maverick, the closest inhabitant to the scene. The men were all knee-deep in the water, stumbling on the slippery stones. Maverick pulled the boat to shore, facing her; two others pushed from the stern. She stretched closer to the precipice on her stomach, flattening tufty grass and loosening shallow-rooted lace plants from the interstices of rock.

When the boat was beached, one of the pushers heaved a body out of the gunwales. The smith, Henry Manning, normally a silent, composed man, was screaming words into the wind, words that she couldn't understand. This was not his part of the town. Nothing but the sheerest tragedy could bring Henry Manning to water, he who despised boats and England and had seen the courtship of Legge and his daughter as an assault upon his dearly held prejudice and authority. And now they were together, for the third man was the mysterious visitor from Ireland, Gabriel Legge, he of the rakish black eye patch, and Hannah knew only one event could bring such enemies together.

She couldn't see the whole body, only a hand. The hand was rigid and got in the men's way. Henry Manning was looking older now, frailer, than she had ever seen him. He leaned his full weight on an oar and instructed the younger men. Suddenly she saw it—stuck like a pennant on a hooked pole that Gabriel Legge was sliding under the body for better leverage—a soggy fragment of Hester's dress. Hannah, keening now with grief, scrabbled down the stony trails.

Hester's corpse was laid out on grass by the time she got close. The arms stuck way out of the body, stiffened in the posture of a woman who had jumped off the precipice, then tried to slow her fatal descent. The two men of her life weighted Hester's arms down with rocks as they looked around for rope or cloth to lash them tight to her body. Henry Manning stood by the boat, mopping his angry, red neck.

She must have bobbed for hours in brackish water. Now weeds twined her body like sea snakes. Bruises the blue of violets blossomed on her face.

"Fine things she wanted!" Henry Manning spat in Gabriel Legge's direction. He heard Hannah's weeping. Hester's eyelids were stuck open. Her lips were twisted into a bitter gaping O. Or "No!" It was as though Hester had changed her mind as the water hit her face.

The stranger deflected Henry's wrath away from Hannah. "Ah, what's wrong with wanting to cultivate yourself?" Then he and Captain Maverick fell to making a stretcher out of oars and a sail. Hannah slunk away. She could not bear to stay and watch them load Hester up, like slaughtered meat, or a cabinet.

THE DAY AFTER Hester's funeral, the stranger, dressed in a cassock of showy blue satin with a matching, embroidered blue silk patch, called on Robert Fitch. He did not come to have furniture made. He introduced himself as Gabriel Legge of Danagadee, son of a shipowner in the business of ferrying families from the Old to the New England. He asked for, and received, permission to court Hannah. She thrilled to his seafaring yarns. He had jumped pirate ship in Madagascar. He had slept in the Garden of Eden, inside an Asian mountain guarded by angels. Children enchanted the deadly cobra with a mere piped melody, the same snake that lurched from its basket and killed an Englishman's servant dead on the spot. He had traveled to Samarkand on camel-back, and he had been to the court of the Great Mughal, whose ostentatious display of gold and jewels made him ashamed of England's shabby pretension. The soil of Hindustan was ground-up sapphire, emerald and ruby; the building bricks were pure ingots of gold. Their food simmered in its own spices, quite independent of the application of cooking fire. The women wrapped themselves in silken winding-sheets, and because of their soft, compliant souls, they yielded their lives to flame upon their husband's death.

She did not believe him, but she, too, longed for escape. And what had become of his suit with Hester Manning, Hannah was bold enough to ask, had he been fearful enough of her broad-backed father not to press his case?

He paid her memory the proper respect. Like many a man before him, he had been led on by her smile, her cheekiness, her apparent boldness. But when the talk had turned to his travels and his dreams, he'd seen her face set in a frown.

"The lass would fair tie me down to England and English ways," Gabriel Legge said. Her passion was more to leave that place, Salem, and the boys around the forge, and her father, than to settle in another place with him. Especially a place of harrowing discomfort, unfamiliar and uncongenial to her narrow sensibilities. She would go only halfway round the world with him, the tiresome, well-trod half, to England. He had not guessed the depths of her fancy, if not for him, then for some of the stories he told.

"My stories all have a grain, a fair grain, of truth to them, Mistress Fitch," he confessed, "and none are spun from whole cloth—"

"You are known for your rampant embroidery, Gabriel Legge. I feared only that you had begun to believe them yourself. I may be a simple girl who has seen none of the earth and its truths, and what you say of the oceans and the mountains may well be true. But, Mr. Legge, I know the heart of womenkind, and none do willingly yield their lives."

"Perhaps this you would believe, Hannah Easton," he said, and with that he took from the watch pocket of his silken vest a small sachet of gemstones, including a ruby more perfect than any she had ever imagined.

"This is yours. This and a thousand more like it are waiting for us."

She closed her fist upon it. A cool fire burned her hand. He wanted an Empress of his own, fit for the Emperor of Dreams.

In the negotiations with Robert Fitch he remained the sober businessman, the shipowner's son. He did not expect a dowry; a healthy, strong, God-fearing woman was all a man could claim a right to, although furniture was always welcome, and the *Swallow* in the harbor was still loading freight. For a cherry-and-maple highboy and dining table of solid cherry, the dowry was set. By the time of the *Swallow*'s sailing, Hannah and Gabriel were married. It would be ten years before she saw Salem again.

WHY WOULD a self-possessed, intelligent, desirable woman like Hannah Easton suddenly marry a man she recognized as inappropriate and untrustworthy? Why would she accept Hester Manning's castoff, or betrayer? Guilt, perhaps, a need to punish herself for the secret she was forced to carry? Unconscious imitation of her mother, a way of joining her by running off with a treacherous alien? Gabriel Legge with his tales of exotic adventure was as close to the Nipmuc lover as any man in Salem; she sought to neutralize her shame by emulating her mother's behavior.

Venn, who listens and is about to get more interested in the tale as it moves away from New England, has his own interpretation. Gabriel was obviously on a wife-hunting mission, the way many Indian students in America go back to India for a week and get married to satisfy their parents, then return with a stranger who can cook, bear children, and, eventually, be loved. In other words, *why not*? She got married because it was her time to get married. Just like you, he says to me, what if you hadn't read *Auctions & Acquisitions* one morning? What if the name Pearl hadn't leaped off the page? You got started on this the same way Hannah did when she walked out along the beach one day and saw the boat and the men hauling the body ashore.

So one morning she was content with her passionate needlework, smugly contemptuous of Hester and her suitor; the next morning she walked to the river because it was her time to be in the path of death, to witness grief, to hear Gabriel's strange defense of luxury, and expose herself to the possibility of life.

We do things when it is our time to do them. They do not occur to us until it is time; they cannot be resisted, once their time has come. It's a question of time, not motive.

10

GABRIEL LEGGE'S father turned out to be an indebted drunk from Morpeth, not a shipowner from Danagadee. Ancestral lands in Northumberland, those that had not been seized by creditors or lost in successive lawsuits, had been given out to Gabriel's far-older brother, the sober but dull-witted Morgan Legge. Gabriel looked upon his place in the birth order—second son, fourth child—as providential. No land to root him, and not a groat's worth of family fortune to tempt him into staying and currying favor.

"Can you imagine me herding sheep? Married to a ewe like my wretched brother?" It was true; Morgan and his wife, named Felicity, whom Hannah called Fleece, and brood of children did come south once to pay their respects and to inspect the homemaking skills of the New World bumpkin their brother had hooked. Hannah had the impression of having been visited by a flock of geese rather than blood relatives.

Homemaking skills, in the world of Morgan Legge, had decided linkages with submission and stupidity. It was man-

dated that the wife should not outshine the husband in anything but parental wealth. In the case of Fleece, a serving girl
on a neighboring farm, this condemned her to permanent
eclipse.

Hannah, orphaned by secrecy and a bee sting, had set great
store by family, having forbidden herself to think too deeply
of her mother. It did not seem possible that actual blood
relatives could not unlock a secret, did not possess in abun-
dance, a side of oneself otherwise hidden or left undeveloped.
Morgan, squat, short, fair and balding, with two eyes and
seven children, wiped that expectation from Hannah's mind.
She was grateful for the absence of family, the absence of
definition and expectation.

She had married a man as singular in his society, as inex-
plicable to Morpeth, as she was in Salem. His life was a mystery
to her, fabulously rich when he chose to embellish it, but
otherwise a blank. He could describe the interior of a Mongol
tent, the smell of camels, the pink flesh inside the trunk of a
raja's elephant, but he could not, or would not, answer the
simplest question about the ships he sailed or the captains he
served. He pointed out to her that his life was provisional. In
the parts of the South Atlantic and Indian oceans that he plied,
the odds were better than even that any voyage he undertook
would be his last. She would be well looked after; that's all
he could guarantee.

W H E N Hannah Easton Fitch Legge left Salem for England
in 1692, the Massachusetts Bay Colony had been in existence
for sixty-two years. Time enough for a full range of political
responses to have evolved. New World Man was either an
ungrateful wretch wallowing in moral regression, or the up-

right angel of God's green promise, reaping the rewards of sober rectitude. Reading those responses today—the charges and countercharges—is a shock: we have not changed in three hundred years. The colonists were not grateful or respectful enough to the Crown and the Mother Country; the colonists were ignorance personified and insufficiently ashamed of their backwardness; the colonists were proud and self-reliant, New World giants to Europe's dwarfs. England's Noblest Party, England's Folly. The New World was hard and savage; it was soft and bountiful. It was evil, it was innocent. England was refined and cultured; it was soiled and sinful. Probably every colonist and every Englishman ascribed to one or many of those views, serially or simultaneously, whatever the nature of their mutual contradiction.

Hannah personally knew many old men and women in Salem who'd arrived on the *Arabella* with John Winthrop in 1630, and who had been intimately involved with every aspect of establishing a colony. It was unclear if by their beliefs they honored more the pristine, God-given nature of the world they first beheld, or their own vain scratchings on its surface. First-ers, she called them, those who believed, passionately, that the first time anything had been made, built, eaten, sold or raised was inevitably the best. They believed that God had guided their hands in those first harsh years, not permitting them to fail; therefore any second-generational dwelling, any frivolous or decorative activity, were by definition the devil's vengeance. She was aware of Firsters' disapproval, the implied fall into sin and perdition that greeted every change. From the Firsters, whom Robert and Susannah Fitch admired, Han-nah had always kept her distance. Each death of an *Arabella* passenger, which called for public mourning and which offered a ritualized occasion for a renewed accounting of the colony's moral slackness, followed by a momentary rededication to values no one intended to live by, struck Hannah as unseemly idolatry.

And there were those in the Bay Colony who counted themselves fortunate to be America-born, free of the taint of Old World strictures, who believed with a kind of reckless arrogance that America had not only purified but also enlarged and redeemed the human soul. The idea of England as a soiled and fallen world, as opposed to merely a savage one, was part of their catechism. They were proud of their backwardness; they mocked the dandies as they disembarked; they reveled in using and broadening their own American accent, which had already ironed out the multifarious wrinkles of British regionalism.

Hannah, though aware of both tendencies among her countrymen, found herself easily embarrassed by their expression. Nothing in colonial society had demonstrated its unalienable claim on her affection. Nothing in English society, or among recently arrived Englishmen, excited her contempt. The English, like her husband, seemed vastly more exciting and knowledgeable and appreciative than the men of Salem; on the other hand, their scrutiny extended to realms of social rank that seemed to her false measures of value.

And England itself, though it might be an exhausted force, as colonists liked to think, still compelled a fascinated study. Like all things fallen, it held a certain attraction. The moral superiority that grew out of the contest with savagery was but one category of excellence. There was wealth and trade and culture, history and the great common pulse of humanity, that surged from the streets of London. That, too, counted.

Always dutiful, she kept a diary (*London Sketches by an Anonymous Colonial Daughter* [University Presses of New England, 1967]) intended—or at least contrived—as epistles to a distant mother, for sharing with Susannah back in Salem. Three were published in Boston papers (heretofore unidentified as to authorship), with some twelve holograph pages having been preserved in the Colonial Archives Wing of the British Museum. They offer as vigorous an assessment of English life in the Dutch King William III's years as any on record. She didn't travel often into the city, saw no plays, had few friends. Her husband was often gone to sea. She was, in other words, an ideal correspondent, the perfect reporter. Seeing no one, going nowhere, doing nothing, she learned to cultivate her own garden.

There were those she had known in Salem who dreamed of a "return" to England, who viewed their years in the colony as a fiduciary sentencing preferable only to imprisonment, an abbreviated means of establishing property and a name for themselves uncontended by a thousand others immediately more qualified than they were. In her letters, she addressed those friends, calling them (in the manner of "Firsters") Desponders. Her letters are addresses from England to Expatriates and Nativists.

> *Consider my old friend, Dr. Aubrey. Thinking himself a superior Specimen of Training & Dedication, most especially to Colleagues (how he grinds his Teeth at the Thought, the Impudence of implied Equality!) trained in the Colonies, he deigns to serve in poxy Boston-town expecting no less than Knighthood for passing two winters apart from the subtle shadings of social Nuance held dear in his native York-*

shire. . . . For Colonial Indifference to protocol, which we might translate as perceiv'd Insults to his imperial Self, our medical Servant closes down his Office and grants Interviews to all and sundry, assuring that his Leavetaking shall be no less attended than his Arrival.

Unremark'd in our obedient and worshipful Press is the fact he had charged his Patients at three times the Tariff of Physicians trained in unsavoury local Colleges like Harvard, and that the perceptible rate of Recovery among his patients is less than the Average that local Sachems might affect from the Gathering and Brewing of Herbs and tree Barks. . . .

But she was no less shrewd in the skewering of colonial custom.

A gentle neighbour, to whom I give the name Mister Mowberry, return'd but a fortnight from the town of Duxbury, has latterly regal'd me with a tale of utter Degradation wrought by zealous upholders of colonial Virtue.

Your gentle correspondent knows well of what she speaks, having witness'd in fair Salem such brazen Gatherings of shiftless Acorns.

Consider a gentleman prepar'd to export to the Colony the purest product of England, namely the wealth of its culture and mental training, who borrows against inheritance in the pursuit of credentials in Land-Surveyance & Committment of Quitclaim, only to arrive in Boston, expecting no more than a civil welcome, to be greeted by stone-throwing ruffians who mock his clothes, his cultivated accent; estate-agents in his chosen City who refuse the Let of lodgings lest he pay a year's deposit in advance; & the Assurance from those court-house Jesters who constitute our native Aristocracy, that no Claim adjudicated by an Englishman has a chance of being Recorded. . . .

GABRIEL LEGGE was a compulsive seafarer, signing on as a mate whenever he could secure a boat. He'd be gone for six months at a stretch, then home for a few weeks, jolly as always, establishing a market for the silks and gemstones he'd secured on his travels. For Hannah, whom he'd wooed with tales of adventure and travel—in some cases transparent with fabrication if not outright fraud—forbearance settled in as the handmaiden of passion. She, who had been raised in a home in which Robert Fitch was never absent, but the income depended upon her sewing for the barest subsistence, accepted the crude arithmetic of survival: *man out the gate, worth the wait; man in the house, mend your blouse.* Lacking a reliable means of comparison, Hannah counted herself a contented wife.

Since she was to write so movingly of sexual passion in her later years, in a voice that is unique among women in her time and place, I have tried to read carefully between the lines of all her correspondence. Her written record is one long chronicle of discoveries, her curiosity extends to every branch of knowledge she ever had contact with. Except sexual love, at least with Gabriel Legge. They lived together in Stepney fewer than three months before he shipped out the first time.

GABRIEL WAS an artful salesman; on each official voyage he did some buying and selling of his own, and always for outrageous profit, and always brought home a pouchful of

Golconda diamonds the size of acorns. He wasn't greedy like the ship's captain, who took with him cargoes of porcelain and cut glass, hunting dogs, horses and cases of rum. The Captain brought back gold-handled flyswatters, brocades fit for duchesses, spices that smelled up all of London. What manner of bejeweled insect earned its dispatch from a gold-handled swatter? Gabriel's tales of the wealth of India, its utterly useless wealth, employed to no end, ignorant of investment, leading to no greater social good, seemed calculated to confront, to subvert, even a reluctant Puritan's finer sensibilities. To admire a thing in and of itself, to honor an activity merely for being, these were alien and uncomfortable concepts.

Gabriel got his kicks from haggling, not from hoarding. He wanted Hannah to overcome her Puritan failing of frugality and spend. And Hannah did, at first to oblige her husband; later, because she loved fine things. She decorated the house in Stepney; she made and sold garments from the exotic cloths; portable curios, like jeweled smoking pipes and flyswatters, she sent to Susannah, Robert and Thomas with trustworthy emigrants.

The maritime trade museum in William Maverick's old house just outside Salem holds many of those objects under glass. Even Mr. Satterfield fails to understand: Hannah's hands are on everything.

For what could Gabriel Legge do in London? He was as much a stranger to the city as she. He saw himself a nectar-gathering bee, bounding from flower to flower, returning to his Queen only when dusted with gold. His name for her was Queenie. He was to her the Jack of Spades, for his one eye, his mysterious and slightly mischievous ways.

And so, the first and second years, 1692 and '93, while Gabriel traveled the Orient, barely surviving storms off the Cape, pirates in Madagascar, an uprising by the bedraggled and degraded dwellers of St. Helena, where an earlier governor had notched the ears of malcontents and threatened to do the same to sailors, Hannah polished her correspondence, observed the world that passed outside her cottage, tended her garden, content, too, with the harmonious arrangement of houses and gardens all around her and with the tidiness of the meadows and the shallow placidity of the little ponds just beyond—and fell, briefly, in love.

So content, in fact, that she did not suffer the despondency that is as much the prelude to as the aftermath of a wayward passion.

11

T H E   N E W S of Gabriel Legge's death arrived loudly and irreverently with a toss of gravel on her sleeping-room window. "Widow Legge, a message." A large, obviously seafaring young man, inebriated but sociable, startled her at dawn as she was poking the grate to light her morning fire. His bulky, uneven body blocked the door frame. He had obviously slept aboard his ship, and the fumes of close companionship and nighttime rum had not yet lifted.

"Widow Legge?"

She blocked the word. The name was not uncommon. Up

close she could see he was far younger than his deformities—
congenital, vocational and accidental—had made him. Probably her own age, younger than Gabriel, but toothless, ill-
fed, with the tops of his ears practically serrated from so many
penal notchings.

"I am the wife of Gabriel Legge," she answered.

"Then double's the loss, I warrant."

He dangled a familiar purse in front of him and dropped
its heavy, metallic contents in her hand. For the first time she
actually believed the unthinkable might have occurred. It was
Gabriel's.

"A good chap, brave and decent to his crew. Died de-
fending King and ship's company agin the Portugee. Most
chaps what dies at sea leave nought but brats and a crone
behind. A less honorable man would not have gold to dispense,
my lady. Many's the last request that goes unhonored, if you
follow my thinking."

She did, sufficiently, to endow his fidelity, and to safeguard
her husband's good name. "Did you see my Gabriel—at the
end?"

"Nae. We, ah, engaged the Portugee ourselves off Zeloan.
The captain at pain of a slow dishonorable death divulged the
names of East Indiamen and English ships he'd boarded and
scuttled and what survived of their crews. None, I fear. He
has a cuttlefish for his confessor now."

Like that, at age twenty-three, she was a widow. Her third
"epistle" to the Salem press was on the comforts of widowhood,
the acceptance of God's design, the smaller pleasures of seasonal
blooms, on attuning oneself to the cycles of nature, the assurance that one's husband had served the King bravely, and
that his contributions and honor had been loyally engraved in
the collective memory.

The letter lacks the bite of the other two. At the very moment of dramatic grief, of total loss, Hannah's spirit failed her. It is a letter no different from any of its time, eloquent and predictable. She had moved on.

AS HER EPISTLES to Salem indicate, she'd never led an entirely solitary existence during the months of Gabriel's absence at sea. I have no doubt of her chastity in the conventional sense; her years in England may have corresponded to the era of Restoration comedy, but Stepney was far outside the drawing rooms of fops and dandies. She confined herself to the bleak society of her fellow Stepney brides, the doctors, the emigrants and repatriates who sought her out for nostalgia's sake. But now, as befitted her new role of widow, she did withdraw completely.

When temptation struck, it would approach by stealth, consistent with her helpful and compassionate nature. In November 1693, during a week of rains that rendered the road outside her cottage a treacherous sea of mud, the axle of a speeding trap broke, spilling the driver and his wife, as well as a boy of seven, into the flooded gully that served as a sewer and lined the roadside. Man and wife survived the accident, she with a broken collarbone, and he with nothing worse than scrapes and bruises. But the boy was thrown onto the stone bridge that spanned the gully and linked Hannah's cottage with the road.

Hannah had been out the door at the sound of the axle's cracking and was already dashing to the road when the child was thrown sharply against the stone bridge. From the sound of the skull's cracking she knew the boy was quite possibly doomed; it was the sound she most dreaded in the world. By the time she reached him, the boy was sitting in the water, attempting to stand, not yet aware of the gravity of his wounds, and the father was shouting against the hiss of rain, "Eh, lad, you took a crack, dintja?" when Hannah gathered the boy in her arms and cried, "Never you mind your trap. Fetch the Doctor for your boy!"

The mother was moaning. The boy turned to his father, smiled and tried to lift his hand, and suddenly stiffened, eyes rolled back, tongue gagging in his throat.

T H E   B L O O D was everywhere, smeared over the dark dining table and cloth she'd embroidered, and deep up her arms as though she had been playing in the cavity of a fresh-stuck pig; when the mother, father and the Doctor arrived half an hour later, wet, mud-plastered from the slick road they'd been forced to walk and the spattering from traps and carriages that had doused them, and the mother, her arm immobilized against her bodice by a torn man's shirt, the boy, whom they'd left in apparent good health with nought but a bruise and a caution, was laid out like a corpse with a blood-drenched witch spooning great gobs of gelatinous blood from a hole she'd bored above the boy's right eye.

"Hag from hell!" the father cried. "You've taken my boy."

"Quick, my leeches," the Doctor commanded. The father had been entrusted with the medicinal bottle of squirming black worms, short, thick and thirsty, tapered at the sucking end for tight body crevices just like this one.

"Yes, the leeches," said Hannah. In her experience treating skull wounds, she'd found more patients were lost to the logic of tightly binding the wounds, attempting to repair the shattered bone and hold it in place by bandaging, than by removing the shards and keeping it open, at least till the bleeding stopped.

The father pushed Hannah aside, threatening to kill her, to expose her as a ghoul and witch.

The Doctor was expert in leech arrangement. Each found a pool of dead blood and began draining it. They elongated and broadened themselves, each tiny black filigree becoming finger-wide and long as the rusty-red pools receded. Then the leeches began their migration to fresh sources of blood, the bright red blood from the tiny vessels prone to easy puncture.

"Pull them off now," Hannah insisted. The father raised his fist at her approach to the boy, and the Doctor hesitated. His tested black beauties had not yet begun to show their ingenuity.

"I have treated these injuries," said Hannah. "You must trust me."

"Madam, I am a physician and bleeder trained by the Royal College."

"And I am a survivor of Indian massacres," said Hannah. "The boy has bled enough. Now we must close him up. Sir, be good enough to remove your leeches."

She refused permission to move the boy, and so he lay on her dining table, the handcrafted cherry table that Gabriel Legge had brought on the *Swallow*; she knew the herbs to boil with the bandages and the importance of changing the dressings and permitting the wound to drain. And all the while, she lectured the Doctor and the parents on the practice of medicine in the Bay Colony, how frontier warfare placed a premium on cranial nurses, how timing was all, how infection wiped out the most delicate surgery, how unpredictable paralyses could result.

None of this seemed logical to the Doctor. He had only his own reputation and that of his domesticated leeches to worry about. As the flesh around the boy's wound turned red and septic, he applied the leeches to the swelling, bringing it down considerably. Then the boy grew pale. If only nature had invented a blood-injecting animal as effective as the leech, something puffed up with blood that deflated itself through a sharp mouthlike organ.

The leeches did their work, Dr. Aubrey (for that was his name) explained several days later when the boy awoke from his coma. His vision was bad; his left arm and leg were numb; his speech was slurred. All in all, the Doctor attested, the results were better than he had expected. Without the prompt intervention of a trained physician with a thorough knowledge of the bleeding portals, however, the boy would have been lost. The housewife was to be congratulated—and forgiven— for her quick, if unconventional, thinking. What she did was instinctual, issuing from a good heart and not, as originally charged, an occult affinity.

It did not end there. Her identity had been discovered. The Doctor sought her out on other cases of head injury. She was not just a sailor's widow; she was in some way a woman blessed with healing powers. People began coming to her for poultices, for bone setting, for the laying on of hands. Yes, it was true: she could regenerate skin after certain burns and other scarring. She knew woodland secrets. Some said she possessed uncanny powers, the sort associated with conjurers and devils (those who heal by suspension of God's law can also inflict injury at long distance through the agency of the Prince of Darkness), and wasn't it passing strange that she hailed from Salem, the very town where the prevalence of witches had called special courts into session and brought down God's severest judgment on the most recalcitrant? She needed Dr. Aubrey's defense and public-spirited protection, and got it.

In Salem, it had taken twenty years before her special qualities had come out, or at least before she began to trust the voices inside her. In England, it had taken only a year. And by the spring of 1694, the voice had found a shape.

The man's name was Hubert—we don't know his last name. Hannah was twenty-four, widowed for a year. He was her age, but in appearance much older, as befit his scholarly bent. His first visit to her Stepney cottage was due to injury —a compound fracture of his left arm—that had grown septic and threatened the need for amputation. He had been bled repeatedly but the reduction in swelling offered no permanent relief. Finally Dr. Aubrey had recommended the Widow Legge and her poultices.

Hubert was a man altogether different from any she'd known. Whereas Gabriel Legge was physically blessed—tall, straight and immensely strong (with the rakish eye patch that added a touch of abandonment and tragedy to all his adventures)—Hubert was bespectacled in the Dutch manner that had become fashionable with the accession of William and Mary. His corn-silk-blond hair was thinning, his ears were long and fleshy, his teeth yellowed from constant pipe smoking. He was educated in Mr. Newton's New Sciences of Mathematics and Physics and held a position as a researcher with the Royal Society. He had traveled to the Continent and met his colleagues in France and Florence, and spoke of them not as rivals in politics, trade or military force, but as fellow discoverers of sacred knowledge.

In fact, Hubert's ignorance in matters of the real world rivaled no one's that Hannah had ever met. She sprang from

alert, educated port-city people. Curiosity, within limits
(which she frequently tested), was a virtue. Until Gabriel
Legge, and then Hubert, Hannah's investment in the word
"discovery" had been limited to people far below her in education, and high above her in what might be called craft,
wile and survival. The discoverers she had known proceeded
not by experiment, like Hubert, but certain knowledge and
unbending ritual, like the forest Indians, or the ministers of
God. Their knowledge of the natural world, or the spiritual
world, seemed to her immense but finite, learnable. Hubert's
knowledge, and his means of gaining even more learning, were
of a different order. She knew many more things than he did.
But what was knowable, in Hannah's sense, was also dis-
countable. He was interested in learning only those things
that his own experiments also created. He could not teach his
methods, or his results, to her.

He devised instead a system whereby her knowledge of
herbs and barks and certain surgical practices followed a logical
pattern. They were not isolated facts. What had seemed a set
of arbitrary facts, that bandages should be clean, water should
be boiled, bleeding should be cauterized and not prolonged
by leeches, that certain natural aids had medicinal qualities,
and that these practices often induced favorable results, pointed
to a larger synthesis of knowledge.

And what could that be? Hubert believed in a medical
heresy so bizarre that even to speak it would imperil his standing as a scientist. Nor was he a doctor. He studied Life Processes, and his observations suggested to him the possibility
that illness and infection and perhaps even disease itself were
not related to spells and self-generated evils, but to invisible
and invasive forces from nature.

Hubert was not disturbed by her widowhood. He saw her

only as a young woman of vigorous mind and spirit in need of more stimulating surroundings and a gentler community of intelligent women. He meant Cambridge, where she could find lodging and employment as a governess. She suspected that he also meant marriage, after a decent interval, but to his credit or his shame, it was never mentioned.

Gabriel Legge had left her sufficient money to indulge her own independence, at least for several years, and the control over it was entirely hers. Eventually, of course, she would have to marry again or find suitable employment, or perhaps even return to Massachusetts, but none of those decisions seemed pressing. She recognized, as Hubert spoke of the Continent and the unfettered life of the mind that he led, so different from the fancies that drove Gabriel Legge's fabulous journeys, that the thought of travel excited her. She was tired of waiting at home, of not bestirring herself in the rich new world opening out at every hand. Even pouches of diamonds did not seem sufficient compensation for idleness.

12

HANNAH'S ALTERNATE prospects of life as a widowed Cambridge governess or as the wife of a placid introvert like Hubert were overthrown just after dawn in late April 1694 by the casual, almost languid, appearance of Gabriel Legge crossing the stone bridge in front of the cottage gate.

He had taken pains over his appearance. Hardly the sailor on leave, he appeared, in his silks and breeches, the gold-crowned walking stick, the powdered wig and the trademark silk eye patch, every inch the imperial magistrate.

"We'll sell the Stepney cottage, of course." It was never suitable for a man of his height. The beams cut across the parlor at eye level. "I presume you'll be ready in a fortnight. We sail for Fort St. Sebastian on the *Fortune*."

"The *Fortune?* The *Fortune!* Whatever happened to the mad Portugee?" She took her cue from Gabriel Legge, for surely had he crawled across the stone bridge begging for forgiveness, seeking accommodation, apologizing for having left her alone and dishonored (which eventually would have been the case), she would have nursed him back to health, forgiven him the hint of deceit in the tale he had told. But he'd rather chosen an approach that admitted nothing, withheld the facts of his past eighteen months and the motives for his cruelty.

"Swallowed by a whale off Grand Comoro and deposited on the Portugee shore. A full desert and jungle year I spent, tearing flesh from the hands of baboons, outwitting the jungle cats, outsmarting the forest savages, joining slavers up the African coast . . ."

The same old Gabriel Legge. He told her that now he had gone down to Leadenhall Street and joined the Honourable East India Company, convinced that his last adventure had exhausted his store of good fortune. His sailing days were over. He'd earned his stake; now was time to think of a career.

"Husband," said Hannah Legge, "the story that was told to me a winter last was most convincing."

"Poor mate."

"You've not just this minute disembarked."

"These trifles? I show you respect by not befouling this cottage."

"I wept for you."

With a smile both amused and sympathetic, Gabriel Legge let her self-pity pass. "You have taken to tobacco in my absence."

"That is unkind."

He sniffed the brocaded cushions, whacking them loudly with the flat of his hand. Dust motes sparkled in the morning light.

"A lingering odor. Madeira soaked. Much affected by squinty-eyed Cambridge swine."

And even as they conducted their interview, the widow and her resurrected groom, Hubert lay in the gutter a few yards below the stone bridge, his fine Dutch glasses twisted from his astonished face, his fleshy ears freshly notched as a slave might be identified by his master, or a common thief punished for a first offense, and a Fornicator's bold *F* branded to the center of his widening forehead. Their morning's work done, Gabriel Legge's mates, including the drunken young man who'd brought the baleful news of Gabriel's demise and then had stationed himself in a nearby public house close enough to watch the mistress's comings and goings, crossed the bridge with the first mate's ornate sea trunks, and one empty locker for the mistress to pack her gear.

THIS IS the best I can do, pulling it together from a hundred sources. I think of Venn, stitching together an October of four years ago, and realize that the most obscure person on the planet today is, comparatively, like a god: observed, adored, commented upon, celebrated. Hannah, whose 1745

Memoirs forms the basis of much of the early life, and only a bit of the middle, the warrant, if you wish, for the linkages in my earlier investigations, still eludes my net. Time has made her free from me, just as an ocean passage made her free of the watchful God who punished every venal sin with droughts, drownings, cripplings. Free from the brutal justice of pious expatriates with confused errands. Out of earshot of the whippings and weepings of Original Sinners.

What made Hannah abdicate sovereign rule of her fenced, peaceable suburban kingdom and sail with Gabriel on the *Fortune*, a four-hundred-ton East Indiaman, in May 1694?

Fear, perhaps, for she knew there was (there always is) a dark side to her husband's rascality. Or simple practicality— she was, after all, a Puritan orphan, strictly raised. She appreciated the value of money. Her widow's subsistence, and with it her freedom, vanished on Gabriel's reappearance.

But there are traits even a modern woman can relate to: her curiosity, the awakening of her mind and her own sense of self and purpose. And I think of Gabriel as well, deceiver, liar, thief and pirate—a gentleman cutthroat with a feared gang to do his bidding—why didn't he kill her, as he had others who displeased or deceived him? Why did he test her, for surely that was his ploy, and why were her indiscretions with doctors, researchers, patients, accusers, not punished?

Venn says he wanted to know if she was prized. If anyone would make a move on her, even more than wanting to test her faithfulness. Gabriel had been in the East; he would know these things.

THE *FORTUNE* was in a convoy of East Indiamen headed for the Coromandel Coast of India by way of the Cape of Good Hope. Hannah's name appears in *Madras Records*, the Fort St. George consultation books, as having disembarked in that English settlement in early 1695. There were three other women on board the *Fortune* on that trip, all three from the same village in Lancashire, and all three single. Their reasons for leaving home were sensible, lucid. The Company paid each of them a monthly maintenance allowance of about fifteen shillings in local currency to provide its bachelor English staff of lonely factors, clerks and soldiers companionship leading, it was hoped, to marriage. Like the Massachusetts Bay Colony, the Honourable Company needed but feared the wilderness, and abhorred miscegenation. Hannah got to know the Lancashire women because, like them, she and Gabriel ate at the third mate's table and grumbled about having to share the decks with livestock that were mainly there as the Captain's and the richer passengers' future provision. A schoolmaster sent out by the Company on the same ship mentions Hannah as being of the four women the only one with comeliness and delicacy. In a letter to his brother started on the *Fortune* and finished in the port town of Masulipatnam, he worried that Mistress Legge will not find any "towne of Moors, fackeers and Hindoos cleane after the manner in England," for "hogs, filth, dirt and swine" clog the streets.

WHAT INTERESTS me about this letter is that the outbound schoolteacher clings to class-conscious perspectives and absorbs Hannah, the flower of the New World Zion, into the Old World hierarchy.

If status had mattered to Hannah, she would have stayed in Stepney. Her curiosity was robust. She wanted to earn, not inherit, dignity. She moved on. Without regrets.

Venn inputs data more boldly, more mischievously than I do. I watch my convoy of East Indiamen voyage across his computer screen, freed of space and time. He compresses by supercomputer Hannah, Gabriel, the schoolmaster, the maiden ladies from Lancashire, caulkers and coopers, soldiers and sailmakers, gunners, cabin boys, two two-headed freak dogs, horses, goats, hogs, sheep, geese, chickens, ducks, plum puddings, vats of pea soup, mutton pies, pork pies, chops, cutlets, potatoes, lemons, rum, beer, dysentery, scurvy, into a one-second-long video model.

Attaining Nirvana, for Venn, is attaining perfect design.

Together and separately we remember what happened to Hannah Easton Fitch Legge aka the Bibi from Salem so that we may predict what will happen to us within our lifetime.

Before you build another city on the hill, first fill in the potholes at your feet.

Heard melodies are sweet, but those unheard
Are sweeter; therefore, ye soft pipes, play on . . .

JOHN KEATS
"Ode on a Grecian Urn"

PART TWO

THE GUIDE, an Indian Christian named Mr. Abraham—I don't know if it's a first name or not— takes me on a tour of the Fort St. Sebastian ruins. Fort St. George, Fort St. Sebastian and all their related remnants of English and Portuguese colonialism are now located in the northern outskirts of the modern city of Madras. This is the place, south of the sluggish Penner River on the Coromandel Coast of the Bay of Bengal, where on a fetid January morning in 1695, from its anchorage on a sand reef half a mile off the shore of Fort St. George, the *Fortune* began its dangerous and laborious unloading of cargo and disembarked Gabriel and Hannah Legge.

The ruins hold no fascination for Mr. Abraham. He is a very thin, up-to-date young man, assiduously elegant in a leisure suit of pale-blue teri-cot, and recently the recipient of a master's degree in commerce from the University of Madras. He listens to test-match cricket from New Zealand on a transistor radio. Free-lancing as a guide for English-speaking tourists is a stopgap. His deportment has in it a protective haughtiness; his dainty, solicitous way of holding a huge, threadbare black umbrella over my melanoma-prone pinkness reveals a man who has greater expectations from life than recycling the faded glories of his subcontinent. He doesn't know it, but his casual graciousness has, in fact, profound historical antecedents. He lets me linger where I want, answers my questions with a shrugged yes and "so they say." Rubble is rubble to him. He lives for development, a South Indian Silicon Valley. He belongs to the future.

I have with me a book of engravings of the original Son-apatnam, and from the fragments of a wall, the rubbled foundation of the customhouse, I can orient myself in time as well as space. I can imagine the customs master, Mir Ali, one of Haider Beg's appointees, spyglass in hand, noting the names and descriptions of all the ships and cargo that sailed into and out of the Bay of Bengal. A loyal man, Mir Ali, without him, Haider Beg would have bankrupted himself a hundred times over. A fifty-yard-long ancient wall of wafer-thin bricks that look, at a distance, like a sheaf of ill-stacked ledger papers once defined the boundary of White Town. Along this wall Hannah Legge would stroll, looking down to the sea and toward forbidden India. And here, still close to the wall, but now crushed for a roadbed, are heaps of white stones from houses that made up the White Town of Fort St. Sebastian. I take up a piece of crushed stone and drop it in my tote bag; it could have been from a wall of Gabriel and Hannah Legge's house. A church and a cemetery overcrowded with sinking headstones still stand, and near the cemetery, a stubby rain-blackened victory tower. Where Mr. Abraham sees collapse, or perhaps even the groundwork for a development scheme, I see the spiderweb of permanence.

A satellite town has grown around, and on, the remains of old Fort St. Sebastian. Settlements here have a parasitic, not homicidal, relationship with nature. Inside the crumbled perimeter of the customhouse, shopkeepers have set up tin-roofed stalls. The whitewashed annex of the municipal school building has usurped a corner of the graveyard. Schoolchildren in sweaty uniforms eat tiffin in the serrated shade of the broken wall. Monkeys leap down from shade trees to snatch food out of their hands. At the foot of the victory tower, a vendor hawks peanuts in newspaper cones.

Whose victory? What led to battle?

But Mr. Abraham forecloses on questions. "These people used to build them all the time only."

These people?

Meaning Muslims and Hindus. Meaning heathens. Mr. Abraham, Christian child of a different intrusion, draws me with a new alacrity toward the cemetery crammed with sunken tombstones. The few stone nubbins still standing are worn clean of inscriptions: each marker carries a typed notice behind a plastic shield. The leaning and fallen stones remind me of conventioneers with name tags clustered by the cash bar. No fence encloses the three-hundred-year-old cemetery. Bony cows graze on untended greenery; pariah dogs doze on sun-warmed headstones.

ISAAC SUCKLING
Death discover'd him
Ere he discover'd Life.

MARY BROWNE
Belov'd wyffe of Col. Josiah Browne
But for whom Vain would be my Toyle
Under this Skye.

On some stones only the name survives. *Clarence Clitherow. Hester Hedges. Henry Hedges. Richard Littleton. Samuel Higginbottham. John Ruxton. James Ord. Count Attila Csycsyry. Michel Joachim Bourguien. François La Touche. Klaus Engelhardt. Antonio de Melho. Francisco da Silva. Ludovico Antonio Apiani. João Muliner. Isabela de Taides. Niccolo Manucci. Hans Van den Brinck. Catchick Sookian. Slaughter Harris.*

One headstone bears no name, only a three-masted pirate vessel and the legend: "Gone off on the account."

Three hundred years ago, Europe converged in a cove on the Bay of Bengal. Today, one person in seven—from Sumatra up to Bangladesh, then back down the Indian coast to Sri Lanka—lives in countries bordering the Bay of Bengal.

I T   I S   a curiosity that Europeans, who'd built the most brilliantly situated cities in the world, should have founded their Indian outposts like Calcutta, Madras and Bombay in the most inhospitable, inconvenient and uninhabitable reaches of swamp and disease on the subcontinent. It is almost as though the Portuguese, French and British, in the same spirit that motivates sweltering vacationers to strip off their clothes and plunge into a surf or mountain lake even before unpacking their bags—or, to extend the metaphor, the heedless sensual expectancy that causes fit young men to dive into an empty pool—decided to dump their cargo at the first available landfall no matter what the draw of its harbor, its hygiene, heat and drainage.

Arriving ships would lose as much cargo in that half-mile water portage across the roadstead as they had in the previous six months and fifteen thousand miles at sea. A graveyard of silverware and clavichords and bobbing wooden trunks full of party silks and fancy linens, bed canopies, spreads, tablecloths, and pallets of heavy formal furniture were slowly filling in the channel between the surf and landing piers of Fort St. George. Every now and then, local women would be spotted in the fort, wearing jewelry crafted of sterling-silver soup ladles and barrettes for their glossy hair fashioned from ivory-handled deboning knives. Storms would toss scroll-top writing desks onto the beach, with deadly sea snakes neatly nested inside each letter compartment.

The Company factors and their wives imported all the impractical trappings of English society, knowing full well that everyday cotton clothes and plain, serviceable furniture were locally and cheaply available. For after all, appearances in the tropics were the first line of demarcation that separated an Englishman from a heathen, and to appear unclean or even unpresentable before one's inferiors merely encouraged the little monkeys, who were, after all, clever and imitative, to strut and mince like popinjays and in general puff up their prices to match their newfound arrogance.

To be accused of dirtiness would be to stand guilty as a buffoon and an amateur. One separated oneself from Them primarily by staying clean and upright: starched, dignified, sober, righteous and faithful. The alternatives were acknowledged to exist, especially among young men outside the ennobling sight of English (or, failing that, French or Portuguese) women, but the occasional misstep was not to be confused with the gleeful wallow of the Hindus and, only slightly above them, the Muslims. It was proven that the most profitable factories—trading posts—were those that enforced the rules of order and cleanliness. And Mr. Cephus Prynne's St. Sebastian factory was the most profitable on the Coromandel Coast.

Perhaps, beguiled by the fecundity, the can't-miss promise of preexistent riches like gold and jewels, the British in India felt no compulsion to search long and hard, as they had in the New World, for ideal harbors and salubrious settings. They had not come to India in order to breed and colonize, or even to convert. They were here to plunder, to enrich themselves (under the guise of a Royal Charter) and pay their fees to the ruling nawabs.

Competing European empires set up their chain of waterfront forts within hailing distance of one another. In Hannah's New England world, French forts even five hundred miles away had been considered too threatening. This commercial competition was something new, a kind of proto–Common Market. In India, the future didn't matter. If they stayed too long they'd be dead and planted in this septic soil; if they devoted themselves single-mindedly to making money, they'd be rich and retired with a safe Tory seat in the Home Counties.

The locals were fisherfolk and boatmen, mostly Hindu with Muslim overlords. Everyone on the Coromandel, Gabriel had tried to explain to Hannah on those endless dark nights at sea, belonged to a caste if he was Hindu, a right-hand or left-hand caste, and everyone was either Shia or Sunni if he was Muslim. They all spoke different languages, they owed fidelity to different masters, they worshiped different gods, and their ancestors had come from different countries.

It had been inconceivable to a Puritan soul like Hannah's. Not just pagans and Muhammadans, but different gods and different ways of worshiping the same gods. Even putting a plural ending on the sacred word God: it became her secret blasphemy. *Gods*. It all went back to her earliest years in the forests.

2

GABRIEL LEGGE decided to join the Honourable East India Company at a time of its greatest upheaval. The Royal Charter guaranteeing a monopoly had been granted by James II in 1686. With the Glorious Revolution two years later, the Protestant William had abrogated it. And so for the decade of the 1690s the East India Company was, to use our term, effectively deregulated. Import values as registered in London sagged from eight hundred thousand pounds in 1684 to thirty thousand pounds in 1695—the year of Gabriel's arrival—due not to a sudden lack of profitability but to a sharp increase in the number of free-lancers, like Gabriel.

(The chaos became exponential—a kind of late-stage capitalism such as America saw in the 1890s, or the 1920s, or, I hesitate to suggest, the late 1980s—until finally all parties had to sue for a kind of peace, new ground rules so as not to exhaust the golden goose. In 1698, William Pitt—known as Diamond Pitt, the grandfather of the great parliamentarian—by force of his personality and his experience as both an interloper in India and a member of Parliament in London, was able to reunify all factions in Fort St. George. The rival East India trading corporations were not merged until the Instrument of Unification was passed in 1701.)

So in the Legges' day, the Coromandel was like Manhattan

in the mid-eighties, like Bugs Kilken's Bel Air. Every interloper set himself up as an independent factor and became the
equivalent of a real estate agent, stockbroker, art dealer, corporate lawyer and investment banker. The value of every commodity was suddenly reassessed with an eye to its resale
potential, a meter was put on everyone's time, and all the
factors and interlopers were down in the pit shouting up, "Buy!
Buy! Buy!"

The chain of multinational factories stretched up and down
the Coromandel like condos on the Florida coast. And the
wealth they generated! Even with the Europeans' enfeebled
head for business, as the nawabs charged (so enamored were
the liquor-swilling *firangi* with legalisms and bookkeeping,
being apparently incapable of keeping accounts in their heads
or of acting decisively in obvious self-interest), they could
hardly go wrong. Everyone grew rich—the shareholders back
in London, the sharp-trading, black-marketing factors, the
various local nawabs and, finally, the Great Mughal himself,
old Emperor Aurangzeb in his Deccan war tents.

I think of those years as being like the last frenzied decade
in the Hong Kong money pits; I think of the factors as the
buccaneers of their day, the arbitrageurs, leveragers, junk-
bonders. The New World was for losers, laborers and farmers
who would never prosper and might lose their scalps in the
bargain. England was dead, finished, washed up, effete and
retentive. Ah, but India! The India trade. An immediate profit
of twenty to one, England to India, and a hundred to one, a
thousand to one, on the way back. And all the women, all
the luxury and adventure, all the hunting, killing, debauchery
a man could dream about.

Money: hand-over-fist money, sweat-of-brow money,

burnout money, finger-to-the-bone money, under-the-table money, black money, dirty money, filthy lucre, money-changing-in-the-temple, thirty-pieces-of-silver money, blasphemous, usurious, treacherous money; profits, taxes, bribes, licenses, fees, levies, octrois, tariffs; middlemen, policemen, watchmen; painters, carpenters, dyers, writers, weavers; doctors, teachers, preachers, judges, accountants, barristers; wives, widows, cooks, servants, slaves, prostitutes, concubines; lewd men, austere men, gamblers, hoarders; Catholics, Roundheads, conformists, Baptists, Muslims, Hindus, Jews, Parsis, Armenians; black men, brown men, yellow men, white; reformers, saviors, visionaries, criminals: all in pursuit of *money, money, money.*

W H A T M I G H T they have seen, that misty January morning three hundred years ago? With no cyclones, although the season was less than a month past, the high surf would have been crashing against the sandbars far out to sea. When Hannah first sighted Fort St. Sebastian from the *Fortune*'s poop, what she saw was an exposed roadstead, a long sand reef, a surf-whipped beach, and dunes no bigger than the humps on camels. She thought herself, after two years in Stepney, a city woman and, thanks to Salem, a townswoman as well.

What must Hannah, a child totally of the North Atlantic, have thought? She had been eight months aboard a medium-sized cargo ship, around the Cape, dodging pirates, weathering storms, eating third mate's rations leavened by Gabriel's light fingers and occasional bribes to the Captain's steward. Any land, even if she'd had to swim to it, would have looked good. Any new human form, after half a year in close quarters with the same scarred, dismembered, begrimed, foulmouthed crew, would have looked comparatively well favored. Even small but well-formed men, like Indians.

The four hundred tons would have to be off-loaded in flat-bottomed masoola boats by local laborers. This was Hannah's first vision of what she was to call the "perfected human form," angelic faces and straight, small-scaled, dignified bodies "as God had draughted Adam, but dipp'd in ebon-ink in place of gilt or blush." She knew she'd been transported to the other side of the world, but the transportation was more than mere "conveyancing," as it was for Gabriel and the others. Many years later she called the trip, and her long residence in India, her "translation."

Of all the qualities I admire in Hannah Easton that make her entirely our contemporary in mood and sensibility, none is more touching to me than the sheer pleasure she took in the world's variety.

The word did not yet exist ("traveler" was in common usage), but if it had, she might have used it: she was, in some original sense of the word (as a linguist is to language), a tourist. She was alert to novelty, but her voyage was mental, interior. Getting there was important, but savoring the comparison with London or Salem, and watching her life being transformed, that was the pleasure. She did not hold India up to inspection by the lamp of England, or of Christianity, nor did she aspire to return to England upon the completion of Gabriel's tour.

If she judged the world from a single, unassailable place, it might have been from a forest in Brookfield, before the expulsion from that New World Eden. Hannah was still alert to the power of the jungle. She did not fear the unknown or the unexplored. Her character was shaped on romps with Rebecca in the woods around Brookfield. And she needed time to sort out her errands—oh, so many errands!—in this vast new jungle.

3

ONCE UPON a time—in 1639, to be precise—today's chapati-flat metropolis, Madras, was a hazardous stretch of beach with a straggly settlement of fishermen's huts. If an East India Company agent named Francis Day had not been in love with an Indo-Portuguese woman living in San Thomé, the Portuguese fort town three miles south, the Company might have situated its factory on a more sheltered dimple farther up the coastline.

Fort St. George, Fort St. Sebastian, Fort St. Joseph, Fort St. Luke: they are monuments to stern-souled, gouty-toed and chilblained Englishmen's sudden submission to the flame-tipped arrows of a dark-skinned Eros. Love dictates the pattern of streets and walls; its aftermath invites demographic up-heaval. White Town, where the factors had their dwellings and the Company had erected its headquarters and church, was a town laid out on the confusing Latin plan, or, worse, followed imperatives known only to a Catholic or Hindu heart.

Like the story of Fort St. George's origin, that of Fort St. Sebastian is apocryphal. In 1684, Clarence Clitherow, a dig-nified gentleman from Liverpool, while working as a factor in

Fort St. George, was discovered to have defrauded a powerful local merchant on a private sale of diamonds. This practice— having been abused by earlier factors and governors, like my relative Streynsham Master, had brought the Company loss of profit as well as embarrassment—was prohibited by the Directors in London. The dignified gentleman, thinking it best to flee corporate reprimand and corporal retribution as swiftly and secretively as possible, disguised himself in clothes borrowed from a Chulia Muslim boatman and sailed two miles southward to the boatman's home. There he stayed while he appealed for reconsideration of his case by the Council.

The Council, prizing knaves above fools and Englishmen over Muslims and Hindus, concluded that the blame was entirely with the plaintiff. The Fort St. George consultation-book entry on "this businesse" and the "accommodation" reached indicates that Clitherow was readmitted to the Company's service at a salary of one hundred pounds and that the diamonds were returned to him. But while awaiting the Council's deliberations, Clitherow, "disordered with country liquor and unnatural potions," had fallen in love with the youngest of the boatman's beautiful daughters, a child of five. He, therefore, asked the Council leave to set up a factory in the very square mile that had provided him love as well as refuge. And when that leave was given, he arranged with the local ruler, Nawab Hasan Beg, to lease and refurbish a broken-down fort, a factory building and a warehouse abandoned by a Portuguese adventurer who had lost a fortune before moving on to Porto-Novo.

What we're seeing is progressive derangement. God-fearing, land-starved, profit-seeking Welsh and English and

Scottish and Irish second sons, jilted by primogeniture, sex-
ually repressed, passion denying, furtively engaging the favors
of native women, girls and boys, all unfolding in the midst
of septic heat, rain, disease, squalor and savage beasts, while
being waited on, cooked for, fanned, massaged by servants a
thousand times more loyal, submissive and poorly paid than
any in the world, in the middle of the biggest real estate
boom, jewel auction and drug emporium of the past five
hundred years. No wonder they went a little crazy.

Eleven years later, when Hannah and Gabriel arrived, Fort
St. Sebastian had drawn, as a magnet might, satellite villages
of weavers, dyers, washermen, artisans necessary for the Company station to carry on its export of textiles to England and
its import of woolens, tin, bullion and brimstone. The new
Nawab, liege of Aurangzeb, was the son of old Hasan Beg,
known as Haider Beg.

THAT HANNAH was not as malleable as an English
factor's wife had to be and that the curbing of her spirit would
require diligence and planning must have been clear to Cephus
Prynne from the moment she, ignoring his steadying hand,
stepped out of the boat that had ferried her—together with
her husband, two junior clerks (known in colonial parlance as
writers), sea chests, cases of liquor, and livestock—from the
Fortune across the roadstead to the sandy strip that passed for
a beach. An East Indiaman of the *Fortune*'s tonnage was obliged
to anchor in the open roadstead. For the Company, the hauling
of cargo to and from anchored ships was a burdensome expense.
But for Cephus Prynne, the Chief Factor, the scary trip in a
fast, open *kuttamaram*, a simple local canoe with logs tied at
a distance to each side, over choppy waves and around sandbars,

was nature's test to see which spongy-souled novice would die or go crazy within weeks.

Cephus Prynne must have seemed to Hannah a man of disquieting miscegenation. Of their first meeting she recorded:

> *This morneing wee went on shoare, Mr. Prynne, Chief Factor, receiving us with civillity but without Kindnesse. "Praised be God, you did not over shoot the Port," Mr. Prynne opined, "but this is the most incommodious place you will ever see." He spared a hand to assist me off the country boate, which hand I shunned. Also present were Mr. Higginbottham, second factor, and Mr. Ruxton, Chyrurgeon. Reverend Colbourn, Chaplaine, sent his excuse, severall Soldyers being sick of feaver.*

Venn leans into my shoulder to read Hannah's entry for himself. I smell cloves on his breath. He chews whole cloves and cardamoms the way we chew gum. *"This is the most incommodious place you will ever see. . . ."* He snickers. He assumes the haughty gait of a British East India Company chief factor and offers me a scornful hand. Like Hannah, instinctively, I back away.

The Chief Factor was probably no more than thirty when he entered Hannah's life on that January morning of 1695, but we know from Hannah's responses that his body was so emaciated and his features so stern that he had the look of a man possessed with the vanity of self-privation. His clothes were from London, Hannah observed, but carelessly preserved through many moldy monsoon seasons. His skin, his hair hanging lank from a receding hairline, his uneven mustache, all were the color of the snuff that dear Hubert had, in another lifetime . . . no, she would not allow herself to grieve for what might have been. Past events surfaced only in images of pale dreary colors. The sounds, shapes and hues swirling around her—the yellowness of the sand, for instance, the hollering of laborers—had a vibrancy that sucked all breath out of her chest.

She moved to where Tamil boatmen and peons were piling up unloaded cargo. The beach was strewn with chests, bales, bleating and neighing animals. Bullion was being inspected by sharp-eyed customs officials in the service of the Mughal Emperor Aurangzeb. Casks of wine were being seized as bribes or gifts of homage. The Company's factors and cash keepers were driving belligerent bargains with local merchants. She heard Gabriel raise his voice against traders, dyers, weavers, as though he had been with the Company at St. Sebastian as long as had Cephus Prynne and Samuel Higginbottham. She strolled away, toward clots of fishermen's children, who watched the spectacle of disembarkation from a cautious distance.

I need to believe that if Higginbottham had not hurried after her with courteous admonitions, Hannah would have kept on strolling, that on her very first morning on the Coromandel she would have made good her escape into the "forest," as had her mother years before in Massachusetts. The second factor coaxed and pleaded with her. "Dear lady, do not stray," he panted. "Dear lady, I commend you to the protection of your countrymen, whom in turn I commend to the protection of the Almighty." Behind the wheezing Higginbottham slid and stumbled his rickety-legged umbrella bearer. The children relished the spectacle; they laughed and clapped each time the Englishman mopped his sun-ruddied face or the umbrella bearer dropped the heavy shade. Hannah might have ignored Higginbottham. She might even have contributed, however circumspectly, to the children's entertainment, had the Chief Factor himself not intervened.

Prynne's intervention involved no clownish movements. His address was laconic and indirect. His gloomy voice reached Hannah all the way from the wharf. "It is not consistent with our interest," the voice rebuked, "to let the people of the land see our countrywomen yield to self-indulgence."

Hannah expected Prynne to come after her as Higginbottham had. She waited for a harsh confrontation of wills. She had intended rebellion, not an accidental breach of Company etiquette. But the Chief Factor expended no further rage on her. The would-be rebel was dismissed. Prynne resumed issuing instructions to boatmen, laborers, scribes and apprentices. His gibes he reserved for the Mughal Emperor's and the Roopconda Governor's officious bureaucrats.

Hannah turned her back on the fishermen's children, startled at her own compliance.

Not far from the wharf, a hound she had grown fond of on the long, sickly trip out to the Coromandel lay stretched at the foot of a dune. The hound, named Tobias, had amused her with its antics of snapping up fish that flew onto the decks of the *Fortune*. Now its eyes were dulled in near death, its flanks twitchy in hyperventilation. Hunched over the hound was its master, Thomas Tringham, a red-haired boy with a sun-blistered face and a high-bridged nose who cursed the unholy heat of the New Year's week in an unalloyed Yorkshire accent. The Yorkshire youth, sent by the Company as a writer, was to be its youngest employee at Fort St. Sebastian.

" 'Tis January!" Hannah kept hearing Thomas Tringham mumble at the hound. She could make out only isolated phrases from his grief's inchoate fullness. " 'Tis January! God ne'er intended it so!"

She tried to comfort young Tringham, but he shook off the sweaty-gloved hand she'd laid on his arm. She didn't misconstrue the rejection. He was wrapped in the surly loneliness of his private sorrow. A stranger's sympathy was intrusive. All the same, she couldn't abandon Tringham. She looked for help from Gabriel, who was surrounded by laborers stacking chests and trunks painted prominently with the Legge name. She called his name twice, halfheartedly, knowing that Gabriel would not come to a dying dog's aid. He was engaged in the cantankerous supervision of bookkeepers who were recording the customs fees assessed on his private goods by the Emperor's and the Governor's men. Boldly, she beckoned Dr. Ruxton. A "chyrurgeon" might still save the hound.

It was Cephus Prynne, however, who responded to her desperate wave. Chief Factor Prynne was lither, swifter, than the portly Dr. Ruxton. He was at her side, his bleak stare fastened on Tringham and the dying hound. "Hyenas love nothing more than tender English cur," he said. He did not hide from Hannah his pale, malicious smile. To Tringham, he said, "Better bury it under a rock."

Hannah understood Prynne's words for what they were: an order, not consolatory counsel. Poor Tringham did not.

"Eight months aboard the *Fortune*, only to die here?" Tringham wept. "Is this land not cursed?"

"Aye, cursed," agreed Cephus Prynne, and scuffed some sand on the hound's flank.

Glittery grains of sand came to rest on Hannah's gloved hands. "Tobias weathered the voyage!" Hannah protested. "So why not the cursed land?"

Prynne's rejoinder shocked Hannah. He said, looking in

the direction of Gabriel and the customs officials, "Mistresses Higginbottham and Ruxton devote themselves to the well-being of their husbands, the keeping of their tables and the education of their children in the Protestant religion."

Just then Gabriel signaled Cephus over. Gabriel seemed to be losing an argument with the chief customs officer. One of the chests had been overturned. Cheese, rum, gloves, watches, spyglasses—valuables he had brought with him for private trade—littered the beach. Hannah had never seen her husband so angry; with his words muffled by the surf, he seemed to be a comedian miming rage. She smiled, then caught Cephus Prynne's cynical stare. He was watching her watching Gabriel. She backed away.

"Mind my words," Prynne said to Tringham before ambling off to Gabriel's aid. "Three feet deep, under a rock."

Higginbottham, Ruxton, soldiers, servants, followed the Chief Factor in showy procession.

"He had no warrant to disrespect his suffering," Tringham moaned. He swiped at the sand with a snap of his hat. Hannah lifted the dog's head for a final view of the sea and three masts that had brought it to St. Sebastian.

WHEN GABRIEL, Prynne, Higginbottham and Ruxton finally returned to where Hannah was cradling Tobias's head, Gabriel was still seething, but this time his rage was focused on "thieving infidels." A porter or boatman, he accused, had stolen one of his chests.

At a deferential distance from the English stood three traders, each with his own retinue. At the edge of the group hovered Kashi Chetty, a small, dark, smiling man in a broad-brimmed, English-style hat. He had dismissed his umbrella bearer, who was left squatting on his haunches near his master's feet. The other two traders sat high aloft in their litter chairs, obliging their umbrella bearers to stand on ornate wooden stools. The lightest-skinned of the traders, the only one not in Indian garments, was an Armenian by the name of Catchick Sookian. If anything, his linen was starchier, his velvet coat more carefully brushed, than the ship's captain's had been at Sabbath dinner table. The third man, Pedda Timanna, was plump, with a plumed and aigretted headgear on his disproportionately small head. He seemed to Hannah to be richer than the others, or perhaps had a stronger sense of his place in a hierarchy she didn't yet comprehend. He sat on a fancifully carved chair and was carried from spot to spot by four emaciated servants. Another servant stood at the ready with a silver spittoon, yet another waved off flies. The lesser traders made do with fanners but no spittoon bearers, and at the edge of the bizarre congregation stood the three decorated hackeries, the hobbled horses and the idle horsemen who had borne the gentlemen to the beach from whencesoever they had come.

Hannah counted twenty-five men in service and a swirling mass of hangers-on, all vying for fanning, swatting and spittle-swabbing duties. Each of the local dignitaries seemed to derive from a different universe of blood, language and sensibility. Each seemed to her, in separate ways, a voluptuary, with bloodshot eyes, a surplus of jewelry, under a cloud of complicated fragrance. It was as though eight months at sea had deposited her on a different plane of existence, a moon, an undersea world in which the last familiar creature, a dog, had just died.

Men with officious faces and ledger books in the service of Emperor Aurangzeb's representative Nawab Haider Beg,

Governor of Roopconda, the large *suba*, or state, in which the English, French, Dutch and Portuguese had gained their small trading concessions, stood watch over the unloaders. Hannah had never seen such display of color: rich silks, brocades, cottons, in colors and combinations of colors that only a garden in high blossom could rival. Despite an inner voice that tried to summon up ancient fears of Turks and Ottomans and infidels, she couldn't quite credit those Christian terrors. In their scarlet uniforms and tightly wound turbans the locals seemed like comedians on stage. They seemed physically weak, no match for the sturdy Europeans, even those, like Gabriel, still groggy from their transit. She had not seen so many people crowded together, ever. The dock in Salem seemed empty, bleached, muffled, in comparison.

"Hannah. Tell this fool—" Gabriel shouted.

She eased the dog's head back to the hot sands. She verified his count of their trunks. It was the green one missing, she remembered, with the brass locks and hinges.

Cephus Prynne spoke sharply to Higginbottham. "It is the duty of all persons in the Honourable Company's employment to acquaint Moors and Gentoos with the Honourable Company's will and power. That is all I desire of you. Less than that I expect not."

Higginbottham reluctantly approached the porters. He put himself through a clumsy emulation of Cephus Prynne's deportment. He threatened whippings and bastinadoes if the thief and the missing chest were not instantaneously restored to Factor Legge. Higginbottham's promise of vicious chastisement, however, intimidated no porter or boatman. The crowd had sized him up. This Englishman was weak. Men tittered; children closed in for better views of the entertainment.

Hannah's journal entry of what happened next is reticent. *"Gabriel acquitted himself fitt to be in the Companyes imployment."* She must have been appalled when Gabriel swatted aside peons and porters, jerked Higginbottham out of his way, then seized Kashi Chetty's umbrella bearer by the hair. Gabriel's hand smashed into the umbrella bearer's face.

". . . fitt to be in the Companyes imployment . . . ," Venn reads aloud.

I detect Hannah's irony, but I, too, had hoped to find censure. I cannot defend Hannah to Venn.

All the same I invent secretive excuses. Maybe Hannah was still unready, unformed. Still afraid to discover herself disloyal. Gabriel was being judged, she must have decided. Gabriel was afraid of losing the respect of the Chief Factor. He did not ever wish to become the laughingstock that Higginbottham clearly was. It wasn't the cursed land that released in him that crude, brute petulance. Prynne and Tringham were wrong about the Coromandel. The land, any land, is no more than catalyst. In England, Gabriel had often shocked her with his violence or enticed her with his unpredictabilities. The Gabriel she knew was at his most angry when he manifested an outer calm, as on his return from the dead. As in his patient questioning about men, every man, who had visited her while he was reportedly dead, killed by the Portuguese. But there was a new deliberateness to this assault on the merchant Chetty's umbrella bearer.

Gabriel raised his hand to strike again. The caved-in face was a randomly chosen target. The victim had been on the periphery of the titterers. His "crime" was that he had been too intent a spectator. Other men in the crowd had smiled at the second factor more insolently, had advertised their innocence more sneeringly.

Hannah shrieked, though she didn't know she had until she heard the shriek herself. This is an incident chronicled in the *Memoirs*. The hand reraised. The face twisted tight in anticipation of pain. The woman's tormented shriek. She is witnessing an unnatural vanishing of justice, an unspeakable new face of violence. She remembers concentrating on the sweat and soil of the ruffled sleeve so she would not have to see nor hear the crash of flesh on flesh. And then suddenly, the tableau explodes into noise and movement. Pedda Timanna, the rich trader with the small head, leans down from his sedan chair, gives the man a quick shove with his umbrella and knocks him out of the hand's range.

"The error is yours," he informs Gabriel, smiling serenely from on high. "The object is not missing. Merely misplaced."

He points his umbrella at the Legges' trunk, which four of his attendants place before Cephus Prynne. To the Chief Factor, he adds, "Please inspect nothing is missing."

Cephus Prynne's blue eyes blanch bleaker. "Mr. Higginbottham, limit your future endeavors to acquainting the unmarried servants of the Company with their living arrangements and with rules of rank and precedence, of sitting at public table, and such sundry matters."

Pedda Timanna's head bows in bitter triumph.

Samuel Higginbottham's shoulders stoop with self-hate.

Only Gabriel misses the merchant's irony and its humiliating consequences. He squats on the gritty wharf and greedily pries open the lid of the gouged, rusty-hinged chest.

HANNAH DID NOT take to Cephus Prynne, but she conceded that he was an efficient procurer of house and servants for his subordinates. The grieving young Yorkshireman and the other two new writers were hustled away to their bachelor billets by Samuel Higginbottham. The Legges were attended to by Cephus Prynne himself. In a procession of palanquins, horses, ox carts and porters who balanced trunks and bundles on their flatly turbaned heads, the Chief Factor escorted the Legges over sandy roadways to the house they were to occupy in White Town, the Europeans-only walled enclave. St. Sebastian, he explained, being a "subordinate factory," did not yet have a Company residence for its married employees. He had plans to buy land from the Armenian merchant, but in the meanwhile the married factors were obliged to live in their separate homes, as did English freemen and European privateers.

The lodging that he had chosen for the Legges, Prynne said, had last belonged to a factor named Henry Hedges, who had died while negotiating an abatement of 8 percent on longcloth in a weavers' village controlled by the trader Pedda Timanna. Hannah sensed there was a story to the last occupant's death. Some hint of fiscal impropriety or at least of behavior inappropriate in an Englishman of rank.

The late Henry Hedges' house was two stories, but in appearance and feel like no home that Hannah had ever imagined. It was a white, miniature palace, modestly plain to the street, but embracing a courtyard with servants' quarters in the rear, a wall, a profusion of flowers and fruit trees, all humming with bloated insects—At last, she thought, the royal bugs worthy of a golden swatter—the branches alive with lizards and gaudy songbirds. Everywhere she looked, reptiles hissed at birds, birds swooped on lizards, and insects formed a gray dome, like a veil, around the head of every worker.

"You will find your *malis* most accomplished, madam," said Cephus Prynne. "I suggest you release them immediately." There were more gardeners and gardeners' children and other unspecified staff underfoot than would make up a small American village.

"But I will need their help—" Hannah was an accomplished small-plot gardener from her spell in England. This garden, she realized the moment she saw it, would be her sanity.

"Dear lady, it is a question of their loyalty. They were recruited by your predecessor. They are like dogs. They know only one master, you see."

"Chief Factor, pardon my ignorance if I find that a most curious way to reward their accomplishments," said Hannah. "I think they might prove their disloyalty first."

"They require but one opportunity. Thereafter, it is quite too late." He bowed and offered up his grotesque little smile. "A friendly warning only, madam."

"My wife is a tenderhearted woman," said Gabriel Legge.

"The Company is not in want of tenderheartedness," said the Chief Factor. "An iron will and a heart of flint, that's what survives on the Coromandel."

Hannah noticed a young woman on the upper balcony, busying herself with brass water pots now that her presence had been detected. She was wrapped in what appeared to be a mustard-colored winding-sheet. Her hair was gathered in one long, thick braid that nearly brushed the floor.

In Brookfield, in Stepney and Salem, a house was a barricade to stop encroachment. Outdoors was the prowling ground for Satan and his companions; indoors was furnished, tamed and therefore safe. But the house that she was to live in, like all houses in Fort St. Sebastian, was built to entice crystal-bright tropical starlight, spume-scented breeze, bugs, birds and butterflies through its huge barred windows. There were terraces shiny as marble, balconies made of hardy woods, a flat roof for evening walks—ground level at night being considered unsafe—and turreted parapets. Behind the main house were the gardens, kitchen sheds, servants' sheds and stables.

Hannah, the new tenant, shuddered. European employers died on duty, or they sailed back home to savor what they had looted. The houses and the servants endured, unless pruned back by prudent management, accommodating to the newest occupants and enlarging their knowledge of human folly and wickedness. She had to admit there was a certain crude wisdom in starting with a clean slate of servants.

Hedges' residence came with a dozen servants, among them the cook, the maid, the groom and valet and the two peons who had served him half a decade. His furniture was scattered through every room; elaborate pieces, some of which had been brought over from England on East Indiamen, others copied in local woods by adventurous Coromandel cabinetmakers.

Cephus Prynne led Hannah on an inspection tour of the premises while Gabriel supervised the unloading of their baggage. She felt the Chief Factor's hand, a little too familiarly, on her arm, guiding her up the dark stairwell. Prynne's voice and bearing suggested he was handing over Henry Hedges' kingdom and subjects to reign over rather than a rented home to maintain. She concentrated on Hedges' furniture so she would not worry about the impression she was making on the servant women with their heavy-lidded, judgmental eyes.

The young serving girl with the long braid, whom Prynne

indicated was new to the premises, hence untainted by too long a service to Hedges, was named Bhagmati. "Means 'Gift of God' or some such," he muttered. "Hindu. Understands some English. Attends Scripture class. Probably honest, so far as she understands the concept."

"You are saying I may retain her, then, Chief Factor?"

"Please, dear lady. Cephus." He laid a cold, reassuring hand over hers. "My intentions are the noblest. If I have experience to share, you may believe those experiences were paid for in hard and bitter currency."

There were carved rectangular center tables veneered with maple wood and parcel gilt, their tops inlaid with silver strap-work, and gilt-framed mirrors carved with putti, acanthus leaves and floral sprays; pairs of matching cabinets veneered in oyster laburnum and mounted on spiral supports; black japanned chairs and white japanned chests; scriptores veneered with arabesque marquetry and folding tops; walnut armchairs and daybeds with carved rails and cane seats and embossed silver sconces and footed silver candlesticks.

"The unfortunate Hedges," Cephus Prynne began. "He did not know where to stop."

"In what manner, Chief Factor?"

"Men too long separated from their home country, from, shall I say, the delicate ministrations of a woman . . . allow their sentiments . . . to spoil."

It seemed a heartfelt observation, but she had no idea of its origin, or of its general applicability. He seemed to be drawing his evidence from the rich collection of furnishings. "They become unmanned. Sentiment, luxury . . . they all gain ascendancy."

It would require a retinue merely to keep salt spray from

pitting the brass and silver, the mildew from attacking the fabrics. Unless the shutters were permanently shut, birds and scorpions and every manner of loathsome creature from outdoors were free to enter.

"A man is judged by the fight that's in him. He yields, or he resists. Your man, Mr. Gabriel Legge, is battle tested, I presume."

"He has ofttimes been to sea, Chief Factor." She followed his lead down the outer, half-covered balcony that Bhagmati had been standing on a few minutes earlier.

"Come, my dear." The exposed side of the balcony, that part lined with brass pots of flowers, ran past rows of bedrooms, all decently furnished in the local style. At the end of the balcony a crude ladder of ship's timbers and lashed-together rope thongs lay propped against the inner wall.

Cephus began climbing to the flat roof. Hannah followed. Bhagmati, the serving girl, stood silently at the far end of the balcony.

Indeed, Hannah had climbed to the top of the world. Not only did White Town command the highest land in the region, but Hedges' house occupied the very pinnacle of the nob. The ocean, broad to its curvature with at least a dozen East Indiamen under full sail, filled the horizon, with the near perspective speckled by fishermen's boats and one-sail dhows. The warm breeze sought out the last pockets of chill and damp from Hannah's bones; it was a glorious moment of January sun and offshore breeze, loud jackdaws circling the rooftops. Potted trees even struggled to give off some shade. She closed her eyes, feeling at last that her travels were over.

He moved so silently, so quickly, his arms were around hers before she could catch her balance. His open mouth was trying to kiss her, to close over hers before she could scream, and she could hear his low, guttural threats and promises. "Saucy wench," she heard, "knowing what's best for a factor," and "He'll be gone, he'll have his bibis, and your nights—" She struggled free now and pushed him away, and Cephus Prynne reestablished his guise of shabby, inoffensive officiousness, casually looking behind him, before she could scream.

"That gardener! Did I not instruct you to dismiss them all? I'll have his hide, I saw him!" Cephus Prynne ran to the roof edge and shouted down, "Stop him, stop him, I say." And he was over the side, down the rope ladder and running down the balcony to the main stairwell before Hannah could catch her breath.

4

ALL THROUGH 1695 Hannah Legge kept a diary modeled on the diary kept by Gabriel in his capacity as a factor instructed by his superior, Prynne, to reform the bookkeeping irregularities in the factory at St. Sebastian. The initial entries are of events; the descriptions of those events cautiously impersonal.

January 8, 1695: The two ships following arrived, vizt., (1) the Loyall Heron *Captain Hope-for Johnson, Commander. (2) the* Pride, *Captain John Bendell, Commander. Though there was a* fresh, my dear husband, accompanied by Mr. Higginbottham, came of to Captain Johnson, and received the Agents Packett from the Council at Fort St. George. Agreement was effected by my dear husband in the affaire of the landing of the Honourable Company's treasure that had come in the two ships.

January 9: We had fresh winds. Mistress Ruxton entertained me last night as my dear husband was on board the Loyall Heron. She is a woman of good humour. Mistress Higginbottham may be of dour disposition.

January 10: We had fresh winds againe. Nevertheless my dear husband and Captain Hope-for Johnson disembarked wilfully and, praised be god, came on shoare. Captain John Bendell, his wife and three daughters remained on board the ship Pride.

January 15: Four days wee had bad weather. George Fleetfax, Apprentice, dyed of sicknesse.

January 17: Mistresses Higginbottham and Ruxton and I welcomed Captain Bendell's wyfe, Harriet, and daughters, Eliza, Charlotte and Anne. Captain Bendell, falling sick while the ship Pride lay in the road, was oblidged to be carried off the country boat and borne by palanquin to the residence of chyrurgeon Ruxton and his kind wyfe.

January 30: The Captain's wife and 3 children were entertained for tea by mee. My dear husband returned from Metchlepatam [Masulipatnam], where hee had been dispatched by the Chief Factor for inspection of the Companyes factorye. Hee sent to desire to speak with Mistress Bendell in the event of her requiring assistance in business with the Companye. Mistress Bendell consenting, he offered her, in her behalfe, to accommodate all necessary affaires if she should give him a Sealed Letter of Attorney.

February 6: Mistress Ruxton confided in me sad news. The chyrurgeon does not live who can restore health to Captain Bendell.

February 14: The Allmighty culled the goode Captain to His bosom. My dear husband shows great charity to the widowe and her daughters.

March 20: Chief Factor Prynne holds the Captain's widow accountable for moneys owed by the dear departed Captain to the Companye. Furthermore, Chief Factor Prynne demands of the widow payment of passages home to be taken by her and her children. The widow sent to for my husband. I offered her comfort while dear Gabriel is in Roopconda conducting inquiries of a poddar, *which is the Gentue word for cash-keeper, concerning the rich merchant Pedda Timmana's ways of tradeing upon creditt.*

March 30: Eliza Bendell was married to Mr. John Harker, freeman, by Mr. Colbourn, the Chaplaine of St. Sebastian. Mr. John Harker offers to cleare the Captaine's debts and make payment in full for passages home taken by his bride's family.

April 10: Concerning Mr. John Harker, Mistress Higginbottham informs mee that the said freeman came into wealth on account of a secret marriage to a Moor woman. Mistress Higginbottham is of the opinion that she should acquaint Mistress Harker with the secret. I am of the opinion that such discharge of duty would inflict on the new bride pernicious suffering.

May 16: This forenoone Mistress Bendell and two daughters embarked the ship Glorious, *Eliza Harker having met with an accident month last. Her corpes was interred in the burying place by the church. Of the circumstances of this misfortune I have no knowledge. Mr. Higginbottham is of the opinion that John Harker, freeman, has sealed up his residence here and has removed himself to the Dutch settlement at Pollicull [Palakollu].*

After mid-May, the diary entries become more disorderly, and personal. Here are just three entries from the winter of 1695:

October 18: Henry Hedges haunts me. He moves from room to room reminding me hourly that the house remains his. I am his tenant.

November 23: Mistresses Ruxton and Higginbottham tease me with talk of black bibis. Their designe is to affright me. They talk of the vanished Mr. Harker. All Englishmen make secret marriages with black girls, they insist. A wealthy Moor or Gentue woman of respected family allowing herself to be a BIBI, that's the only exception. They remind me that John Harker was not held accountable for poor departed Eliza's accident by the Chief Factor. No Englishman here accepts any connection between Mr. Harker's keeping a BIBI and Eliza's falling off her horse.

December 24: I know Henry Hedges kept a secret wife here. I feel his bibi's presence in this house as much as I doe his owne. May God forgive mee for entertaining thoughts of spirits and phantoms.

5

WERE THERE no relatives in England to send the heavy furniture to? Hannah wondered. Or had Henry Hedges, a man so strange and tragical—or mild and farcical—to judge from his abandoned projects of sketching and poetry, his notebooks of descriptive accounts of village life and the forests, his long comparative lists of words in Persian, Tamil, Telugu and English, transformed himself so completely from a modest Shropshire lad content with his lowly station in the English hierarchy to such a displaced, self-indulgent nobleman that his collection of native artifacts and furniture would have embarrassed his relatives?

I am aware, as I write this three hundred years later, of the greatness of Henry Hedges. His accounts (in four thick volumes) are the core of nearly any serious study of South India in the early British times—but what it must have felt like, to have been a twenty-five-year-old Salem woman, discovering them for the first time, digging them out of folded silks in the drawers of those hand-carved dressers, along with the folios of the bright, unappreciated court paintings of the Mughal masters?

Henry Hedges was a man of the New Science and of the Old Humanism. How, or why, he chose to ship out to India as a Company man he never explained—perhaps he saw it as the Peace Corps of his day (although his collection of furnishings indicates he was no mendicant-scholar). He was shrewd, curious, brilliant and passionate, a man of that extraordinary time, and slightly unbalanced.

Hannah had never seen such possessions (they are housed today in the Victoria and Albert, and in several Continental museums). Most factors lived frugally, within their Company means, hoarding their Indian wealth for an early retirement. Theirs was a conversion society, calculating every purchase, every expenditure, every sale in local *tars* and pagodas, against "real" money, bullion, in the real home country. In Henry Hedges we have an early appearance of a Sir William Jones or a Sir Richard Burton, a true eccentric English expatriate.

That the acquisitor suffered in Fort St. Sebastian is incontrovertible. While going through Henry Hedges' ledgers of household accounts, Hannah came across a startling line. *I am sick, I must die.* Hannah doesn't appear to have recognized this as a line from Thomas Nashe's "A Litany in Time of Plague." Nor did she see it as part of Hedges' indictment of Company society, its studied ignorance of the people it traded with. Hedges was a pedant—he served without extra pay as Company translator merely for the practice it offered him— and he must have been, like Burton, insufferable. His interest in India was too acquisitive; he felt he owned it by dint of his own efforts and suffering, and that partial ownership conferred upon him a benevolent proprietorship. Like certain missionaries who combined selflessness and spiritual arrogance, Hedges found himself dissatisfied with both sides, neither of which manifested the pure essence of their cultural selves. The Indians, especially the "Zentoos," meaning Hindus, were already losing their integrity. He felt he had known the last generation of noble practitioners of the ancient Vedic rites.

Hannah cited these ruminations as proof of his breakdown, which, in a sense, they were. One more Englishman snared by the Company and destroyed by the tropics.

In the small circle of Englishmen and Englishwomen within which Hannah's social life was confined, she saw many variations of Henry Hedges' ailment and many strategies for its management. The most effective cure was to fabricate a fantasy England, in which life had been idyllic and would be again on retirement. Even the young recruits of nineteen and twenty wore their Englishness as indelibly as a criminal in Salem or London had worn the branded letters of his sin: *E* for English, Extraordinary, Ethical.

The fort was Little England. The Fort St. George Council's penal code encouraged straight and narrow living. Uncleanness, lying, cheating, drunkenness, swearing, missing morning or evening prayers, using seditious words, mutinying, dueling, all were punishable with whippings, mountings of the "wooden horse," confinement and fines. When caught. When admitted. When they spoke to their servants and mistresses, to shopkeepers and clients, they spoke as though theirs were the bell-toned sweetly patriotic voice of a homogenous sovereign nation. Hannah with her stories of wigwam burnings in Hopewell Swamp discomfited them.

Early signs of the self-pity and contradictions that would result in the twisted logic of the white man's burden were already evident. The factors knew their lives in India were extraordinary and, by most standards of the day, debauched. The Company code they lived under placed inhuman limits on even routine freedom. At the same time, their personal code was Excess in All Things. And so they recast themselves as capital's little pilgrims, forgotten victims of England's indifference to their sacrifice. Self-pity, unaccountability and hypocrisy were recast as virtues and renamed forgiveness, solidarity and tolerance.

The household ran itself—Hannah didn't think of it as being run by the servant woman and the peons—leaving her time during the day to visit or be visited by the fort doctor's wife, Martha Ruxton, and the second factor's wife, Sarah Higginbottham. She kept a journal of events, a protection against a jealous husband's ferocity. Through her embroidery, and much later through her stealthily penned *Memoirs*, she revealed to herself her deepest secrets. She was without Gabriel's company for weeks at a time while he toured smaller factories, scouted dyers' villages and indigo plantations for the best dye roots, and *mittahs*, or village markets, for the most skillful artisans. She didn't trust Martha or Sarah as confidantes. What she wanted from them was their gossip, their history in the place.

Over two years she elicited from Sarah the story of Martha's courtship and marriage. In 1681, the last year of my ancestor Streynsham Master's governorship, John Ruxton had arrived in Fort St. George, a thirty-year-old bachelor. Cholera, dysentery, typhus and lash ulcers had preoccupied him through Nathaniel Gyffords's harsh governorship. Then, midway through Elihu Yale's term, in June of 1690, as the monsoon broke and the very bowels of the Bay of Bengal were churned as though an elephant had tramped through a paddy field, the *Golden Bliss*, carrying Martha Ord, a comely girl of fourteen, and her mother and five younger sisters had docked. The thirty-nine-year-old bachelor doctor had discovered his need for golden bliss.

The mother and sisters had gone on to Masulipatnam, where Martha's father, Grimston Ord, was third in charge of the factory. Martha Ord succumbed to the doctor's fevered courting, insofar as an experienced and out-of-practice expatriate could mount it. In actuality, it had more to do with a strict accounting of his holdings and the assurance that upon his demise—which could happen sooner rather than later, given the precarious age and profession—Martha (and her parents and unmarried sisters) would come into one of Fort St. George's tidier fortunes.

Immediately after the wedding on a September Sunday in 1690, the doctor, thinking ahead to the marital pitfalls that awaited young brides and old grooms in a fort filled with lonely, lustful soldiers, sailors, factors and clerks, moved to the more remote Company outpost at Fort St. Sebastian. The old physician—for he thought of himself, unfailingly, as elderly, as did his patients and even his postpubescent bride—had stories to tell of sturdy-souled Englishmen in desperate need of healing.

I have studied Dr. Ruxton's death certificates. He was a great medical metaphysician; the deaths from Despond, Despair, Ingratitude and Melancholia outnumber those from the pox, consumption, syphilis, dysentery or ague.

Martha Ruxton had never lost the chubby contours of childhood. Now in 1697 an old married lady of twenty-one, she had been seven years in White Town and had developed neither the gaunt angularities of the fever-prone nor the cushiony complacency of the Company wife. Nor, apparently, had the tropical sun met her face or arms head-on: she was still pink and blond, easily flushed; daily she applied pastes of milk curd and lemon juice to her pretty face.

Sarah Higginbottham's story came from Sarah herself. She confided to Hannah that she had arrived on a Company allowance to find a mate. Hannah remembered the Lancashire women on the *Fortune* and wondered about their fates. Sarah had accepted the hesitant Samuel Higginbottham's offer of marriage at the end of a fifty-one-week stop-and-start courtship. (One more week, and she would have been obliged to return.) She was older than Martha and Hannah, thirty-five at least, and had the resignation of a woman who had tried other lives—dairymaid in Devon, barmaid in Bristol—and hated them profoundly. She, who had known servitude as a girl, now had a retinue at her command.

Martha and Sarah savored their roles as guide and guardian to Hannah. They never let Hannah forget that they were truly Englishwomen, while Hannah was tainted because of her long residence in primitive New England.

"I suppose Mr. Legge has found himself a bibi," Sarah began, always with a smile.

Hannah knew the word, but did not let on. Bibis—their

uses, their place, their importance and the need for tolerance thereof—constituted the opening lecture of old Company wives to Company novices.

Martha's and Sarah's smiles exasperated Hannah. Their smiles suggested that there was no choice for white men, not when the heat of India fired the brain. The very thought of an Englishwoman attempting to satisfy a rampant Englishman brought out the freckles in Martha. Every English husband strayed into infidelity. Gabriel, too, would find himself a bibi. The term, as employed by Sarah and Martha, meant a healthy young black girl, a native woman in Black Town, or some servant of the English or a slave of one of the Muslim nawabs, or a girl of low morals still living in some mud hut with a widowed mother who could be counted on to look the other way. To Hannah's friends a bibi was an annoyance, but not a threat.

"Whatever you do, you will of course never confront your husband's bibi. You will never acknowledge her," said Martha.

"She does not exist," said Sarah.

"But she must exist, surely," Hannah protested. It seemed to Hannah that bibis, suspected and real, were at the center of most female conversations in White Town. Any servant with a new sari, any cheekiness detected, anything missing, meant a good serving girl had passed over to bibihood. Bibis were simultaneously beneath notice, no more than cute little pets like monkeys or birds (although considerably less trouble), and devious temptresses, priestesses of some ancient, irresistible and overpowering sensuality. Wise husbands did not seek bibis on their own serving staff, but could easily be distracted by some wench hanging the wash on a neighboring balcony. Each White Town wife, therefore, had a vested interest in keeping her neighbors' servants as old and shrewish as tolerable. Maintaining an appropriately large staff of women servants of insufficient comeliness was a domestic virtue that Company wives appreciated.

"Your maids should be ugly as jackdaws," advised Martha. "Their voices should rasp like rooks, their skin should hang in black wrinkles . . ."

"And be poxy," Sarah added.

"Are the women of the Coromandel Coast otherwise so alluring to Englishmen?" Hannah asked. "If there be choice, surely—"

Hannah was not that innocent of the male entitlements, but she had never learned the code of female accommodation. To accommodate meant to demonstrate an intention to please, even on occasion to yield, but with a view to establishing control. "Why would our husbands? Are the women in this land more beautiful?"

Perhaps she was still thinking of the men she'd witnessed that January morning she had landed on Fort St. Sebastian's beaches. The men were small and finely made, wrapped in the same half sarong as the women. She reckoned that young women fashioned along the same lines as the men (young women were not easily encountered; fully 90 percent of Indians one saw on the street were male, or shuffling old widows) could well be irresistible to white men.

In fact, whenever Gabriel was away inspecting factories or villages, Hannah spent her days in a dream of sensuality. She walked the streets and even the back lanes of Black Town, just as she had walked in Salem. She heard music from the upper floors of the sheds that passed for their housing and smiled back at the faces of youngsters as they gathered to

watch her. Some children followed her, pulling at her clothes
as though she were nothing more than one of the wretched
cows that wandered everywhere, sometimes garlanded in flowers, their horns painted a garish red and purple and yellow,
to be touched on the forehead as they placidly munched refuse
in the gutters. Men passed the cows, walking, on carts, or
being carried in litter chairs, and touched their own foreheads
after touching the cow, as though releasing and preserving
some sort of religious essence.

"I do not know of their beauty," replied Martha Ruxton.
Martha boasted that she had never scrutinized a young Indian
man's or woman's face. Too close an inspection, she felt, might
engender uncharitable thoughts.

"Have you never really looked at Bhagmati?" Hannah per-
sisted. "Do you find her beautiful?"

"It was all right for a bachelor like the late Mr. Hedges
to hire that maid," Sarah answered for Martha. "In my household she would be inappropriate."

Martha Ruxton's instructions and Sarah Higginbottham's
confessions stunned Hannah. These women, the only women
she could call friends here, accepted cups of tea and biscuits
from Bhagmati without seeing her. Bhagmati was invisible to
the women of White Town. This explained why Martha
knew—and refused to know—that her husband, the good
doctor, had a sizable family from his bibi, accumulated over
the years. Some of his children were ten and twelve, and already
married. Little mongrel curs, Gabriel had joked to Hannah,
whom the doctor shooed away from his compound with a cane.

Martha's teaching was indirect. Black bibis know their
place, so a wife's safety lies in assigning them a place that is
harmless. Perverse pleasures could be demanded of them and

satisfied without harm to anybody. Accommodation was synonymous with expatriate femininity. Mating happened fast on peninsulas at the world's edge. These bibis had only a few months in them—they didn't retain their desirability through the years like Englishwomen. The swift deterioration of their charms had to do with the flora and fauna surrounding them, with their spicy diets and gaudy garments, with their summer-scorched, monsoon-drenched climate. India heated up the senses. Every glance and nod smoldered into overtures of carnality. Men and women succumbed to primordial impulses. And when instinct subsided, sober single Englishmen and women tied the knot; adulterous Englishmen and women stalked their prey.

Sarah the realist's lesson was dour. Her lesson had to do with the unpleasant inescapability of death in the tropics. No one could say if he or she would be alive next week. India was a permanent plague, and the possibility of death sharpened everyone's drives.

"And did the late Mr. Hedges have a bibi?" Hannah asked in all innocence.

Martha Ruxton bowed her head. "Mr. Hedges' acumen was doubted on—"

Sarah Higginbotham objected. "His reputation was impeccable."

"But in the matter of furniture? In the matter of finery? In such matters was his acumen not—"

"I heard it said that Mr. Hedges had been a voluptuary," Sarah conceded.

"But not in the carnal sense," Martha added.

Hannah asked, "What other sense is there?"

"When you have been here longer, you will not have to

ask. There are as many occasions for sin as there are birds in the trees. Or trees in the jungle. Or monkeys—"

"A voluptuary," said Sarah, "according to my husband, is a man distracted from the Company's business by the lure of personal pleasure."

"Look about you." Martha laughed. "Is this dwelling not popish?"

"Mr. Higginbottham likens this dwelling to the Sun King's summer palace." Then Sarah grew suddenly serious, reaching out to clasp Hannah's hand. "I should not wish to live here, not if Mr. Higginbottham were away as much as Mr. Legge appears to be."

Martha dropped her voice. "This house is said to have hauntings. Tell me, do you hear a gentleman's feet on the roof? He is not an Englishman. Many have seen a gentleman in Mughal robes smoke his *huqqa* and pace in the moonlight."

Hannah felt called on to defend her mastery of the premises. "There are no ghosts on my roof, I assure you." But she knew that hauntings were for blistered, sunlit tropics as well as for dark woods near Salem. That's why she had Bhagmati sleep on a pallet in the middle of the balcony, just outside her bedroom door.

The sinister talk of the roof, however, reminded her of her first day's unpleasantness, the touch of madness that she had experienced and that she dared not share, not even with Gabriel lest Gabriel challenge the Chief Factor to a duel. "And what of Mr. Prynne? How do you judge his acumen?"

Martha stiffened. "Mr. Prynne is the very model of a Company man. He dedicates himself entirely to profit."

"But he is selfless," Sarah protested. "If he dedicates himself to turning a desert into a garden of riches, it is for our welfare and not his."

At that very moment, the tinkle of Bhagmati's bangles alerted Hannah to one of her servant's silent communications. She seemed to understand English, but did not speak it, nor did Hannah speak more than a word or two of the local languages. But through her eyes, and her body, Bhagmati communicated. Some guest was downstairs. That guest was Indian and male, therefore not to be shown upstairs unless specifically invited.

"Who could it be?" Hannah turned to her guests. "An Indian visitor?"

Martha Ruxton rolled off the cushions to her feet. Again, for an instant, the freckles flared. "I thought you might profit from acquainting yourself with the trader Pedda Timanna." She led the way out of the overdecorated room.

The Englishwomen were now in a group walking to the archway that opened on the balcony. It was a radiantly bright, Mughal evening, the moon lighting the sky like a blue-gray curtain. The trees and outlines and vague shapes of Englishmen stood out in black profile against the late twilight.

"A horrible man," Sarah Higginbottham cautioned.

Martha laughed. "But he too turns deserts into gardens of riches."

The visitor was the small-headed trader who had recovered the Legges' missing trunk on the day that the Legges had disembarked at Fort St. Sebastian. On that first, confused morning, Hannah had read arrogance and insubordination in his halting the contact of Gabriel's fist with the umbrella bearer's face. Now, two years into her Indian years, she felt a certain admiration for the wizened man who sat in his palanquin outside her door, still borne on the shoulders of two old men shorter than himself.

Pedda Timanna brought his hands together and bowed his head to each of the ladies. And to Hannah's surprise, Martha Ruxton reached into a small purse and extracted five heavy pagodas, as much money as Hannah had seen at one time. And Pedda Timanna slid open a small drawer built into the footrest of his palanquin and dropped, one by one, a diamond, two rubies and an emerald into the pink, soft waiting hand of the fort doctor's wife.

Martha turned toward Hannah, suddenly an older, worldly-wise expatriate. Even her voice was deeper, and resonantly resolute. "My advice to all English wives in this cursed land, Mistress Legge, is this. Let your husband provide you all necessities. You provide yourself the amenities. Acquaint yourself with a trader." She held the diamond up to the moon. "Jewels travel with ease."

It was not a simple matter of profit for Martha Ruxton. Hannah guessed Martha was a voluptuary.

N O , I D O N O T think the diamond that passed from the richest trader to the sharpest buyer was the Emperor's Tear. This was a provincial gem, a Coromandel beauty, a Burton-to-Taylor bauble. There is no evidence that the Emperor's Tear was ever out of Emperor Aurangzeb's clutches, and he was waging border wars against Raja Jadav Singh a few miles to the north and west. But the fate that brought Hannah Easton to India and, finally, briefly, put her in contact with India's most perfect diamond, so improbable in its Brookfield origins, had already consumed 99.9 percent of the distance between them, and she was only twenty-seven years old.

I am thirty-two years old, and I have devoted eleven years of my life, off and on, to the reconstruction not just of a time and a place, but also of a person. She and I, New England and India, Venn and—no, that's not fair. I will not reveal her life before she leads it; that feels like a violation of the respect I feel and the methods I have chosen. It feels, frankly, too much like the methods and wishes of Bugs Kilken.

Venn, I know, is amazed. I may not have the National Weather Service and satellite-tracking data to feed into my little model of Fort St. Sebastian, but I do have the daily meteorologic observations of Mir Ali, the customs official who logged the contents of every ship. I have the sales receipts of every licensed store in the fort, and a record of official exports.

"Venn," I plead, "tell me when I have enough. Make your next program X-29-1695." He's supportive; he's impressed. Maybe, he says, studying the original engravings of "White Town, Fort Sebastian," and the layouts of both Black and White Towns, and the punishment records, with every house demarcated as to owner and function, he could begin to create a very bare stage, a kind of Beckettian rendering of seventeenth-century South India. It would have the specificity I require, and a diamond might still be lost, but in the fullness of time, he says, computer-assisted time reconstruction will be possible. It will be, literally, the mother of all data bases. It will be time on a scale of 1:1, with a new concept of real time. He won't call it time-travel. Neither we, nor time, will have traveled an inch, or a millisecond.

6

THE COMPANY'S regulations required Chief Factor Prynne to keep an official diary and consultation books of meetings with his subordinates and with visiting members of the Council at Fort St. George. But Gabriel Legge, too, maintained a diary, which for a man as restless as he was seems surprising. Perhaps Gabriel distrusted Prynne to provide for Leadenhall Street truthful summaries of daily business conducted in St. Sebastian, its small, dingy subordinate factory. Or perhaps he was contemptuous of the young apprentices and writers, like Thomas Tringham, who had wept like a woman over his hound's carcass in full view of local mobs on the beach.

Gabriel Legge's *Diary* is useful in that it unintentionally discloses how often he deserted Hannah in Henry Hedges' eerie house, with no company other than the maid Bhagmati.

At least in the first year and a half of his tenure of the Company's junior factorship in St. Sebastian, he seemed to have enjoyed good relations with the difficult Cephus Prynne. Here are some of his *Diary* entries:

February 11, 1695: Obtained orders from Chief Factor Prynne to vissit the factories south of the Penner River and conduct inspections concerning improprieties. Sett saile on the small English Pinck, called the Little Teresa.

February 20: Very foule weather.

February 25: A Dutch Fly-boate wee found rideing, its foretop-mast crackt. We invited its Commander, Senr. Hartsinck, on board the Little Teresa, *whereupon the Commander informed us that in its passage the Fly-boate lost a man overboard. We demanded as gift from Senr. Hartsinck refreshment of fruite, Hoggs And water, which gift the Dutch Commander was happy to relinquish.*

February 28: Wee came on shoare at Sadraspatam, the Agent receiving us with respect.

June 30: Wee are informed that our factorye at St. Andrews is frequently home to Romish Priests. Our Affaires here are in foolish Posture. Wee have little confidence in the ability of Mr. Richard Ruckle, who was re-entertained as Chief at a sallary of 100 LI per annum.

August 26: Wee advise you to see to the sending home of Mr. Richard Ruckle, and to appoint a more fitt and faithfull person as Chief at St. Andrews.

October 18: Wee are informed of complaints concerning Our Cloath which merchants here in St. Catherine describe as being full of Mothes. Wee have also been in receipt of complaints concerning white Ants in some of Our Cloath.

November 29: Wee noate that the Counsell at Fort St. George recommends me to remaine at our factorye in St. Catherine and to use my utmost endeavors to discover whether the fault is in the Maker of Our Cloath or in the Warehouse.

January 18, 1696: Wee have the Nombers of the bayles and peeces of Our goods in which wee have ascertained defects. We shall advise you of such goods. We inquire Liberty for the Selling of such goods cheape.

March 20: On retorne to our factorye at St. Andrew, wee are sorry to find that Mr. Ruckle continues to proceed in irregular actions.

If he stay longer, he may doe the Honourable Companye mischiefe.

June 6: Wee do hope you will permit us to present the requested Pesh-Kash *to the Nawab's uncle that wee may obtain greater accommodation in Our Trade from the said Nawab.*

July 24: As to the matter of Mr. Richard Ruckle, wee have proofe that he behaves in scandalous fashion on Sabbath daies.

August 1: Wee are very glad that you have inquired yourself into the unfitt conduct of Mr. Richard Ruckle and have graunted us our desire to send Mr. Ruckle home.

There were two Gabriel Legges, the wild and expansive Gabriel Legge who'd shown up in Salem with his tales of mountains and camels, deserts and lakes; Gabriel Legge the jealous lover and husband; the democratic Gabriel Legge who, alone among Company factors, seemed to enjoy the hardship postings, the company of rough and low-born privateers, local traders and artisans. And then there was the cautious Gabriel Legge, who worked grudgingly under Cephus Prynne and Samuel Higginbottham, men of small compass and meager imagination, whose grasp of profit was dictated by turnover and not investment.

Hannah watched her husband retire early behind his bedroom doors, ledger books open, cursing the failed opportunities and drinking until spilling the ink pot or losing the thread of commercial narrative. His eye patch was no longer dashing and touchingly vain—it was the curse of the record keeper. The logbooks of the factors are models of scrupulous entries and veiled discontents; I have pored over Gabriel's accounts for mention of Hannah, "my goode wyffe," and found only paltry recognition of the woman sewing just a few feet away.

He would be gone, weeks on end, into the jungles and up the coast as far as Hughli, now Calcutta, and down to Lanka.

"My goode wyffe tonight entertained women in my absence. My goode wyffe bade accompany me to the *mittah*, but was dissuaded. Incommodious facilities for whytte women of gentel byrthe," writes Gabriel Legge in defense of his decision; the interior, or the smaller stations up and down the coast, untouched by European influence, must have been brutal tests of stamina and resistance. Factors came out of those encounters with village India reeling with fevers, distempers, malaria, fatigue. Malaria carried off half the factors and probably left the survivors victims of fevers the rest of their lives. Many didn't make it back to the fort at all, dying within hours from generic "tropical plagues," which must have encompassed the full range of viral disease from rabid-bat and -dog bites to polio, the full rainbow of waterborne dysenteries (they had as many euphemisms for diarrhea as Eskimos have for snow). The head aches constantly, cuts suppurate, the bowels—well, the bowels come in for obsessive chronicling, which would indicate the commonness of defecatory commentary, like sports chat around the watercooler. Even the happy or melancholy outcome of other factors' daily bout with the thunder mug are jealously or gloatingly recorded in Gabriel's logs.

To his credit, whatever we may say of Gabriel Legge, he was a man capable of great loyalty, but he placed his faith more in ideals than institutions. The ideal of England in India moved him. The idea of spreading enlightenment, science, sanitation and, as he understood it, Christian tolerance, and of absorbing the best in the culture around him, was a continual delight. His practical nature was not at war with his lust for maximum profit, and both dictated the keeping of an open mind. But the idea of the "glorious enterprise" being the exclusive reservation of the Company and of posturing little potentates like Cephus Prynne and Samuel Higginbottham reduced him to rage and, finally, treachery.

I mean, of course, a treachery even greater than the relatively straightforward murder of the Chief Factor. Greater than the marital infidelities, the parallel families he had fathered and for whom, honorably enough, he provided. Internecine homicide among East India factors, which could easily be blamed on tropical passion, drink, brigands or the depredations of local highwaymen, were not uncommon. "Fevers" is a blanket term, and who is to say, three hundred years later, that murder was not the dark companion of many deaths? These were adventurous men with nothing to lose, driven by mercantile lust, in a time and place that provided cover for base designs. You set aggressive men on a course of unstructured competition, and they soon become desperate men in unscrupulous battle. It's a wonder they didn't destroy themselves utterly.

He was a man perched on the edge of some great cataclysmic upheaval, I think now; a man of thirty-five—which was borrowed time in that place and century—though of course still vigorous. A desperate man faced with a gray, careworn future of subservience. Or a man waiting to make a leap.

The marital relations of Hannah and Gabriel are an area of mystery today, because they were areas of discretion three hundred years ago. Abundant evidence exists as to their sexual natures, which were vigorous. It would seem that Gabriel enjoyed the favors a white man felt his due in an Asian culture. Where he traveled, he planted his seed. That Hannah felt herself exempt from the bibi jealousies of a Sarah or Martha also appears self-evident. She was not raised, or trained, in garrison expectations of male infidelity. She had not led the desperate sort of life, like Sarah, that substituted gratitude for tolerance. She was a faithful wife who had attracted her share of suitable beaux and suitors, and who resisted courtings and temptations even when expectations and opportunities presented themselves.

Hannah convinced herself that Cephus Prynne conspired to keep her husband from her, but conceded that Gabriel Legge relished his travels up and down the Coromandel Coast, exercising power over the Company's agents and chief factors in tiny outposts. If Gabriel missed Hannah's companionship, he kept all yearnings to himself. He sent her few messages while away, but he regaled her with outrageous stories of impossible adventures when he came home.

The falling out between Gabriel Legge and Chief Factor Prynne didn't happen until the winter of 1696. It started with a public notice that the Company's Seal had been misused for private business by a junior factor and that from now on the Seal was to be kept in a box with three locks, the keys to which were to be in the sole possession of the Chief Factor. It escalated when Gabriel ordered repairs on a warehouse that had been damaged by floods. It exploded into a scuffle when the Chief Factor humiliated Gabriel by reprimanding him in front of young Tringham and a freshly arrived apprentice for having bound a cash keeper with the man's own girdle and delivering fifty crippling blows with a stick to the man's soles. The cash keeper had died later that evening. Of a heart attack in his hut, according to Gabriel's report. "In future be frugal in your hate as you are in your love," Cephus Prynne had mocked, "so we may not have to disburse grand gifts to the Nawab's minister to halt the police report."

After the scuffle, Gabriel Legge spent more time drinking with freemen and privateers and less time reforming the conduct of Company employees like Richard Ruckle or reorganizing the subordinate factories' books. The "*poddar* (cashkeeper) affaire," in fact, made Gabriel a hero among Europeans who were not in the employment of East India companies owned by rich men in London and Paris and Amsterdam and Copenhagen.

7

AT ATTILA CSYCSYRY'S Suchikhana, the stuffy, smoky, infernally hot den of male privilege in Fort St. Sebastian, the men were drunk and complaining. Pedda Timanna had been spotted in White Town, bold as you please, riding in his palanquin despite traditional prohibitions against black trespass and ostentation, and stopping briefly at a white man's house.

The ban against the baboons should never have been lifted, said the men as one: Chief Factor Prynne said so from the front table where he was served his single glass of claret; so did his chief detractor from the rear table, the Alsatian gunner of promiscuous employment who called himself the Marquis de Mussy but had been born a baker's son from Aachen named Klaus Engelhardt; so did, with greater or lesser enthusiasm, Dr. Ruxton, Higginbottham, and some young factors, some foreign visitors from the Portuguese or French forts, some

English travelers or interlopers and other free-lance traders. It
had taken Gabriel Legge several weeks to finally join the drinking contingent at Count Csycsyry's Suchikhana; he'd gone there
as a guest of the cynical and disaffected Marquis de Mussy.

It had started as a typical night at Count Attila's, with
the usual crowd seated in their rigid hierarchies, reflecting
their usual animosities. The Marquis was a pirate, as were
many others. A liquor concession in an abstemious country
under the grip of the orthodox Grand Mughal Aurangzeb
himself is an oasis open to lions and gazelles alike, and not to
be lightly barred on grounds of moral repugnance.

In Black Town, the Muslim overlords tolerated so-called
punch houses for the Christians and gentiles, meaning Hindus
and various forms of unacceptable half castes, so long as no
araq, the staple English arrack, a potent rice or molasses liquor,
was sold to the faithful. Attila Csycsyry, an oft wounded, now
philosophical Transylvanian Protestant who'd followed the
Turk-hating mercenary trail that led, finally, to the Coromandel Coast, did not, exactly, run an arrack house. To his
thinking, arrack houses were notorious bhang dens, where
alcoholics spiced their drinks with hemp and opium, where
knife fights broke out and ended in murders.

He was, to himself, a publican. But on Company land,
public houses were not permitted. And so, an ever-resourceful
immigrant in a concession of traders, he had appropriated a
name known to all, Suchikhana, meaning "water room." Attila
was a water bearer, an honorable profession in the land of a
desert-bor   faith. He was a purveyor of civilized European
wines, brandies, beer, whiskeys and, for habitués who tasted,
then tolerated, then demanded, the barbaric local brews: rums,
palm *tari*, which the English called toddy, and the deadly

arracks, which he brewed in his own distillery on the cleared
land just west of the fort. He drew the line at bhang.

The Suchikhana was part social club and part meeting hall
for those who rejected the Company's paternalistic and poorly
rewarded attentions. Freemen, pirates, interlopers, adulterers,
dropped by early in the afternoon when they were not sacking
Surati merchants' ships or bribing the Nawab's men, and they
were transported home in carts or litters by Csycsyry if they
couldn't stagger to the door. The Suchikhana was a place for
privateers to barter information on schedules, routes and flag
protections for ships laden with enough gold to be worth their
taking.

What to Cephus Prynne and the Company Council was
piracy was to Gabriel and the more disaffected factors a kind
of zesty entrepreneurial initiative. He enjoyed his evenings
drinking with YellowBeard Huyghen, ThroatCut de Azvedo
and Cutlass da Silva, men who had made themselves over.
Once upon a time, de Azvedo had been a physician and rabbi's
son. YellowBeard Huyghen had been a butcher in Batavia.
Over liquor made from palms, from rice, from molasses, they
told stories of sea voyages too fantastic to have occurred to
men with tame names like Samuel or Thomas or Cephus. Even
Gabriel's own tales, those that had astounded the hidebound
Puritans of Salem and won the hand of Hannah, he now saw
as secondhand. In the story competitions Gabriel remained
silent, remembering the better ones for retelling at home.

One such traveler was an Antonio Careri, a Venetian au-
todidact and physician who claimed he was following in the
footsteps of his uncle, Gemelli Careri, who had experienced
many marvels in the jungles around Count Attila's Suchikhana.

"Seems there was this woman, you see," the Italian began,

"washed up on an island. No human beings around, only this lovesick buck baboon . . ."

The men started laughing; they knew the joke or many like it.

"So the weeks go by, and she yields, and the months go by and she has a half-monster child, and then years go by and a second comes along, hideous as the first. . . .

"Then one day, a ship passes. The baboon and the pups are in the cave where he keeps them. She signals and they save her. Seems the baboon wakes up from his toddy drinking and looks out just as the lady is being rowed out to the ship. So what do you think he does?"

"I know what I'd do," said Dr. Ruxton.

"What about you, Mr. Legge? What would you do?" asked Cephus Prynne.

"If I were a baboon?" He didn't like the question, the pointedness of Prynne's interrogation. The Chief Factor's verbal amusements all held implicit threats, or testings.

"I should have no choice, Mr. Prynne. A baboon cannot speak, cannot swim, cannot fire a cannon."

"Perhaps throw a coconut out to sea?" Mr. Prynne laughed.

"Or resign himself to loss," said Gabriel. "Raise his pups with hate in their hearts."

The Italian picked up his story. "In rage and grief, it is written, the baboon carried the unnatural issue to the beach and sacrificed them in her sight. So horrified were the sailors at the vision that they threw the woman overboard, lest her corruption damn the ship's body."

It was for Dr. Ruxton to provide the moral. "And so again she is washed up on the beach. The baboon forgives her. They go back to the cave. Such is it ever with those who step over the border."

"In a kingdom west of here," the Italian visitor began again, "a great baboon much attracted to a serving girl began courting her at night. So persistent was he that finally her father yielded his permission, thinking he would soon tire of her, or she of him. But passion did so infect the beast he could not navigate soberly in the dark. Every morning, upon awakening, the girl's father found his tiny hut a shambles of carnality, and the girl helpless to forbid it."

"Aye," agreed Samuel Higginbottham, who had heard many tales of baboon bibis, and was glad to have his suspicions about local women once again confirmed.

"A Portugee happened to pass through the village one day, and spotted the wench bathing in the river. Much attracted to her, he lingered nearby until after dark, thinking to seize the maiden for himself—only to see this great lurching beast burst through the window with a loud crash of pots and breaking tables.

"The young man was much offended by the girl's poor taste in lovers and so demanded of her father the meaning of such outrage. But you know the Zentoo mind—"

"Slaves of the basest passion—"

"Pariahs, excrement, devil's spawn—"

"Doubtless, good sirs. But I refer only to their cowardice when confronted by their clearest duty. The father holds out his hands and says, 'What can I do? This creature has taken my daughter's honor and makes all this noise when he does not find her at home.'

" 'Why don't you kill him?' the Portugee demanded."

"Indeed, as any man would do," Cephus Prynne opined. It was generally agreed that therein lay the difference between European, even Portuguese, and Asiatic sensibility. The Asiatic, without a concept of manhood, lacked all notion of patriotism, loyalty, honesty, decency and honor. No honor is taken where none exists. God would not permit the theft of what He intended be preserved.

The group had now warmed to a congenial topic. The Asiatic mind and its failings.

Antonio Careri was not to finish his story that night. How might he have ended his "Portugee-Bests-the-Baboon" yarn? I have read endless variations of these racist anecdotes. The white man, being more manly, easily disposes of the dark-skinned, subhuman competitor. But he does not live happily ever after with the distressed damsel whom he has rescued. He discovers just in time that she has been tainted by life among the baboons, and he throws her—this time to drown —back into the sea.

The baboon stories swirled around Gabriel Legge in the smoky Suchikhana. The storytellers indulged in asides on Pedda Timanna and Henry Hedges. Pedda Timanna was crafty and dishonest, they claimed; an ingrate, a braggart and a traitor; a leech, a parasite, a scorpion. It was the view of Chief Factor Prynne that the Company coffers in Fort St. Sebastian had been depleted through the self-aggrandizing ventures of Henry Hedges, the late factor whom Gabriel had been dis-patched to replace. The results of Henry Hedges' submission to luxury—some claimed for love of a woman—were certainly plain to see. A badge of shame, some drinkers hissed; the moral fiber of the Company would be strengthened by a show of mass arson.

Gabriel Legge, who was the new man in the post, hence the beneficiary of collective wisdom, took from the storytellers' spite his own determination to rise above it. He would assem-ble such a fortune that he would not have to spend his evenings ranting about the depredations of a black merchant or a white sensualist. He would buy his way out of the petty hierarchies.

That evening a misguided concept of personal liberty fueled Gabriel Legge. He would never exhaust the space provided by the half-filled drawers of the carved dressers and armoires at his disposal, nor could he ever in twenty years wear all the clothes that Hedges had left behind. But that was personal folly. Prynne might claim that Hedges had appropriated Company funds to indulge his weaknesses, but as Gabriel had studied Company records, he had perceived the shortfalls were more ingrained in the system. The real trouble lay in the mismanagement of Cephus Prynne himself and his inability to drive the hard bargains with local suppliers upon which Company profits rested.

While others joked and gossiped, Gabriel thought of ways to make an ally of Pedda Timanna. Since Pedda Timanna had his eyes and ears in every *mittah*, he had to know how weak the Chief Factor's hand really was and how desperate he was to show even short-term and empty profits to deflect the pressure he was under from the Council at Fort St. George. *Do not show fear or weakness in your dealings*—that was drummed into the head of every young factor even before leaving Leadenhall Street. So Timanna was pressing Prynne hard for greater trade concessions, demanding higher cash advances for procuring the quantity of salampores and embroidered muslins that London wanted. Worse, he was refusing to accept in full or partial payment the unsalable European goods—woolens, brimstone, tin, gloves—that Prynne had foolishly imported.

Timanna had just returned from Pondicherry, where he'd been scouting better deals with the French, probably so he could buy more ships and more houses. He already owned,

Prynne had had confirmed, in Black Town, eight gardens, five houses—two of which had spectacular views of the ocean—two lots, three godowns, or warehouses, four shops and two ships. His ships carried export cargoes of textiles and surplus English woolens to Malacca and Acheh. Moneylending to him was a hobby, and he indulged it with dedication. At least one European, a woman now dead, was rumored to have mortgaged to him a pouchful of diamonds and invested in his Malaccan trade.

India hands like Prynne and Ruxton hated Pedda Timanna not simply because he was wealthier than they, but for something far worse: he flaunted his self-respect.

He was a merchant-adventurer, not a beholden middleman like Kashi Chetty or Catchick Sookian. His power came from his indifference to European factors and the frugality of their Europe-centered trade. The Fort St. George Governor, John Goldsborough, and Council treated Cephus Prynne, who'd been banished to a nowhere post like Fort St. Sebastian, with disdain. Prynne, in turn, treated Indian power brokers with condescension. Scorn made them intimate.

"He seems a most formidable adversary," said Gabriel.

"Then I hope you were listening, Mr. Legge," the Chief Factor announced with practiced emphasis, "for the dwelling in White Town that Pedda Timanna stopped at last night was none other than your own."

"I believe my wife was entertaining Mrs. Ruxton and Mrs. Higginbottham. I shall inquire as to the nature of his visit. If such occurred."

"I was taking tea on my terrace last evening. The moon was full. Quite full enough, Mr. Legge."

And so saying, bowing courteously to one and all, the Chief Factor took his leave.

HANNAH SLEPT ALONE; Gabriel was on one of his walks, to clear his head after drinking. He and his drinking companion, the Marquis, had stumbled home in the dark— a familiar pattern these last few nights—wakening first Bhagmati, who slept on the terrace outside her mistress's door on a rolled-out mat. She slept in her working clothes and was up at once, rolling her floor-length hair in a loose braid, then pinning it on top of her head in the few moments it took Gabriel to climb the stairs. Then she managed to disappear, leaving the terrace and the opened bedroom door to Gabriel and Hannah, with the Marquis standing at a distance behind.

Hannah had been cautioned by Martha and Sarah to avoid the Marquis. He was a man of sinister plans, a mercenary who had fought for fat fees on behalf of any Muslim nawab or Hindu raja who had enough jewels to hire him. The querulous subcontinent had made the baker's son immensely wealthy. As a hand-me-down, a belated wedding gift, the Marquis had passed on to Gabriel a *huqqa* of solid gold enameled with garnet-dark poppies and azure-winged butterflies, an amber-embedded alabaster carpet weight as tall as the cook's toddling child, a leaf-shaped mirror of jade and rock crystal, a sword inscribed in a curly alien script with an invocation to fight or die.

"Wife!" She knew not to answer.

"I say, my good Christian Massachusetts Bay Puritan wife. Have you missed me?"

"Of course, my husband."

"Have you entertained yourself in my absence?"

"Only with my sewing."

"Your sewing! You hear that, monsieur le Marquis? Every night more sewing, more embroidery."

"A most fortunate man, M'sieur Legge."

"A black man named Pedda Timanna did not visit?"

She knew the uselessness of lying. But she had nothing to hide. "He had business with Mrs. Ruxton. I believe he sells her diamonds."

"In my house?"

"He is not permitted in Dr. Ruxton's house. I believe they must arrange their meetings thusly."

She answered in a clear, forthright voice. Gabriel Legge knew from the example of the unfortunate Hubert and of doctors in Stepney that men were attracted to his wife, and, furthermore, her power of attraction was no matter of shame or embarrassment to her. In the mood of the time, which is barely changed, *she bore watching*. And Gabriel was possessed of more than a jealous streak; unfaithfulness he might have accepted before deception. His wife had presented him with the occasion of the former—though never acted—but never a hint of the latter.

"And Mr. Cephus Prynne—has he visited as well?"

"Never after the first day. And I do believe he regards himself as unwelcome here."

And with that, Hannah had returned to her bed, leaving the door open should Gabriel, even in his drunken state, choose to visit. Bhagmati stood at the far end of the terrace, waiting either to scurry to distant quarters, should Gabriel claim the marriage bed, or to again unroll her mat as a sentry outside her mistress's door.

SHE AWAKES with the first streak of dawn, the twittering of the first birds. The house seems full of noises, but not of voices or movement. The echoes, it seems, of great events. Bhagmati's mat is still unrolled, but the girl is gone. Gabriel's boots are lined up on the terrace at the top of the stairs. Gabriel is asleep, loudly and drunkenly, in his room, still dressed but for his shoes and belt. He has fallen across the width of the bed, the very picture of exhaustion. Hannah knows from the snoring he will sleep the Sabbath away, another small demerit that will be administered by the Company Council.

At the edge of the fort, in the still-dark west, jackals howl and hyenas chuckle like cardplayers in a room next door. Buzzards circle. The noise is coming from overhead, and the sky is turning pink over the ocean; dawn will come quickly.

The rope ladder to the roof has been moved into climbing position. She doesn't know whether to climb or to watch, but soon the indecision is taken away, for the ladder is adjusted ever so slightly by invisible hands and slowly a regal form descends in a white shimmering material and gold ceinture, her ankles and wrists jangling softly with gold. Hannah ducks behind her door. It is that two-dimensional time of the dawn, or of history, the light not yet able to endow shape with form or meaning. The woman's long black hair looks at a distance, in the pale light and against the white silk, like a giant fissure cut across her back. The white-wrapped arms seem to move separately, severed from each other by the hair, and she dashes down the far end of the terrace, entering a room behind a splintered door that had always been locked. It must be, she knows, Bhagmati, but a servant transformed. Hannah watches, and watches, but no one emerges from the storage room, and now the sky is morning bright though the sun has not yet risen above the ocean's far curve. By this time, Chief Factor

Prynne is usually pacing his terrace, offering his profile to the sun, but not this morning.

She will try to sleep an hour or two and rise in time for services. No reason for both of them to be fined. Maybe she'll screw up her courage to beg the Chief Factor's forgiveness for her husband's indisposition.

But she finds she cannot sleep. She has lost control of her house, as though its complicated history, its artwork, the convolutions of its predecessor's fancies and obsessions, were all coming out this morning to claim their inheritance. The simple servant girl returned in her familiar sleeping-and-waking clothes, rolled up her mat and began the light whisking of the terrace with her stick-bundle broom, leaving no trace of the queenly vision that had descended.

"Bhagmati," Hannah called.

The girl presented herself at the opened door. The morning light behind her was blinding white, and she merely a slim black cutout against it.

"I saw you. You were on the roof terrace. You were dressed in white silks and gold. You went behind that door."

The girl said nothing.

"Bhagmati, what are you?"

No, she did not believe in ghosts and witches. Those were the primitive beliefs of the world she had come from. But she did believe in evil, and in possession, in falsity and magic. She could not hold with poor Hubert that the world was explicable by formula and experiment. That was the faith of an Englishman who had never seen America, and never seen India. And having seen India, and America, Hannah knew she could never be content in England. The girl continued sweeping the terrace, opening the bird cage and feeding the parrot, singing softly to herself.

She knows that men have died for her. She knows that the world that seems so calm and peaceful this Sabbath morning is full of furious meaning, but refuses to reveal itself.

AT THE INQUIRY later, all attested to the fact that Cephus Prynne had left alone. None were seen to have followed him. The walk up the hill from Sonapatnam wall to White Town was considered an evening's constitutional stroll, indulged in safely by one and all, except of course the women. It was not unknown that jackals prowled the trash pits and hyenas inspected the burial grounds; both those areas were, by mutual agreement, far outside the perimeters of civil protection.

Of course, on the field where the body of Cephus Prynne was found, three days later, in the most deplorable condition of tropical decomposition, bandits and brigands of every persuasion had often wielded uncontested power. Very little flesh remained, but for the tight skin of the forehead, upon which the letter *H* in a Roman script had been slashed. And on parts of the body the pariah dogs and buzzards and hyenas had not carried away, other letters were faintly discernible—an *A*, a *C*, an *E*—as though the Hindus or Muslims had thought by a promiscuous imitation of the English alphabet they were pointing the finger of guilt away from them, instead of directly at their hearts.

8

IT HAD RAINED steadily for three days from a high, bright sky the day that Two-Headed Ravanna and his three sons were impaled for the murder of Chief Factor Cephus Prynne. Ravanna, a well-known local cutthroat who had never before attacked a white man, earned his name for the goiter that extruded from his neck and lay on his shoulder like a second head (which in jest he often emblazoned with eyes and a mouth). He went to his agonized death slowly lowered upon the sharpened *shul*, surviving to hear loud cheering as the gory spike burst from his bowels and out the very eye socket of his phantom head, and lasting with sufficient strength to curse the Mughal Governor, Haider Beg; the Company Governor, John Goldsborough; and the motley assortment of traders and factors who had sworn to his presence outside the gates near Attila Csycsyry's distillery the night of Cephus Prynne's disappearance.

All *firangi* men and women participated in the credible lie that Chief Factor Prynne had been slain by highway bandits. These are times of famine and skirmish! Bolt your portals against Zentoos and Moors! The jungle is no place to turn the other cheek!

Fearing a correlation between plunging morale and plunging profits, the Fort St. George Council met in extraordinary session and unanimously promoted Samuel Higginbottham to chief factor.

There were some rumors that weeks before his death, Prynne had accused Higginbottham of deceit or theft and had asked for insulting clarifications on several entries of prices of goods and costs of sorting, weighing and packing them for shipping home. To counteract these malicious rumors, Sarah spread rumors of her own: Pedda Timanna's hired assassins were behind the incident. John Ruxton told the young writers that he had seen enough curious deaths on the Coromandel Coast to know for sure that fools expired of cholera, lunacy and flux, and knaves were killed by daggers, garrotes and poisons. Martha Ruxton convinced herself that the mutilated corpse recovered near the distillery was not Cephus Prynne's at all.

Nawab Haider Beg was not disconcerted by Prynne's precipitous removal. *Firangi* factors were expendable. The institution of bribes-for-influence would endure. The weaker the English Company, the stronger the competition from privateers. The more cutthroat the rivalry, the richer the coffers of the Mughals. He arranged the magistrates' ruling: the Englishman got drunk as Englishman were wont to do and was set upon by idol-worshiping robbers who owed their political allegiance to the Hindu Raja, Jadav Singh, who lived in the sandstone hill-fort beyond the jungle.

The evening after the body was recovered and buried ceremoniously with gun salutes, Gabriel took Hannah for a ride along the surf-scalloped shore. Beyond the sand reef a two-masted Dutch hooker flying the Marquis's flag of scarlet crossed cannons on an onyx field was unloading its cargo into *kutta-marams*. On the beach fishermen were spreading torn nets across the dunes; children were teasing sand crabs out of their holes; gulls, crows and pariah dogs were picking through entrails of discarded fish.

Twilight is so fragile in the tropics! Nightfall so sudden and unequivocal! I can see Hannah, taut spined on horseback, and Gabriel eager, impatient, riding ahead to meet the piratical Marquis. In every lungful of velvety night vapors, Hannah tastes the warmth and wetness of the Coromandel Coast's peculiar fecund mortality.

We know that Hannah and Gabriel Legge were on the beach on a June night in 1697. We know that Hannah suddenly let go of her reins, that she twisted impulsively, violently, in her saddle, and kissed Gabriel. We know this because recent scholarship about the Company's trade is finally retrieving the communal and individual memorial of the "Hindoos and the Coromandel Moors." All the stories are there, scattered in a thousand libraries and a million scraps of information. Put them together, as Hannah's life does, and a consistent story emerges. In the consultation books of the Company's factories and forts, the story of the Coromandel Coast is the story of Europe, of white nations battling each other in outposts paved with gold. It is the story of North America turned inside out.

A fisherman's child, crouched behind a sand dune, witnessed Hannah Legge's kiss. Reared in an overcrowded shack where sexuality was furtive, a fierce, efficient grab and shudder and nothing more, he watched, mesmerized, the beautiful white woman seize her man right there on the beach, *his* beach, and vent on him without coyness and without shame her wild *firangi* passions and selfish wants, and as he watched the woman greedily, shamelessly, he saw a vision of himself on another shore by another ocean, an adventurer without family, without caste, without country, cantering into worlds without rules.

An asset hunter knows when to continue digging long after economists and historians have stopped.

That fisherman's boy found his way to William III's court in London. There he chanced upon John Dryden's *Aureng-Zebe* and was incensed by its Eurocentric falsity. That fisherman's boy composed his own heroic play, *The World-Taker*, in rhyming couplets as a corrective. In the extant fragment, the anonymous fisherman-poet claimed that when he first came upon Dryden's confession that "true passion is too fierce to be in fetters bound," he was wracked by the vision that had befallen him years before on a sandy strip in neglected Fort St. Sebastian.

FOR HANNAH, too, that night served as a diving board into the Unknown. For there on the night-kohled rim of a seductive ocean, as the beach children hooted and giggled and threw fistfuls of sand, Gabriel announced to her he was joining the Marquis as a pirate.

The Marquis, in his honorable youth, had been a gunnery mate for the British in battles with the Spanish. Then he set himself up, *à la pige*, free-lance, for anyone who paid. There was no dishonor in being a mercenary or of working for the natives. A fractious subcontinent had made all of them rich, traders and militarists alike. Hindu against Muslim, Muslim against Sikh: it was a paradise on earth.

The dishonor that had banished the Marquis from Compagnie Royale service, and from respectable fraternity in all but Fort St. Sebastian, had been over a woman. As a rising young officer in the French outpost, then known in his Alsatian guise as Klaus Engelhardt, he had presented himself one morning half an hour late for dress parade. It was known he had been with his bibi. The young lieutenant had been offered a gentleman's choice, which he failed: ride the spindle-backed, blood-encrusted wooden horse for an hour with legs weighted down with iron for maximum penetration and possible permanent damage, or watch his bibi ride it before his eyes, and those of his mates, until her certain death.

A factor finds his true self by becoming a freebooter. There's no stopping voyages of self-discovery. Ditto for voyages of self-destruction.

Hannah, a foster child twice over, could inherit full knowledge of the world's wickedness, but she couldn't bequeath it to Gabriel. Gabriel was impulsive, charming, jealous, violent and generous. He had a democratic spirit; he worked well with blacks—better, in fact, than with whites. He truly did not understand the bargain of the world: the principle that Hubert had tried to teach. The equal-and-opposite reaction. So she let Gabriel sail on the *Esperance*, the Marquis's sloop. She did not ask him whose vessel he planned to plunder nor for what treasure he longed to risk his soul. He was not a pirate of simple rapacity as was the Marquis's second mate, Cutlass da Silva. And he was not like Captains John Avery and William Kidd, who relished harassing haj-bound pilgrims in order to enrage the Grand Mughal. Gabriel wouldn't, he couldn't, do what Pirate Avery had done in the winter of 1695, seize the proud, pious Emperor Aurangzeb's most prized vessel, the *Ganj-i-Sawai*, torture its passengerload of devout Muslims, violate veiled women from the imperial family and harem, then gloat off to Madagascar or the Mascarene with a booty of beauteous Turki slave girls and five million rupees in bullion.

Covetousness was not Gabriel's sin. He was a stubborn dispenser of unprincipled justice. He was a rash romantic with ungovernable yearnings. Hannah didn't plead with Gabriel to take her back to England. She was not ready to entomb herself in Morpeth or London. She didn't feel bereft—of roots, of traditions—as Martha and Sarah professed to feel. Instead she felt unfinished, unformed.

She was, she is, of course, a goddess-in-the-making.

The Coromandel had started something as immense as a cyclone deep inside her body and mind. To let Gabriel go was also to let herself expand.

Two weeks later she waved farewell to her husband as he sailed with the Marquis and Cutlass da Silva on his tyro mission. The goal was modest: harass the wealthy backers in Paris, Amsterdam and London. The prey, too, was modest: an English ketch, *Clyde's Folly*, which had been captured by the French at the mouth of the Palk Strait and was being escorted into the French port settlement of Pondicherry with a cargo of fifteen barrels of brandy and ten chests of crude coral. Hannah waved and waved until the *Esperance* pressed its prow through the gauzy lavender horizon.

HANNAH LOOKED on Cephus Prynne's murder as emancipation. Being rid of a sexual tormentor was the least cause for her new sense of liberty. In murder she saw the workings of an alien providence. She had no doubt that Gabriel had killed Prynne. Her conscience could not condone acts of murder—the teachings of Robert and Susannah Fitch were deeply embedded—but she was glad that for the present at least her Puritan conscience was aflounder like a Coromandel *kuttamaram* in a typhoon-churned sea.

If Cephus Prynne had died prematurely and precipitously,

but of natural causes, she and Gabriel would still be enmeshed in the corrupt embrace of the Company. Under Prynne, the satellite English in Fort St. Sebastian had begun to think of themselves as patriots planting the flag for King and Country, as missionaries of commerce martyring themselves for holy profit. The truth was, Hannah felt herself no more at home in England than she did in the Coromandel. She was deficient in that genetic impulse toward teary-eyed patriotism.

Piracy, in fact, seemed to her a normal outgrowth of the unnatural conditions of plunder and violence that were otherwise condoned, and even lauded, by the Company and its factors. The outrageous act of murder, conceded by no official but condemned by the Fort St. George Council, simultaneously cast the Legges out of Little England and bound them to it with the fastness of unconfessable guilt.

To Hannah emancipation meant she could stay on in the house that Henry Hedges' ghost still roamed and ruled. Once upon a time the creaks and moans had terrified her; now the house seemed as vast and as stocked with mysteries and wonder as the woods of Brookfield, as the universe of laws of the New Science that poor Hubert had tried to explain. Like Henry Hedges, she put herself in the hands of an Indian woman. Perhaps the same Indian woman. Ostracism opened up unwalled worlds for her.

She was taken by Bhagmati behind the splintered door where the white sari was kept carefully folded on top of a brocaded man's silk jama, to a makeshift shrine where an oil lamp burned. Flowers were arranged around a painting done in the court manner, of an Englishman in modified Mughal dress.

"Hedges-sa'ab," said Bhagmati. And another portrait of a

serving girl holding her arms out as a parrot perches on an overhanging branch. The bird cage is open. The girl's face— Bhagmati's face, obviously the painters had sat on this terrace under Hedges' patronage—registers sheer terror, but Bhagmati laughed.

"Bird-come-back," she said.

WHEN GABRIEL LEGGE was offered a way out of the Company, he took it. Emancipation from the Company meant signing on with the dead Chief Factor's most hated competitor, the Marquis, and organizing the coast's stateless *firangis*, cynics and rebels into a joint-stock association with a huge common fund for outfitting piracy against the Indiamen of all European-chartered trading companies and against the fancy fleet of the Grand Mughal. Rich men like Count Attila Csycsyry subscribed in shares; brawny men like YellowBeard Huyghen, Cutlass da Silva and ThroatCut de Azvedo contributed some dormant image of themselves, for they were not born to plunder, nor were they born with the names they adopted. Perhaps piracy on the Coromandel Coast—going to sea, raising a flag of one's own, being the boss and dividing the loot, scuttling the sobersided sons of sea cooks who stood in the way—was the seed of the frontier dream, the circus dream, the immigrant dream of two centuries later. Gabriel invested all his hoarded capital, but was treasured more for his imagination, his genial leadership, his quick intelligence.

Soon the Marquis enlisted the embittered Pedda Timanna's support to buy, in exchange for tin, musical automatons, French wines and cheeses, two Coromandel-built three-masted vessels. For reasons of sentimentality and superstition, the *Esperance* remained the flagship, but Gabriel took over as its captain from ThroatCut de Azvedo. Through Pedda Timanna's influence with the Grand Mughal's representative, Nawab Haider Beg, Gabriel was able to acquire for the new joint-stock company of privateers an imperial *farman* to raise revenue and administer justice in a square mile of rough coastal land within Fort St. Sebastian's shadow.

This square mile he rechristened New Salem as a tribute to his wife.

GABRIEL CAPTAINED the *Esperance* on seventeen expeditions, each of them an adventure that put his earlier tall tales to shame. Legend credits Gabriel with having sacked the *Humility*, a Mughal pilgrim ship more richly laden than the *Ganj-i-Sawai* and the *Queddah Merchant*. He shipped his booty—the ingots, the pieces of eight, the Arab gold and Christian gold, the Moorish and the Burmese stones—to accomplices in New York, where, again, legend obscures its eventual disbursement. Some say the old friends could not resist the temptation; others say his loot lies just within the continental shelf where a corsair went down. He survived shipwrecks, cyclones, duels, whippings, at least one mutiny and two heartbreaks. There are handsome clans of Legges in Madagascar, Mauritius and Réunion. I've received a letter from a Vyankoji Legge of Bombay inquiring if his "sinister blood bondage to the aforesaid Gabrielji" qualified him for citizenry in the U.S. or the U.K., or a share of any recovered treasure.

Every now and then, a Legge Reclamation Project is announced. A parapsychologist and a credible-looking ex-SEAL in a wet suit and an Atlanta Braves cap come on CNN and announce the discovery of a Mughal pagoda off Marblehead or Truro.

I know who's behind it.

"Bugs," I say, "give it a rest."

"It's off Marblehead, I know it is," he tells me, sipping his Evian. *It, it, it,* the Emperor's Tear. He's in Aspen this time with the discard of an Asian dictator. Though our professional relationship has been over for years, I'm still the only person he can talk to about it. And he's the only person who knows nearly as much as I do.

"Don't confuse some crystal gazer with a diamond cutter, Bugs."

9

EVERY NOW AND THEN we hear of a gentleman robber, a polite soft-spoken white-collar wannabe who enlists respect from his victims and sympathy from the public: Gabriel Legge, the Robin Hood of the Coromandel Coast, seems to have been that kind of pirate.

On one expedition in the Laccadive Islands, legend has him holding Captain William Kidd's feet to a cookout fire to inflict on Kidd the same pleasures he had on the islanders, forcing them to dance on hot coals or to water wrestle with sharks in a shallow pool.

At St. Mary's in Madagascar, where freebooting New England slave traders had their headquarters, Gabriel is known to have bilked the gentleman slaver Adam Baldridge of eighty thousand pounds destined for his bank account in London, and to have humiliated him soundly by stripping him naked and tying him to a mast to be jeered by two hundred freed slaves destined for the American market.

In Zanzibar, he gambled for and won a Frenchman's ship, *Le Rêve Doré*, and discovered, in its airless, lightless hold, footed chests of jewels and gold urns and a writhing, moaning cargo of freaks and monsters—three-eyed maidens; identical jugglers joined in the head, the chest, the back; two-headed, four-armed girls who spoke separately, even in different languages; a three-headed youth with seven arms who made love to three separate women simultaneously; six-legged goats; old women with necklets of youthful, breast-shaped goiters—waiting to be shipped to the Sun King's court in Versailles. "Twynnes and monsters," he wrote, whom he dispatched mercifully by sword, "lest their deformitie rowse unseemlie lust."

The expedition that Gabriel liked to recount to his friend Attila "the Turk-hater" Csycsyry involved Peter the Great's "grand ambassador," Golovin, and a ship's carpenter, Pyotr Mikhaylov. Gabriel had met the two Russians when he had been shipwrecked off the coast of Java, and he had been picked off-sea by a Dutch East Indiaman carrying the two Russians on board. The carpenter, a jolly, gigantic man with a reformer's fiery, violent ideas, had ranted against the boyars, the landed aristocracy of his country, against the clergy of all nations, and especially against the Turks. He had dreamed of exterminating the Turks. It seemed strange indeed that a carpenter and an ambassador should be traveling together, and that the ambassador conveyed a worshipful attitude toward a simple tradesman.

Pyotr Mikhaylov, agreeing with Gabriel, had been for the

freeing of the slaves, and for the stringing up of the slavers' captains. "Free them all!" he shouted, sloshing the potent clear liquid into beer-sized mugs, "bring on the carpenters, the builders, the sailors, the poets." True to his word, he had freed and Russified an Abyssinian the Dutch had bought for resale.

The story always came to a climax with his assertion that the young carpenter, drunk on what he called "little water," had said, "Someday you will tell your children you drank vodka with Peter, Czar of all the Russias."

GABRIEL'S SEVENTH expedition is written up in many histories, French, Dutch and English. In keeping with the bilingual nature of his partnership with the Marquis, the caper goes by two names: Sauvez le Singe! or Save the Monkey! Pedda Timanna had let drop to Gabriel, while bartering diamonds and wild cinnamon for bullion, that the Dutch East India Company had just seized a fort on the Coromandel port islet of Vishnuswaram, and that the Hindu Nayak who ruled this islet, fearing ouster or at least humiliating subjugation by the Dutch, was hiring mercenaries and promising them a percentage of his gold-filled coffers. The Nayak, it was rumored in punch houses like Attila Csycsyry's and in the high-ceilinged chambers of Fort St. Sebastian, was an easy-to-fleece "heathen foole," who saw as his only mission in life the saving of a temple that his ancestors had built to a "heathen devyl with animal bodye" they called Lord Hanuman.

The Company consultation-book entries on Sauvez le Singe! go into some detail about both the Nayak's military vulnerability and the Dutch motivation. The Nayak, a profoundly, or shortsightedly, religious man, had spent little on fortification and much on temple beautification. His one decrepit fort, situated at the mouth of the one easily navigable channel that separated his islet from the bigger, stronger island of Ceylon, had fallen easily to the Dutch Company's soldiers, who had courted Ceylon with generous trade treaties in exchange for a temporary base to launch their Vishnuswaram operation. The prize the Dutch were after was the revenue of lavish donations collected each year from the more than two hundred thousand pilgrims and miracle seekers who came to pray to Lord Hanuman.

The Nayak, though resigned to the immutabilities of fate, was desperate to save the sacred temple from spoliation by infidels. Samuel Higginbottham had it on good authority from a Portuguese interpreter, Antonio de Melho, working in San Thomé, that the Compagnie Royale de France's factory in Pondicherry, too, was casting a rapacious eye on the temple coffers in Vishnuswaram. Saving the islet for England was an act of high patriotism.

B U T   W H A T   mesmerized Hannah more than the profit-hungry *firangis'* motives was the sturdiness of a religious faith that allowed hundreds of thousands of devotees to worship a godhead that chose to reveal itself as a scarlet-faced, yellow-furred, long-tailed monkey.

On the long nights of Gabriel's absence, and the long days of her newfound isolation from the society of Company wives, it was Bhagmati who became Hannah's only link to the outside world. And that outside world, increasingly, was a world of stories and recitations, for Bhagmati was as unwelcome on the streets of Fort St. Sebastian, and especially White Town, as the wife of Gabriel Legge had become.

It started with a simple request. She could not sleep, the moon burned brightly through the coir-matted window, and she knew that Bhagmati, too, was lying awake on her mat outside the door.

"Talk to me, please," she said.

They now spoke a common language, she and her servant, which the Company women had warned about. Bad enough, they said, when you can't understand what they're saying in that yanna-yanna-yanna language they speak, but it's worse when you *do*. They should of course understand simple English, but on no account should you permit them to address you in their chatter. Should that happen, it means you've lingered too long in the halfway house from home, all the accommodations you've made are suddenly manifest, your blood has thinned, your brain and your palate have made some sort of infernal adjustment. You can eat their food, endure their weather, tolerate their heathen ways. You find yourself getting ideas across to them, somehow, and comprehending their responses.

"Who is this Hanuman I've heard about?" she asked. A simple question with military and economic implications.

"Lord Hanuman?" the servant asked. She squatted in the moonlight in her white sleeping sari. In the semidark, her voice was deeper, not that of a twenty-year-old, or however old she was, but of a storytelling mother putting a child to sleep. With Bhagmati as guide, Hannah felt she had tumbled headlong into a brilliantly hued subterranean world peopled with shape-changing monsters and immortals that exaggerated or parodied hers. But thanks to Gabriel's voyages, she knew it was real.

Bhagmati could neither read nor write, but she was so

agile memoried and charismatic tongued that she could recite
to Hannah hour-long fragments of the epic poem she and her
people lived by. In the epic, the god Vishnu comes down to
earth for the seventh time to save mortals from demons, assuming on this seventh descent the bodily form of Prince
Rama, the rightful heir to the throne of aged King Dasaratha,
and worthy husband of a beauteous orphan named Sita.

"Bhagmati—did all this happen, exactly as you're telling
it? Or is it just a play, a poem?"

"Exactly as I say, *memsa'ab*. The place he came to earth is
known. The forest is marked."

"All right."

Like a child, she wanted reassurance. The Bible, too, was
very specific. It was said you could trace the cities in the Holy
Land in a few months if the Ottomans permitted. Every place-
name in the Bible. There were pious men in Salem who had
done it.

Bhagmati began her telling: In the course of Prince Rama's
tribulations on earth, he is unjustly banished to a forest for a
term of fourteen years. While in the forest with Sita and a
loyal younger brother, Lakshman, he comes home from his
food-gathering errands one day to find that the demon-king
Ravanna, the ten-headed, twenty-armed cruel and lustful ruler
of Lanka—Ceylon—has abducted the beautiful Sita.

Ten heads of course were possible. Two-headed men were
often paraded through town; two-headed cows and six-legged
goats wandered the streets of Black Town at will. She had
watched the impaling of Two-Headed Ravanna. Two-headed
babies frequently washed up on the beach. Gabriel had carried
on conversations with the ghastly three-headed man with seven
arms. The Coromandel was madly fertile. Where three is pos-

sible, somewhere there is ten. In Massachusetts Bay, life had been so hard, the summer so short, that freaks of nature were given less opportunity to emerge and no comfort to thrive. And, of course, the authorities would not permit it.

In the long battle to free Sita from captivity in Lanka, Prince Rama is given crucial military help by General Hanuman and his monkey warriors. Hanuman, born of the wind god Parvana, has the power to fly, to seize clouds, uproot trees, relocate mountains. He can cross the waters that separate the tip of India from Lanka in one vigorous leap. He can torch the demon capital with his burning tail.

She had seen the rolling fire spreader those nights of her earliest memory. The stories of Bhagmati ignite the memories she has tried to suppress. Abduction, betrayal, vengeance. Like the Nipmuc, Hanuman can cure burns and battle wounds with his knowledge of the pharmacological properties of rare herbs, and he can sooth anguished hearts with his poetry.

If Hanuman was an artist-physician, Hannah is glad that Gabriel was fighting for, and not against, the temple-defending Nayak.

But more than the story of Hanuman, it is the story of Sita's captivity that consumes Hannah. Rebecca had embraced her alien lover. Rebecca chose to stay in her Lanka with her Ravanna. But Mary Rowlandson, the virtuous Puritan woman, had been dragged from Lancaster. Did Sita step out of her fenced garden because she heard, as Hannah herself had only faintly heard in Salem but now heard louder on insomniac nights, a knocking on her door, as though every bird, every flower, every sail at the horizon's edge were calling to her?

In Bhagmati's honey-toned recitation Sita is the self-sacrificing ideal Hindu wife. But the shape she assumes in

Hannah's fantasies is of a woman impatient to test herself, to explore and survive in an alien world.

Hannah finds herself attracted to the events in Sita's life. Like Hannah, Sita was a foundling. The Fitches recovered her from their doorstep; a childless king, Janaka, had unearthed the girl infant with his plow and named her Sita, or "furrow." Sita adjusted to life as a king's adopted daughter and a prince's wife as willingly as Hannah had to her girlhood in Salem. And then, because of machinations against her husband, her life changes abruptly. She has to choose between continuing her life in a palace wracked with malice, jealousy and intrigue or breaking away and trying out new surroundings and whatever they will bring.

Sita chooses the new, and new temptations. She banishes herself from court life and sets up pastoral domesticity free of court customs and taboos. But one day she sees a beautiful deer grazing outside the hut. She has to own that deerskin; it is a passion such as she has never known.

Bhagmati had her way of stopping the tale, of extending her fingers in every direction as if to say, "Hedges-sa'ab. He had to have." And Hannah got the intended message: in attachment is death.

Sita pleads and nags Rama into pursuing the animal deep into the forest. Rama, ever alert to dangers, even, perhaps, aware that Sita's lust is unnatural, makes his brother pledge himself as Sita's protector. And, of course, the deer *is* a demon in disguise dispatched by Ravanna. As Rama's arrow pierces the demon-deer's throat, it utters a cry for help in Rama's voice so loud that it is heard by Lakshman and Sita in the hut. Sita, again driven by new emotions—this time fear and rage rather than greedy longings—forces Lakshman to break his pledge to protect her and go off to Rama's rescue.

Before leaving, Lakshman draws a white circle around the hut within which Sita is to confine herself, and be safe, while she is alone. White Circle, White Town, Hannah thinks. As soon as Lakshman is out of earshot, Ravanna, assuming the shape of a holy wanderer and alms gatherer, appears just outside the white circle. Sita brings the holy man water and food, but in her dutifulness steps out of the white circle. Ravanna seizes her by her long hair, hoists her into a flying chariot, and carries her off to Lanka.

Ravanna's simple lust for her grows into love so potent and humbling that he offers to rid himself of his other wives, his riches and his monumental ego just for her acceptance and approval. Sita tells him that she scorns him as a swan scorns a crow. She negotiates a twelve-month moratorium, at the end of which period she knows that she will either be cannibalized by Ravanna or rescued by Rama. And Rama, with the able help of Hanuman and his monkey warriors, does rescue Sita. But while Mary Rowlandson's freedom had cost twenty pounds in goods, Sita's freedom is dearer. Scores of mortals and demons are slain, the villain is felled with a weapon borrowed from the gods, and a kingdom is laid waste.

The real difference between Mary Rowlandson and Sita, perhaps, is that Sita's story doesn't end with her rescue. The complications, the variations, are only beginning.

Sita's reunion with Rama is brief and unhappy. To Rama her claim that she guarded her wifely honor from the attentions of her captor is not sufficient to absolve her of her crime of having allowed herself to be kidnapped and imprisoned. Worse, Sita chose survival instead of suicide while in prison. *Ravanna has desired you and gazed upon your beauty. Honor has required me, your husband and king, to avenge this evil. Now the same honor requires me to renounce you.*

Sita proves her purity to her husband and to her society in a trial by fire. The god of fire, Agni, embraces her and expels her unscorched.

Bhagmati always halted her recitation with Sita, embodiment of wifely virtues, stepping triumphantly out of the flames. It wasn't censorship; it's all that Bhagmati knew, or had ever been taught. Hannah couldn't visualize the family reunion after that fiery ordeal. Did the Hindu Sita, like the Puritan Mary Rowlandson, question the rules that her husband had pledged to uphold? Could a woman who had strayed leagues and sea channels away from the restrictive protection of the white circle, who had traveled in flying chariots, resisted the heady courtship of a ten-headed demon, discovered the potency of self-reliance, return to the passive domesticities of her very young girlhood?

O R A L I T Y , as they say these days, *is a complex narrative tradition*. Reciters of Sita's story indulge themselves with closures that suit the mood of their times and their regions.

Venn's mother, (Mrs.) Padma S. Iyer, M.B.B.S. (Vellore), M.D. (Johns Hopkins), who now operates her own fertility clinic in Boston, was born a half hour's automobile ride from the old White Town of Fort St. George. Her version of Sita's story ends with Sita throwing herself back into the fire (in Padma's newfound vocabulary), "to spite Rama and the hegemonic rules of Rama's kingdom, Ayodhya."

Venn's friend Jay Basu, who came from Calcutta to MIT only last year to work on the X-2989 project, was taught a more drawn-out conclusion by his grandmother. In his version, too, Sita passes the trial by fire. Rama, relieved, installs her in the palace as his queen and gladly fulfills his conjugal duties and passions. At night he lies awake torturing himself with imagined violations Ravanna may have committed on Sita. No, it's worse: he can forgive Ravanna his rape. His fear is that Sita might have enjoyed it. After the first, no future lover leaves a mark: *Rama doesn't know.*

Distrust, his own and that of his advisers, drives him to banish Sita, now pregnant with twin sons, to the forest. Years pass. Sita makes a life of pastoral contentment for herself. The twins grow up regal and strong. Remorse and loneliness bring Rama into the forest where he accidentally rediscovers Sita. Eager to restore serenity to himself, and his family to the palace where it belongs, he begs Sita for one more trial by fire.

This time Sita refuses. If during her first exile, the forest had disclosed to her only its dangerous blandishments, then during her second exile the forest has disclosed to her its wise secrets about eternity and redemption. This time she stands up to Rama and the unfair institutions of Ayodhya. She flings herself to the ground. And miraculously the Mother Earth that had given her birth now swallows her whole, leaving no trace of Sita the mortal.

I MAKE ONLY one demand of Venn and his mother, and of Jay and his grandmother. Where is Sita's version of her captivity in Lanka? I want to hear Sita tell me of her resistance to or accommodation with the multiheaded, multilimbed carnivorous captor. Did Sita survive because of blind or easy faith in divine Providence? Or did she genuinely believe that deprived of Rama's protection, she'd transformed herself into a swan whom a crow wouldn't dare touch? I may not have Sita's words, but I have the Salem Bibi's; I know from her own captivity narrative what Sita would have written.

10

HANNAH WAS on the roof of her house scanning the waves for the *Esperance*'s press of jaunty white sails when Samuel Higginbottham, whom, since Cephus Prynne's demise, she had gone to great lengths not to run into on her provisioning trips, dismounted in a pale haze of dust at the edge of her garden. She moved back from the roof's parapet; she intended not to be at home to any factor or Company agent in Gabriel's absence.

She called Bhagmati to help prepare a lie: Mistress Legge was feeling poorly and could not come down. Gabriel had instructed her to isolate herself from Martha and Sarah, from anyone with Company associations who might grill her about the Marquis's missions. But Bhagmati, she could see, was out in the courtyard, arguing strenuously with a dark young woman in cream-colored clothes.

From the arm gestures, which practically shouted "Be off with you, fly, fly!" Hannah assumed the woman was either an acquaintance of her servant's who had gained admission to White Town under false pretenses, or a vague relative of Bhagmati's, someone she didn't want around. This woman, at a distance, at least, looked saucy and self-confident; she stood with a hip crooked, one hand resting on it, leaving the other free for gestures. And her gestures seemed to take in Hannah up on the balcony, who had thought herself unseen. But Samuel Higginbottham had also caught sight of her pacing the roof before he had dismounted, and now ordered her down with a presumptuous slap of his fist on his open hand.

She leaned over the parapet and took her time scrutinizing the dusty Englishman. Promotion to the position of Chief Factor had given his florid round face a new square-jawed sobriety. She remembered him as he had appeared to her that first day on the beach: a slow clumsy man, overtly fearful of Cephus Prynne's caustic tongue, and fitfully arrogant with Pedda Timanna, Kashi Chetty and Catchick Sookian. Was promotion to Chief Factor in a Coromandel outpost what he had dreamed of and prayed for all along? Was this the dusty fate he had plotted to embrace? She felt grateful for Gabriel's wildness.

From the roof she taunted him. "And what business might the Chief Factor have with a married woman?" Let him think her rude. She was no longer a factor's wife. Why should she rush down, offer him water and food, make him welcome? She remained within the protective magic circle she had drawn for herself. If she stepped outside that invisible circumference, if she raced down, she would lose her advantage. Sarah and her husband were adversaries now. Fate had changed alignments.

"This business concerns your husband," the Chief Factor retorted.

"Then you ought to return when my husband is present."

His jaw lost some of its chiseled sternness. She noticed how contrived his stiff-spined deportment was and pitied his desire to appear authoritative for people he considered his subordinates. His features—the thinness and straightness of the nose, the arch of the brows—were in such prim and agreeable alignment that in spite of the grim expression he had assumed they gave his pale thin face a near prettiness. (The portrait of Chief Factor Samuel Higginbottham, mounted on horseback, in full imperial glory [c. 1699] with ships' spars and bales of calico in the background, was personally commissioned by the Company's own master portraitist and today is in the special collection of the National Portrait Gallery, London.)

"What business takes your husband away?" He glanced away from her.

"I'm not a fool, Mr. Higginbottham. I do not disclose my husband's affairs. And . . . my husband is not a knave."

All at once, in a reproachful monotone, the Chief Factor unburdened himself of the message he had come to deliver to Gabriel. The Company, he informed Hannah, was pledged to protect, on pain of severe chastisement of its personnel, all ships belonging to the Emperor Aurangzeb.

Hannah stopped him. "Gabriel Legge is not adverse to helping the Badshah should he require help."

But it was as if she had not spoken at all. Samuel Higginbottham continued to recite his message. The Company was pledged also to protect the ships of all Indian merchants, be they Muslim, Hindu, Armenian, Christian, if they had the Emperor as their liege lord. Any piracy of the Emperor's fleet would therefore have to be considered a hostile act against the Company.

Gabriel was fighting Europe's war, saving the monkey on a tiny island off the Pamban Channel. But why allay the Chief Factor's fears just yet? Why allay them at all? He was right to dread the Mughal Emperor's rage. Martha Ruxton had told her a hundred frightening anecdotes about the Emperor. After Captain Avery, the English pirate, had sacked the *Ganj-i-Sawai* off the Malabar Coast, the pious Muslim Emperor had put all Englishmen and Englishwomen in Surat in irons. And when men like William Kidd or Cutlass Culliford harassed haj-bound shiploads of the Emperor's dearest subjects, the Emperor had had Company agents whipped and threatened to cut them out of trade. Where men like Higginbottham and other factors saw damnation in the ebb and flow of profit margins, the aging Badshah talked only of vengeance and sacrilege.

It was unthinkable that a noble Englishman, the fairest of God's creatures on earth, should be stripped and tied to a post in the middle of a public square and flogged by men under a distant authority, more practiced in carving the entrails of goats than the chastisement of a gentleman's shoulders. The first condemned Surat factor, white skinned, blue veined, suety from long hours in some local punch house, had died of apoplexy when the flogger raised his arm.

"Day and night our men and women suffer tyrannical insultings at the hands of these slavish heathens."

"And you seek to alleviate suffering?"

The Chief Factor flinched. Hannah was grateful that it was the uneasy Higginbottham and not the cold, self-possessed Cephus Prynne who had borne the warning for Gabriel. "Commerce is our mission. Conquest the necessary means."

"You have delivered your message," Hannah said. "The response will be conveyed by my husband himself, when he sees fit."

When she regained her shaded post behind a pillar, she commanded visions of the sea and of the now-vacant courtyard where Bhagmati directed boys in the watering of trees. The cheeky interloper was gone, and Higginbottham was but a dusty dot on the southern horizon.

T H E   N A Y A K kept his word on rewarding the Marquis's mercenaries. Gabriel came back with sea chests filled with riches. He came back, but Hannah didn't see much of him. He was traveling the hinterland with Pedda Timanna. Count Attila and the Marquis dropped titillating hints of business deals; Gabriel and Pedda Timanna were bribing washermen and bleachers to boycott the Company; they were seeking an audience with the Nawab for trade concessions; they were closing deals that would cut heavily into Catchick Sookian's, Kashi Chetty's and the Company's textile-exporting profits. Especially the Company's.

When she delivered the Chief Factor's threat to the Marquis, he gloated and preened. Hannah understood that the threat had had everything to do with diminishing profits and nothing to do with privateers sacking Muslim pilgrim ships. Would Higginbottham develop the backbone to become another Cephus Prynne? Men like Higginbottham and the Marquis had no home, no loyalties except to themselves. Their homelands were imaginary. For them there was no going back, and no staying on. They were in a perpetual state of suspension, which was not the same as floating free. They were ghosts, trapped in space meant for full-fleshed and warm-blooded humans. She would need to root herself, she was not sure where nor how, before she too became ghostly.

I H A V E C H E C K E D the consultation books of Fort St. Sebastian for this period. The entries are in the plump, passionate handwriting of Thomas Tringham, the writer whose beloved hound Hannah had helped bury on that first day on the Fort St. Sebastian beach. The handwriting reveals the panic that the frugally worded summaries are intended to conceal.

The summaries are of the Chief Factor's separate consultations with "Kasey" Chetty and Catchick Sookian about the appointment of a chief merchant with whom the factory would deal exclusively and to whom the Chief Factor would delegate the authority to settle trade disputes among the "natives." Kasey Chetty is led to believe that if he can influence Nawab Haider Beg to arrange for the English an imperial *farman*—a land grant decreed by Emperor Aurangzeb himself—he will be favored above other candidates. Catchick Sookian is led to believe that the Company automatically ranks Armenians higher than natives because Armenians are Christian-born and vehement in their faith and perforce more reliable and manly; and that if he can organize a joint-stock association among native merchants who traditionally resist commonly held stock and commonly run trading operations, the position of chief merchant is guaranteed him. The Chief Factor impresses upon Sookian the Company's paradoxical need both to increase the volume of exported textiles and to decrease its outlay of cash credits.

The negotiations with Pedda Timanna were clearly unfriendly. The entries are mainly lists of debts owed to him by the late Cephus Prynne and Samuel Higginbottham in their official and personal capacities. These debts total 250,000 pagodas, exclusive of the four diamonds and six rubies mortgaged by Martha Ruxton. There is a summary of the debt-settlement proposal made to Pedda Timanna originally by Prynne and later amended by Higginbottham. This proposal requires the creditor to forgive 40 percent of the sum owed and to accept English woolens as payment of the remaining 60 percent.

Higginbottham's amendment promises Pedda Timanna a permit to buy one residential property in White Town and to enter Fort St. Sebastian in a palanquin. Pedda Timanna's response, too, is summarized. He thanks the Chief Factor for his "generous application" and "blushes that he must needs decline it." There is no mention of the fact that he has been entering White Town by palanquin at his will for a considerable period. His circumstances are too humble to permit high discounts and the Coromandel climate too brutish for the resale of woolens. He expects that the Company being "honourable" and its factors "noble" his application will be "well received and will terminate agreeably." Meanwhile he is considering an offer from the Compagnie Royale de France to remove himself and his family to the French settlement of Pondicherry. There is no specific reaction recorded to Higginbottham's amendment, whether he considered the invitation to own a house in White Town an insult or merely insufficient.

Higginbottham took to his bed for six days when he heard that Pedda Timanna was moving to Pondicherry. Sarah had to petition the Fort St. George Council for special exemption from the Council rule that required the Chief Factor to be on the premises of his factory every day. She gave out that Samuel was "indisposed by the insupportable heat." But her husband's ailment was graver than sunstroke or dysentery. He accused himself of the crime of "tameness" in dealing with Indian merchants. Cephus Prynne would have threatened and blustered his way into restraining Pedda Timanna from moving his assets to Pondicherry.

The French were a more hated enemy than the Dutch or
the Danes. Capitulation to the Compagnie Royale was tan-
tamount to personally handing William III's head on a platter
to Louis XIV. Higginbottham's self-doubt atrophied into a
suicidal melancholy. Sarah could not get him to eat or bathe
or make love to her. On the seventh day in desperation she
visited Hannah in the hope that she could talk Pedda Timanna
into accepting the Norwich woolens in spite of the Coromandel's heat.

She appealed to Hannah. Samuel was fast becoming a
broken man, she sobbed. If she, Hannah, had any influence
with Pedda Timanna, whom she, Sarah, had never spoken
against and always considered a higher sort than other natives
. . . then now was the time. They have had their differences,
but after all, they were all English, all working for the Crown.
They had that, didn't they? Thank God, they had that sense
of belonging.

Perhaps she looked closely into the eyes of Hannah and
saw no blazing insignia of attachment, no Cross of St. George
reflected in them, no light from a higher allegiance. She realized she had humiliated herself needlessly, fallen back on her
serving girl's faith in her wheedling good looks and other men's
power.

"Let me see the woolens," said Hannah. They were fine
and high-quality gray woolens, light by New England standards, and for a moment she held them to her face and bare
arms. Woolens like this in Salem would belong only to
the merchant aristocracy. Sarah misinterpreted nostalgia for
commerce.

"You will do it, then?" she asked.

"I will take a dress length off this bolt," said Hannah.
"On personal consignment."

With a shipload of Norwich bales, and her husband's future riding on their sale, two yards at a discount price had not been Sarah's intent. In fact, she took it as an insult and hurled the entire bolt at Hannah.

With that bolt of gray wool, Hannah turned out a somber wardrobeful of Puritan outfits: a coat for Gabriel, tunics for herself, complete with white-lace trim.

Hannah pleaded with Gabriel and later with the Marquis not to let Samuel die of despair. Wasn't Cephus Prynne's death enough revenge? There could never be enough revenge; the Marquis laughed. But he was charmed by her concern. He called it her womanly aspect. He promised he would help Samuel out of his difficulty. And then he laughed again. His help would make the vengeance all the sweeter.

He bribed or bullied Kasey Chetty and Catchick Sookian into forming a new joint-stock association and lodging the common fund of a paltry seventy-five thousand pagodas in the Company's treasure. Zentoos, he joked, don't like to trust their money to anyone outside the family. This mixed-caste and multiracial association would be catastrophic. They would bicker and squabble over who was to sign contracts, who to keep the books and disburse the money. By helping Higginbottham he was ensuring Higginbottham's inglorious ruin, brought on not by external agency, not by external assault with its possible recourse to glorious defeat, but by glaring incompetence in the area of his greatest vanity: knowing the locals and how to outsmart them.

The two merchants, one a Telugu of the balija right-hand caste and the other an Armenian Christian, each bought seven shares of one thousand pagodas. Three shares of one hundred pagodas were bought by Thomas Tringham, who appears in their bookkeeping as Tomma Trinamma, perhaps as a protection. (Until Bugs Kilken lured me unwittingly into the pursuit of the Salem Bibi, Tomma Trinamma was thought by scholars to be the mistransliterated name for another Telugu merchant of the same right-hand caste as Kasey Chetty, and who, like Chetty, had moved from the golden kingdom of Roopconda after the Sunni Emperor Aurangzeb had defeated its Shia king. Thank you, Bugs.) The bookkeeper's phonetic misrendering of Thomas Tringham is no more grotesque than the Company's conversion of Kashi Chetty into Kasey. The remaining two shares, also of one hundred pagodas, were subscribed to by Rezabeebeh, wife or perhaps daughter of Catchick.

The Chief Factor recovered as soon as Thomas Tringham brought him word of the joint-stock association. To prove to himself that his recuperation was complete, he humiliated Tringham for lazy record keeping in front of the junior writers. The youngest writer noted duly that Samuel Higginbottham "was in sufficient repossession of his natural unkindnesse to heape a parcell of indignitye on all and sundrie." Thomas Tringham was so disillusioned by this unprovoked malice that he disclosed nothing about his own small part and investment in the formation of Sookian's and Chetty's company. The Fort St. George Council commended Higginbottham for restoring "stabilitie and respecte to the English nation" and ordered him to procure through this new association twenty thousand pieces of Guinea cloth and twelve thousand pieces of salampore cloth without advancing credit to the merchants. Higginbottham, not to be outdone by the ghost of Cephus Prynne, promised to deliver on his own recognizance thirty thousand pieces of Guinea cloth and twenty thousand pieces of salampore and better-than-ever quality.

The catastrophe that the Marquis had predicted came very quickly. Sookian's and Chetty's weavers missed the date for delivery, forcing the Chief Factor into criminal alterations of dates in the factory accounts. When the two merchants finally did haul the goods to the factory for quality checks, the sorters discovered that only a third of the orders had been filled, and the balance made up with bales of ginghams and sailcloth dungaree.

In his rage—or perhaps in his desire to emulate the demonic furies of Cephus Prynne—Samuel Higginbottham is recorded as having seized a sloop belonging to Kasey Chetty and personally supervising its dismantlement. For years after, he talked of this as the one glorious moment in his long service to the Company. When Samuel Higginbottham died in Fort St. Sebastian, Martha Ruxton (who by then was Martha Ord Ruxton Yale Hartley, having long outlived Doctor John and stayed on) had a piece of that sloop's mast and a scrap of one of its two sails buried with him. She also commissioned the stonecutter to etch a sloop on his headstone.

I have traced that sloop with my fingers. Mr. Abraham, my guide, saw it as a worthy mercantile symbol. "Higginbottham," he says, telling me there are, with appropriate fracturing of the word after nearly three centuries of Tamilization, a number of place-names, streets, even families perhaps, carrying versions of that glorious name. Those who came out from England and died and left their bones in the English cemetery occupy a special place in Mr. Abraham's litany of heroes. A corner of England forever goat trampled, vine tufted, sun beaten and salt encrusted.

It seems a fitting commemoration of impotence. I had to shoo a goat off the mast tip.

11

HANNAH LEGGE might have lived out her life in India, in the new palace Gabriel was building in New Salem. Her bones might be resting in St. Mary's Cemetery of Fort St. George. Wherever she stayed, I am convinced she would have changed history, for she was one of those extraordinary lives through which history runs a four-lane highway.

There is some evidence from his logbooks that Gabriel Legge intended to retire from piracy—the capture and hanging of Captain Kidd had a sobering effect; the increasing ferocity of Deccani wars between Hindus and Muslims put several delicate financial relationships in question, and the increasingly erratic behavior of both Chief Factor Higginbottham and Nawab Haider Beg made continued dealings a less stable prospect than when the association had been formed.

Between Gabriel Legge's sixteenth and seventeenth voyages, Samuel Higginbottham unintentionally incited a riot that ended with Nawab Haider Beg assigning exclusive blame to the English East India Company and dispensing justice by cutting off the nose of the young factor Thomas Tringham with solemn ceremony in a public place.

Eventually, because everything in history (as Venn keeps telling me) is as tightly woven as a Kashmiri shawl, Higginbottham's riot changed the course of history.

The riot had its origin in one fateful glance that the Chief Factor cast out his bay-facing office window on an amber-gold, honey-sweet late September afternoon. A Coromandel-built two-master with a decked poop was being rowed ashore by a dozen *firangi* sailors in scarlet tricornered hats and silver-braided blue coats. Seated on a throne under a gaudy roundel, being fanned with peacock feathers by servants, was Gabriel Legge, the pirate resplendent in Norwich grays and gold braid. On the beach an escort of forty lance bearers and four *firangi* musicians and an equipage curtained with red silk and valanced with brocade and lace waited to transport Pirate Legge to the fort, factory and his New Salem palace.

Higginbottham at once dispatched young Tringham and the factory's dubash, or interpreter, to Nawab Haider Beg's gold-domed palace. The dubash was a man capable of simultaneous guiltless loyalties to the English Company's friends and foes. Knowing that, Tringham had been sent along to rally the focus of the interpreter's promiscuous affections. Dubash Ali, who also went by the names Oliver and Ortencio, was a handsome black-haired, green-eyed, peach-skinned consumptive of thirty. Many stories circulated about his provenance; he was a Baluchi whom a Dutch slaver had bought and abused; he was an Arab seaman for Pirate Avery and had jumped ship on the Malabar Coast; he was a Spanish don's son whom Moors had captured and hauled eastward. The one constancy in Ali's life was concupiscence.

In the letter to the Nawab, after he had stated his name, nationality, profession, and made the required Mughal epistolary self-deprecation of describing himself as His Highness the Nawab's least worthy servant, Higginbottham demanded that the Nawab cast out of the great state of Roopconda all interlopers, namely Gabriel Legge and his diabolic cohort of brigands and pirates who owed allegiance to none other than Lucifer, and who, if not restrained, would soon seize Emperor Aurangzeb with gory force and lay Hindustan waste.

Perhaps in Leadenhall Street—but certainly not in Fort St. Sebastian—there existed a Company officer capable of appreciating the rich ironies, even the grim humor, of Higginbottham's dilemma. He might even have called it theatrical, operatic, this clash of competing, profit-driven opportunists. Haider Beg was no less an underling than Higginbottham, serving as he did at the sufferance of Emperor Aurangzeb, although he exercised untrammeled authority over a broader area. The Nawab knew that a significant, and potentially vast, portion of his wealth derived from playing off the European powers against one another, and in further encouraging the breakup of European concessions into smaller and smaller, and ever more efficient and ruthless, competitors. Assuming, of course, that in their single-minded pursuit of profit they did not forget their nominal obedience to Mughal authority. He was more than willing, on occasion, to inflict that sharp blade of remembrance when the European authorities allowed their underlings to drift.

A summary of Nawab Haider Beg's response is entered in the Fort St. Sebastian diaries. The Nawab's letter, too, begins with the usual courtesies and invocations. In the name of Allah, who is most kind and most merciful, Haider Beg assures Higginbottham, Englishman, valued friend, fortune's favorite, esteemed Chief Factor, that his concern for the Emperor's well-being has been received. However, out of his affection for this Englishman and his great respect for His Royal Highness William, monarch of sovereign England, he has stopped the epistle's farther passage; his fear is that the Englishman's generous concerns could be cunningly misrepresented by English-hating or less tolerant courtiers as the English Company's arrogant refusal to pay the Emperor and the Nawab their modest and much-deserved increase in tariff and customs duties.

After all, new money is needed. The Emperor, defender of Islam, protector of the Holy Word, is waging an expensive war against that flea of an infidel, that idolatrous Jadav Singh. The Nawab and the Emperor understand the English as fellow monotheists, civilized members of the great fraternity of empire builders. Imagine the alternative, business contracts written in sand by monkey-worshiping savages. He therefore directs the English Company to arrange for the immediate settlement of its debts and to increase its bullion investment in Roopconda and so outbid all competitors, namely the Hon. Marquis de Mussy, who is a spirited practitioner of the art of free trade.

Young Tringham and Ali-Oliver-Ortencio ferried this correspondence over hillocks and through jungles, crossed rivers in flimsy barks, waited out highwaymen in hollowed tree trunks and moist caves. (The series of miniatures chronicling the dangerous day-and-night journey is in private collections.) Tringham carried the Chief Factor's letters to the Nawab in a taffeta-lined leather pouch stamped with a tiny gilt knight spearing a tinier dragon. Instead of flames, the dragon breathed out a curvaceous grace of floral trellises. The Nawab always slipped his responses in silk or brocade cases made especially for the portaging of proclamations. During their journey, while Tringham slept, the dexterous dubash extracted the precious letters from their pouches or cases without fissuring the official seals, copied them on his garments with an invisible unguent, then sold the copy to either the Marquis or to the Compagnie Royale de France for a brace of Madagascar slaves to pleasure his jaded flesh.

Higginbottham wrote more letters, to the new Governor, Thomas Pitt, at Fort St. George, and to the Directors in Leadenhall Street. Each letter was more urgent than the last, but each response seemed cooler, less committed. He could not wait the months necessary for the Directors to receive his complaints and then the many more months for him to receive their response.

These letters took over his life. The factors were demoted unofficially to writers and enrolled in his epistolary campaign. He was an early victim of primitive communications, and to give him credit, his letters to Leadenhall reveal the insights of a man born two hundred years too early. Communications create trade, he argues, not the other way around. He sketched in plans for an overland route to England, or at least to the frontiers of Europe, that could cut two months off the Cape route to England, where horses and camels might be pressed into service, where diplomatic links might guarantee safe passage of documents even through hostile territories. But he was a man born to frustration. An ineffectual, embittered visionary, lacking Cephus Prynne's sordid force of character.

The India trade, wrote the Directors in response, has achieved on the English market an enviable level of acceptance. In fact, so successful is the integration of India cloth, the double calicoes, the lighter flannels, the new dyes and colors and stripes, that the spinning mills of Norwich have registered their complaints to the King and the House of Lords. The reexport of East India fabric to the West Indies and America has practically closed the traditional mills; the cotton stockings of India are held in such esteem that the English manufacturing may never recover. Tradesmen need only advertise "India silk!" to have their doors assaulted by frantic buyers.

Higginbottham read the reports with mounting excitement. It was unimaginable that rising demand would not be met with augmented supply. This child of free enterprise then learned the bitter lesson of political reality: expanded export from the factories of India was problematic. At the time of imported cloth's maximum popularity, voluntary curbs were being proposed. Thus, the prudent course, Higginbottham was told by the Fort St. George Council, would be to starve supply to guarantee a bloated price. No further communication on this subject was contemplated.

In the first year of the new century, blocked in the expansion of his trade, the destruction of Gabriel Legge became his life's end. Legge did not have to answer to Leadenhall Street. Legge and the Marquis were thick as thieves—no surprise there—with the suppliers and artisans, with their fellow defectors from the French and Portuguese factories, and even enjoyed a favored status with the Nawab himself. It seemed that a man who played the cards that were dealt him, who met all his quotas and returned decent value, who tried to rein in the rapacious tendencies of his underlings, was not sufficiently treasured by Pitt or London.

And then, in October 1700, his only helpmeet, Sarah, out for a stroll with Martha in the Ruxtons' garden, one minute was sharing delicious gossip that she had just heard about the notorious traitor, Gabriel Legge, and his bibi, and the next instant was bitten by a rabid flying fox. She died within two weeks, spitting out her pitiful hydrophobic curses those last days and nights, lashed to a string bed in a distant corner of the courtyard.

MAYBE IT WAS Sarah's sudden death that unhinged him. He saw himself as St. George, the Company's knight-errant dispatched to destroy the reptilian Legge. Letters were no longer sufficient. He needed to slay the enemy.

On Guy Fawkes Day, he sent Thomas Tringham and the dubash to New Salem with an ox-cart load of fireworks as a conciliatory gift for Gabriel Legge. Tringham was to deliver the fireworks to Legge himself and was not to trust any servants. Only the reliably treacherous dubash was taken into Higginbottham's confidence: the fireworks were really disguised explosives. The dubash was to deliver the crates of fireworks to Legge's new warehouse and then, before leaving, ignite one charge, and flee before the reaction sent the waterfront complex higher than the circling buzzards, and Legge and the Marquis with it.

Some men are poor conspirators, others simply unlucky. The dubash was impatient to collect his reward, and Higginbottham was fated to a life forever unfulfilled and unhappy. On the afternoon of the fifth of November, 1700, the distraught widower Samuel Higginbottham had expected Gabriel Legge, the rich entrepreneur, to be working as assiduously in his warehouse by the wharf as the Chief Factor did in the Fort St. Sebastian office of the Company. The fireworks were meant to do grave damage to Legge's bales of cloth waiting to be shipped. But it so happened that on Guy Fawkes Day, Gabriel was visiting Zeb-un-nissa, his black bibi, in her hovel in the qsba's most crowded alley. The dubash had heard stories of

Legge's capacity to prolong his pleasures; he set fire to the explosive-packed cart, without waiting for the pirate to bid goodnight to his bibi.

It was she who had put on her fine cream-colored silks— gift of Gabriel on the occasion of their first son's birth—and visited Gabriel's home, to test the fortifications of servant defense and white wife against her, and found them laughably weak.

The ox cart blew up half the alley. Shops and huts blazed. Men, women and children sprouted wings of flame. Their screams and curses were heard, soon enough, in every village, every factory, every home in Roopconda state. The Hindu Raja, Jadav Singh, meditating on the roof of Devgad, his hill-fort, heard the cries and pledged revenge. Nawab Haider Beg, distracted in midpleasure with an acrobatic Abyssinian slave, dreamed up deserving new chastisements.

Whole villages of dyers, washers, bleachers, rope makers, sail riggers, boat builders and repairers, fishermen and ferry-men converged on Zeb-un-nissa's burning alley and rioted. They rioted against the Nawab's avaricious tax collection, against the poor wages promised and not always paid by *firangi* traders, against the acceptance of hunger and disenchantment. For three days, the rioters sacked, ravaged, pillaged. They trussed Thomas Tringham with rough ropes of hemp and transported him, kick by kick, to the magistrate's doorstep. He pleaded his innocence, in the most perfect Persian any Mughal had heard from an Englishman, his red hair flaming with sincerity. Poor Tringham claimed to have discovered his true calling in the Nawab's Roopconda: he wished to learn languages, to study Islam, to teach Persian and Telugu to the unappreciative factors of the Company. Falling on the Nawab's and the Great Mughal's infinite mercy, he would resign his commission in the Company and join the service of the court, acting as its official dubash to the English.

So impressed were they with his eloquence that the death sentence was commuted and extended to dubash Ali instead. He was stoned to death.

The Nawab's mercy came at a price for Thomas Tringham. The magistrate, on the Nawab's personal orders, chose to teach the *firangis* a lesson for having incited a revolt against taxes. In the past, when the English, the French, the Dutch and the Portuguese trading companies had sinned against the Nawab, he had been content to whip or shoe beat or impale the companies' Indian servants. This time, the Nawab eschewed all such mercy. Thomas Tringham was tied to a post in New Salem's gutted marketplace; his nose was sliced off with a sword, and the bleeding, fainting noseless factor was hoisted backward on a washerman's donkey and paraded through thirty villages.

Gabriel Legge was not fated to be killed or maimed that day. Lust and luck had always governed his life. Though Zeb-un-nissa's hovel was badly charred by Higginbottham's obsessive loathing, and her thatch roof entirely burned, the lovers copulating in a cement bath tank filled with star-chilled water and floating lotuses were spared all but a shower of sparks. Villagers still tell of an eight-foot naked *firangi* giant who was seen in the alley, glistening, tumescent, blister backed, hurling brick walls and burning buffalo out of his way.

MONTHS LATER Hannah would realize that while she'd wept and raged over the confluence of Gabriel's lust and Higginbottham's obsessions, Destiny was ensnaring her life into Roopconda's larger history.

A true Englishman owed his wife discretion. So discreet

were long-term residents that their half-English children grew up within sight of their fathers' wives without ever being acknowledged. Bibis were at times emboldened, like Zeb-un-nissa, to pay visits to White Towns and to White Houses, under the guise of milkmaid or washerwoman, just in the hope of capturing the *firangi* wife in a kind of paralyzed tableau.

Hannah was a stranger to all these conventions. The explosion and the indisputable disclosures in its wake shattered her marriage as definitively as a bat bite had ended Higginbottham's.

All around her now, she saw chaos. New Salem, shared with an arrogant wench who had fathered Gabriel's son, in a society that had effectively turned on her for her husband's piracies, was a prison that no amount of riches could soften. She had lived with, and accepted, the possibility that Gabriel might never return from any of his voyages, and that uncertainty had bound her closer to him. But the certain knowledge of his unfaithfulness, his preference of a bibi to her, was a matter that her pride would not permit forgiveness.

We might call the explosion, the attendant shame and the arrogant visit of the bibi a very loud wake-up call, a sign to Hannah that tolerance and patience and even a pragmatic trade-off between luxury and uncertainty were no longer sufficient, no longer bearable.

She made up her mind that she would be gone from the Coromandel on the next appropriate sailing, for London. She asked Bhagmati, her only true companion, to make the voyage, but the servant would not cross the dark waters, would not desert the small shrine she kept for Henry Hedges. Bhagmati still walked the parapets, now in the empty palace home in New Salem, dressed in her silks and sometimes dressed in his.

Until the passage could be arranged, Hannah moved back to Fort St. Sebastian, to stay with Martha Ruxton, while her trunks could be packed. It would be, she felt, a clean break. Service in India was a well-known widow-maker, and that was the status she intended to claim in England. She was an alert and accomplished woman, thirty years of age and childless. Hubert had long before sewn the idea of Cambridge, of domestic service as a governess.

It would be a bleak, gray, dismal life, she feared, after some of the excitements and colors and violence of the Coromandel Coast. But a life without treachery, without killings. Her life would reside in other people's stories; she would have stories to tell someone's children.

Tringham was brought to Dr. Ruxton's house after his penitential tour of the outlying villages. The excision was clean—thanks, perhaps, to the high-bridged, prominent nose of the young Yorkshireman that had given the butcher an adequate target. But what a ghastly sight it was, how casually cruel to inflict an unavoidable, undisguisable mark that serves no purpose and threatens no life, in the center of a face.

Hannah remembered the scalpings, the brandings, the blown-away faces of Salem, and the surgeries she had practiced to good advantage. She remembered the injured boy in Stepney, whose wounds were incomparably more serious. Ruxton had only heard of the various dismemberments wrought by native laws—they seemed bent on excising every limb or digit for one offense or another, including the ears and eyes, which made crude sense—but a nose, an English nose, was a gratuitous insult to England, to manhood and to a surgeon's skills.

"I can help," said Hannah. It was to be her final act in India. Tringham, too, rebuffed by the Mughals and now humiliated before his countrymen, had decided to book passage with Hannah on the same packet ship to England. But he intended to disembark in the Cape.

Calling on her knowledge of suturing, and of the skin's ability to bond to itself, Hannah convinced the doctor, and the patient, that a nose of sorts could be fashioned from a flap of skin cut like a wedge from the forehead, twisted in a fashion to suggest gristle, then joined again to the cheeks.

He would look syphilitic, perhaps, the doctor opined, but otherwise improved. Hannah had a surgeon's touch, but it was all he could do to dissuade her from sacrificing a joint of the wretch's little finger and grafting it to the stump of bone already exposed. All in all, the Cape might be a solution. Despite the red hair, he might find a home among noseless people.

12

WITH TWO WEEKS to go, and the December cyclone season upon them, Bhagmati made her to way to the Ruxtons' house and begged her mistress to reconsider. The master was drinking heavily, he had grown careless and abusive, and now he was at sea in a dangerous season, in a bad temper.

She had had a dream. The dream was about Gabriel. Within hours he would be back home again. She had seen him in a masoola boat heavy with chests. There hadn't been room in the boat for sailors. Not even for the Marquis. But she had also dreamed of corpses. Bodies bobbed like gulls on the waves. The bodies, impaled by Mughals' spears, shriveled like fallen fruit in the forest.

"Please come home. One last time," she begged.

Hannah took the dream to be Bhagmati's euphemism for gossip overheard in the marketplace. Fishermen must have spied the *Esperance* on the open roadstead. Boatmen were unloading booty even now, and ferrying in small portions of it to the customhouse. The rest of the loot, the Marquis and his sailors would load with weights and dump in the shallows until retrieval was safe. Haider Beg maintained a reasonably efficient but still bribable force to round up beaching pirates. The Marquis was wily about local ways. He knew whom to bribe and whom to intimidate. It was all part of the Great Game. And she was sick of the Great Game.

There were trunks to pack, friendships to end with promises of letters, and so she went back to New Salem, hoping to avoid her husband. Gabriel had been sullen but fair-minded. She would have resettlement money, and he agreed to forward cash to her at regular intervals for the next few years, or as long as his business prospered. She would miss the warmth of his returns, standing with him on the roof as he pointed out the whirlpools and sandbars he'd braved, and thrilling her with his gargantuan tales.

From the roof, the sky seemed unusually bright, unusually high. The domed sky bounced giddy rays of light off fishermen's sails. She would not allow herself to think of typhoons.

She would not get over the fear she herself had felt when those short years ago the *Fortune* had anchored in deep waters offshore, and she had had to lower herself into a *kuttamaram* crammed with Lancashire maidens, most of whom had now married and scattered like buckshot across the Coromandel and Malabar coasts, the spaniels, a harpsichord and a cherrywood cabinet. She would not let Martha Ruxton's stories of "country boates spleet into peeces" repeat themselves, over and over.

She discerned a pinnace far out to sea. Not the *Esperance*. The *Esperance* could not show itself during the day.

Toward dawn, in an eerie dream, Gabriel cried to her for help. She ran to the balcony, pulling the rusted latch off the door in her anxiety. Again she heard the moan of someone in pain and need. But it was only the rough wind scraping seas and forests. The wind blew from the northwest; it blew with such fury that it tore thatched roofs off fishermen's huts; it lifted oxen and horses from their tetherings and hurled them in the surf-striated black waves of the churned-up bay.

THEN SHE SAW the light boat by the sandbar. It was the kind of boat that Martha Ruxton, always scornful of local skills, had derided as "a country boate fit for Moores, Zentoos, hogs and swine and coolies." But this boat's sail riveted Hannah's attention. This sail was not of patched and moldy canvas that local fishermen and ferriers dried on dunes between trips. Scarlet silk glowed against the sapphire sky. This was a boat fit for the most audacious New World fortune builder or the most disdainful Old World pirate king. She prayed that the Nawab's troops hadn't seen what she'd seen.

She watched and waited impatiently for the craft to grow

larger, splash closer to the shore. But it remained tiny, its movements erratic and jerky. Sailors were trying to pole the craft away from the bar into deeper waters. But sand sucked their poles and swallowed the prow. Gale winds snapped the mast and loosened the blood-red flag of silk.

It happened so suddenly that Hannah wasn't sure if she had seen it or imagined it. The wind caught the boat atop a sandy crested wave, lifted it, spilling all deckhands into the water, then turned it over and dashed it on the heads of the sailors and beasts before they'd even oriented themselves in the water. She saw the bobbing and sinking of spheres (human heads?) and of rectangles (chests of silk and brocade?). Men struggled out from under the upturned craft and were swept away by ferocious currents.

In the quickly lightening dawn, she watched the boat crumple like straw with each crashing breaker. And then she saw a force of destruction gather upon the beach that she had never seen and always feared: a crowd, a small army, an armed guard of the Nawab's men making their way across the wind-torn roadway to the half-beached hulk. The bodies of *firangi* sailors, most of them drowned but some still struggling, were chopped and speared as the soldiers passed. It was a scene of mass murder on top of a furious cyclone.

Bhagmati tried to pull her away. Bhagmati took charge; Hannah was shaking from the cold and wind, the sight of men she now recognized being hauled upon the beach and stabbed some more. She let herself be draped in lengths of coarse cotton such as Bhagmati wore. Tough-palmed hands daubed muddy brownness on her white forehead and cheeks. White Town, Bhagmati urged, was a place to flee. The mobs were stoning the enclave walls. The rumor had started in the *qsba* and spread, fueled by the Nawab's men. His soldiers were already patrolling beaches and trails for *firangis* who had sacked another Mecca-bound pilgrim ship. Muslim boatmen, pilots, traders, were spilling infidel blood to avenge sacrilege. The Nawab had received word of the piracy from the Company, from Higginbottham himself. The Company intended to show no mercy to *firangi* interlopers like the Marquis and Gabriel Legge.

The Marquis had left instructions with association wives for just such precipitous escapes. They were to get in touch with Count Attila Csycsyry at his punch house, and he'd billet them in safe huts until enough of the Nawab's men could be bought to look the other way. But Bhagmati could not place her faith in dishonesty, nor in a drinker's promises. She had her own getaway plans. She hustled Hannah down the hill, over the bridge and into a shaky settlement of washermen in Black Town. So Hannah did not witness the Marquis's drowning nor Cutlass da Silva's mutilation.

BUT THERE WAS a witness to the beach happenings. The fisherman's child who had watched the lovers in happier times, years later, in a cold, lonely attic in London, retrieved the memory in rhyme. The manuscript fragment of *The World-Taker* that has survived opens with a shocking soliloquy summarizing that night's events. The manuscript's current owner in Calcutta, a Marwari businessman of taste, will not permit any portion of it to be copied. The prohibition derives from his nationalism. He has no wish to expose the fragment to Western scholars who will note in it only a sad mimicry of lesser Dryden and Pope. An asset hunter thrills to the chase. The few lines I remember verbatim I remember for the clues they contain:

O, how I dread to tread again
Sonapatnam's shores of blood and pain!
Cursed was that day when I
Spied the slain Marquis ascend the sky.
One cruel death ought reveal lessons wise,
But the celestials dispensed one more prize.
Cutlass da Silva's tongue to a board was nailed;
Justice is e'er meted, dear and bejewelled.

So the Marquis died that night. Cutlass da Silva had his tongue cut out. That gruesome soliloquy does not mention Gabriel.

THE DETAILS are given to me by Mr. Abraham as we walk around the ruins of the customhouse. That night of massacre became a guidebook's lore.

Mr. Abraham says, "These chaps suddenly found themselves between devil and deep blue, if you get my drift only. One sec they are discoursing so merrily, dividing up their loot, and the next sec they and their belongings are all tumbling topsy-turvy in the drink. November, December, are very bad months here, you see. Very treacherous. So what is happening is this. The boat is sticking in sandbar. You know the Lord Tennyson poem, 'Crossing the Bar'? Tennyson is thinking of this Madras-side sandbar only. The pirate chaps are huffing and puffing but nothing is happening. Then suddenly wind is dislodging the bloody boat! The boat is now like an upside-down bowl. The de Mussy fellow and that Portuguese chap, they are good swimmers, isn't it? They are somehow managing to struggle from under the boat, they're managing to wade neck-deep on sandbar. All is well for them, you are thinking. In the meantime the English fellow is sitting tight inside the upturned boat. He is thinking, My God, am I in a cave or a whale's belly or what? The good Lord is listening to him and the good Lord is creating an air pouch in the water for the Englishman, this Legge. And the boat is hiding him from the eyes of the angry Muslim mob. But the other two chaps are not so lucky. The good Lord is always finding jolly good means to punish sinners and devils. An arrow is piercing de Mussy's skull. So de Mussy is dead on spot, which means he is luckier than the Cutlass fellow. Cutlass is not bothering to see if he can give succor to his wounded friend. Oh, no. He's a selfish fellow. He is just running and running. And wham! He is running into the mob. The rest is not a pretty story."

Cutlass da Silva, Mr. Abraham confirms, had his tongue cut out, but the tongue was not nailed to a board as described in the soliloquy. The tongue was actually nailed to da Silva's chest and da Silva himself then nailed to a plank and dumped into the Bay of Bengal, where he was accused, falsely, of having dumped three hundred haj-bound pilgrims.

"So you see, there could be no moaning of the bar as he put to sea, clever, isn't it? No tongue, no moan."

And what happened to Gabriel? Knowledge, as Venn would say, comes from purity of design. Data without design is a muddle. The data on Gabriel's death had been given to me the day I stumbled on Hannah's things stuffed in a cardboard box in the hallway of the maritime museum in Marblehead. I just didn't know where the data fit, it was so long ago. Gabriel Legge lived a comparatively long life, dying in 1720, and is buried in the British Cemetery in Calcutta.

THE FOREIGN TRAVELER

from the "Salem Bibi" series

c. 1700

9.5 cm × *11.3 cm*
Provenance: The Museum of Maritime Trade
Anonymous Loan

This is the starkest in the series. The artist executes his vision in frugal lines. An emaciated *firangi* in a Muslim ascetic's garb stands beside a low white wall. The dense, almost-black forest backdrops the figure. Actually, there are two figures; a seductive, veiled, dark-skinned woman extends a gold-bangled arm toward him. In the woods, we see the eyes of demon forms, tigers, half-human, multiheaded monsters. In the pigmentless area behind the wall, I make out no path or road that a traveler might pursue. The traveler's eyes are sunken; blue pits in a bony gray oval. He stares straight at the viewer, or at the artist, who might well be sitting in the courtyard of a half-completed palace. A cap of embroidered cloth sits too low, too loose, on a shrunken forehead. Wisps of mustard-yellow hair hang limp over a saggy, wrinkled earlobe. The chest is bare, long, narrow. The ribs bulge through the tent of gray-blue skin. The wrists are opalescent, crisscrossed with lapis capillaries.

There is little doubt the figure is Gabriel, and the painting a concentrated story of how he survived the drownings and butcheries of December 1700. If I had to title the painting I might call it *Entry into the Garden*. It seems in every way a reversal of the familiar expulsion myths of Adam and Eve from Eden, Adam's fall, sinning all.

In December 1700, Hannah became, to her satisfaction, husbandless.

History was already rewriting her fate. Her passage to England was nearly complete. Face smudged with lampblack, wrapped in white khadi, shivering in a servant's hut, Hannah was still retrievable. Poor Tringham, after all, was packed, partially healed, face wrapped in a scarf, waiting at the docks. And Hannah, rather than waking up and fleeing for her freedom, felt a heaviness in her bones, a fatigue, that wouldn't go away.

Shock, depression, rejection—we have words for it now. The fatigue that doesn't lift. A moral collapse. Or a vision of the future that the body refuses to endorse.

All she wanted was sleep. She didn't care who came and went; she slept like a local through heat and light and noise. The packet ship came and loaded, and went. Hannah Legge did not board and was thought to have died in the riots, and her piratical husband to have drowned.

Who are these coming to the sacrifice?
To what green altar, O mysterious priest . . .

JOHN KEATS
"Ode on a Grecian Urn"

PART THREE

IN THE CARNIVAL CROWD that had gathered to witness the cutting off of Thomas Tringham's nose stood a sturdy mendicant in soiled khadi cotton, with a begging bowl and a long staff to lean on and the holy wanderer's saffron daub on his forehead. He was deep inside enemy territory, not because of his obvious Hinduism—the vast majority of inhabitants of Muslim lands were Hindu—but because this master of guerrilla strategies and of incognito disguise was Raja Jadav Singh, King of Devgad, a Hindu-ruled disfigurement on the Muslim map of South India, and a deeply embedded thorn in the flesh of Emperor Aurangzeb.

Devgad was an oblong parcel of swamp, jungle and Deccan escarpment that cut a narrow swath a hundred miles long and fifty miles wide, from the arid highlands of south-central India, east and south to the Coromandel Coast. Revenue from the various European factories within its territory, as well as tributes from the dozens of vassals and the thousands of individual villages, kept the Raja rich and able to wage, in turn, continuous war by every means possible, except classical confrontation, against the Emperor. His successes against the more powerful Aurangzeb had forced the aged and arthritic Mughal to abandon his palaces in Agra and Aurangabad in order to come south and personally direct the fighting.

Devgad had resisted the Grand Mughal's designs for inclusion only because of the Raja's unswerving hatred of all Sunni Muslims. He had himself been raised in the palace of a Shia king. His father, though devoutly Hindu, was the King's *subedar*, a kind of fort commander, who took to calling himself a king. It was a small, obscure fort and efficiently run; hearing no objection from the Shia overlord so long as he remained loyal and productive, he, his wife and the boy's tutors taught his son to *be* a king.

The text that was pounded into him by his tutor was the Sanskrit classic, Kautilya's *Arthashastra*, the *Art of State-Craft*. In deference to his concept of patriotism, the young Jadav Singh struck the coins of his realm in Sanskrit, not Persian. From Kautilya, he learned the art of survival in a ruthless but elegant age: the weaker king, in order to survive, must seek the protection of the more powerful, or he must strike an alliance with his equals, or he must retire behind fortified walls and wait him out. If defeated, he accepts the most humiliating terms, suffers silently, then plots his revenge. Defeat and humiliation, and the thirst for vengeance, he learned from the fate of his father.

When the young and intolerant Aurangzeb, the Great Mughal, had defeated the Shias, he proved to be less forgiving of heretics and infidels than any of the five previous emperors in the hundred and seventy-five years of his illustrious lineage. Even minor forts were cleansed of subversive elements. He installed Hasan Beg, the father of the current vassal-nawab, Haider Beg, to take over the Coromandel Coast of Roopconda, and to kill or drive from power all Shia sultans, and to expel all Hindus from positions of assumed power. Jadav Singh's father had been turned out of the fort, humiliated. The son had sworn revenge and had carried the pledge forward to the Nawab's son, and to the Grand Mughal himself.

Raja Jadav Singh had not come down from Devgad to

witness an English factor's punishment, though he never forgot the expression of disbelief on the pale *firangi* face just before the sword came down on the stately triangle of pinched flesh. Months later he confided to Hannah that in the moment before Tringham's grimy white shirtfront exploded into glistening scarlet, he understood something about the *firangi* arrogance, which enabled even flawed, pathetic little men like Tringham to dream of plundering lands they did not know, and did not hate. They really didn't think that laws applied to them. They tried to walk the world like gods, without armies or servants or gold to protect them, and without the principle of vengeance to ennoble them.

That day, Jadav Singh, exercising the eccentric right of a holy man, had stepped in front of the washerman's donkey upon which the poor, accommodating but denosed Tringham was forced to ride backward, and whispered into his ear, "Turn your hate into action, friend. Join the enemies of your enemies. Avenge this day!"

The Raja's reason for billeting himself in disguise in the nearby fort of Panpur (the seat of a vassal who, after the slaughter of his sons and the enslavement of his three wives, had fled Roopconda for the protection of the Raja) was to harass the *firangi* trade in the weakly defended coastal outposts of Fort St. Sebastian and New Salem, to stir up resentment against the Company and thus, eventually, diminish the revenue the *firangi* paid the Grand Mughal Aurangzeb.

The Panpur vassal had proven himself loyal and reckless, capable of sufficient vengeance to recommend him as a *subedar*. While Higginbottham plotted only the death of Gabriel Legge, Raja Jadav Singh had been waiting in Panpur fort, almost within sight of Fort St. George, for just the right moment to hurt Higginbottham, the Marquis, Legge, the Nawab and the Emperor.

2

IT'S RAINING. For weeks without break it's been raining. I couldn't have imagined such rains in Cambridge or Boston. Venn says, looking through all my notes on Hannah, Gabriel and the Coromandel Coast, that a perfected X-2989 program, sucking all data into itself like an informational black hole, might be able to generate three milliseconds of virtual reality running time.

Life is extremely wasteful of data, in other words, says Dr. Venn Iyer.

Mr. Abraham is reluctant to be outdoors in this muddy season. He takes off his squeaky-new leather sandals, rolls up the flared legs of his made-to-measure trousers and leads me down a flooded alley. Only mad dogs and American scholars, Mr. Abraham sighs. A cycle rickshaw whizzes by and spatters mud on his starched and ironed shiny garments. I offer to pay the dry-cleaning bill and realize at once from the jerky way he pulls ahead that I have offended him.

We are in this alley because three hundred years ago, when this busy, built-up mile was just sandy seafront, a washerman's hut stood near here. Hannah lay in that hut, enfeebled not quite by fever but perhaps by a premonition that her time on the Coromandel was not yet over. The present moment, however perilous, could not equal in terror the premise of her return. (Like Venn, I believe less and less in accident, more and more in design. She did not make the boat's sailing because it was not yet time for her to return.)

It was a cyclone that finally awoke her. A cyclone with the fury of divine judgment lashed the tiny port village. Around nine o'clock in the morning, the high winter sky precipitously blackened. For two hours or more, winds from the north sucked birds out of trees, blew thatch off the huts, then attacked the remaining walls, washing everything into the sea. Houses toppled off shaky foundations. Paddy fields turned into salty lagoons. Then winds from the east more malicious than the winds from the north lacerated the coast. Ships tore free of their anchors and beached themselves in jungles leagues inland. Water rose as high as a cliff and swallowed dunes. Within moments, the water cliffs flooded the customhouse. The river surged over the bridge and swirled into the crowded alleys lined with stalls. By noon the sea spread itself over five villages and three market towns in the hinterland. That afternoon the winds blew first from the south, and then from the south-southwest, and carried debris-loaded seawater back into the Bay of Bengal.

The harsh, gritty wind lacerated her face. When she covered her cheeks with her hands, she felt warm blood on her palms.

"This is no country for Christians!" she cried. This was not the place she wished to be entombed. But where could she run to? She saw the folly of a governess's job in Cambridge. There would surely be no welcome there for a pirate's widow, and no place in old Salem for an Indian lover's daughter.

An angry mob was already within earshot. Bhagmati hurried the grief-dazed Hannah, no longer disguised as anything but a half-dead *firangi*, around uprooted trees and waist-deep mud pools. They had to make their getaway before the pathways were flooded. They found a donkey, braying senselessly for its lost master. Bhagmati prodded the beast, with Hannah's body upon it, toward the bridge.

That night the bridge broke. An Englishwoman on a donkey and her servant were on the bridge when winds wrenched it off its base (Coromandel consultation-book entry, but never confirmed), lifted it and dashed it back into frothy river water. That bridge has been rebuilt and broken and rebuilt many times since. The bridge has been officially named and renamed over and over again. One of its longer-enduring names was the Robert Clive Bridge. But among local people, since the night that Hannah and Bhagmati sailed downriver on broken-off waterlogged planks, it has been called the Bridge of Drownings.

I visualize the sundered bits of barks and timber, bodies of victims and animals swirling downstream. The stone bridge is forever collapsing. The "Widow" Legge is forever cut off from White Towns on fortified hillocks. She floats, cold numb fingertips clinging to a splintered bark. The donkey eddies with desperate velocity until the waters suck it down. Men with hysterical faces in flimsy boats grab at her. How insulated her life has been that she has not witnessed such hate before!

"Bhagmati!" she screams. "You, the Lucky One! Make me lucky!"

Hands hurl a jute sack over her head. She hears herself scream, feels herself hauled into a country boat like a fisherman's catch and dumped on top of other bagged and wriggling humans.

3

HANNAH CAME TO on a low divan in an airy tower room in a hill-fort. The divan was the only piece of familiar furniture in the room. There was a large wooden chest with iron clasps pushed against one wall and a silken carpet patterned with hunting scenes on the stone floor. Heavy bolsters and outsize cushions were piled on an embroidered floor rug, and brass urns, pitchers and spittoons ranged in neat rows under a high window slit.

After the grand excesses of Henry Hedges' English furniture, the dark austerity of the tower room—she would not allow herself to call it a prison—startled her. She would have to accustom her limbs to fold and her spine to flex into new positions so she could recline, lounge and squat like the locals. In hallways and courtyards out of her view, soldiers and servants were issuing instructions in a language that she hadn't heard before. She squatted on the thin rug, cheek pressed into the stone wall, knees drawn up to her chin in despair. For the first time in her life she longed for the rule-bound sternness and security of the Fitch household.

Bhagmati's soft singing seeped into the darkening room. Hannah pushed the portal with her shoulder; the portal gave way, revealing Bhagmati in the circular landing of the turret. She had her back to Hannah, her eye to a musket chink in the pocked stone wall.

"Whose prisoners are we?" Hannah asked.

Bhagmati swiveled around, startled by the panic in Hannah's voice. "We are not prisoners," she explained, calming Hannah. "We are in Panpur Palace. We are the guests of Raja Jadav Singh. The Lion of Devgad. Panpur is his vassal."

Hannah had heard Cephus Prynne and Samuel Higginbottham speak covetously of the quality of indigo grown on Panpur plantations. She'd associated Panpur exclusively with squalid villages that somehow harvested a valued commodity that Gabriel, the English Company and the Compagnie Royale fought over. That Panpur had a fort, a courtyard with fountains, landscaped gardens with canals and a monarch capable of inspiring apparent devotion made her realize how myopic had been her life in Fort St. Sebastian.

"A raja?" She was used to saying "nawab."

"The Grand Mughal calls Raja Singh the Rat of the Coromandel."

"What do you call him?"

Bhagmati laughed. "My lord."

The servant woman appeared young and beautiful, regal in her posture! She had changed into fresh, fragrant garments. The bared lustrous skin of her arms smelled of floral oils and woody essences. Her hair, still wet from a bath or from the rain-churned river, cascaded in raven waves. Even her voice had a new confidence.

In the formal diplomatic dealings on the Coromandel Coast, English people were most often in contact with Muslims, who ruled in the name of the Emperor Aurangzeb through their nawabs and their laws and customs agents. Muslims seemed a more knowable people than Hindus; Muslims' aversions and their attractions struck familiar chords with devout Christians. They had a heaven, a hell, a book, a leader, a single god; they knew sin and tried to repent. Their dietetic codes were harsh, but logical.

The idea of Hinduism was vaguely frightening and even more vaguely alluring to Hannah. English attitudes saw Islam as a shallow kind of sophistication; Hinduism a profound form of primitivism. Muslims might be cruel, but true obscenity attached itself to Hindus, whose superstitions and wanton disregard of their own kind—burning young widows, denying humanity to those they called untouchable—excited contempt. Muslims had restrictions, which were noble and manly; Hindus had taboos, which were superstitious and cowardly. Hindus were unreasonable, and unreachable, so tradition-bound that their minds were considered undeveloped, except for a wily ruthlessness among the trading castes. What little good she knew of the religion came from Bhagmati's stories; what little she saw in practice alarmed her. It seemed to feature the worship of various horrific and comic images. They worshiped the male sex organ; they worshiped an elephant-headed, fat-boy god. They had more gods than people, and, God knew, they had enough people.

Venn bristles at Hannah's misconception of Hinduism. He believes in a cosmic energy that quickens and governs the universe. He explains to me impatiently the Hindu concepts of Brahman and Atman. "Not gods," Venn protests, "but vivid metaphors. The 'gods' are visualizations of the Brahman's aspects and attributes." I simplify the concepts for myself into Cosmic Soul and Individual Soul.

The antagonisms between the three religions naturally reinforced each other's prejudices of the other two, but Christians and Muslims tended to concentrate their opprobriums against the common Other. If anything, Hannah had a Christian's skepticism about other faiths, bolstered by a Muslimized intolerance for idolatry.

And now she was in a totally Hindu world. Bhagmati seemed no longer a servant. Perhaps she, Hannah, was about to become one.

In other words, at the age of thirty, Hannah was a pure product of her time and place, her marriage and her training, exposed to a range of experience that would be extreme even in today's world, but none of it, consciously, had sunk in or affected her outer behavior. I want to think, however, that the forces of the universe (for want of a more precise concept) were working within her. I don't have any other way of explaining what she was about to do, or become.

4

THE PANPUR FORT was protected by a steeply built-up embattlement, a brick wall and a moat. The Bay of Bengal was in view and offered protection on its eastern flank. A wide river separated the nominal jurisdictions of Muslim Roopconda and Hindu Devgad, to which the Panpur fort and outlying villages paid their levies. English factors passed easily over these religious and political borders, enjoying trading rights in both jurisdictions, but among locals the borders were strongly defended.

Hannah could look out of the high window and see crocodiles bare their immense jaws in the green water of the moat.
At a distant line of trees, and across the swollen river, Nawab
Haider Beg's soldiers in their showy Roopconda uniforms were
cutting down trees and setting up their tents. Cannons were
trained in the fort's direction. Gunners, most of them *firangi*,
directed the cannons' placement. Horses and elephants were
being exercised by stable hands. Eunuchs carried caldrons of
water into the women's tents. Sword sharpeners enjoyed a lively
business. Slaves were setting up clay ovens, and cooks lighting
fires to feed an eventual army.

"The Nawab's men?" Hannah asked, astonished.

"The Nawab's men are also the Emperor's men," Bhagmati
explained. "He knows the Lion rescued the English widow."

She felt a shudder of wonder, that the life of Emperor
Aurangzeb, the Seizer of the World, was crossing the life of
a Brookfield orphan. She understood; somehow she was the
cause of the Nawab's encirclement. Bhagmati explained the
strategy: the Nawab would wait. He wasn't sure if Jadav Singh
was inside, and a full-scale assault on a modest fort was un-
manly unless the prize was worthy. To wage war simply over
the rumored presence of a white woman was ungallant. This
was a war of intelligence, of spies, of courtesans and servants
and eunuchs bribed, of notes passed across lines under saddles,
inside bodices. Hannah looked down at her clothes. The coarse
khadi and veils were stiff with dried mud. Her feet were black,
bruised, naked. A smell of slime and rot came off her wet,
weed-tangled hair. She felt herself the servant woman.

"They say the Badshah came south to fight the Raja himself," Bhagmati said. She laughed a brief bitter laugh. "But
even in wartime you want to bathe and change."

She put on a clean sari, the same as Bhagmati's. That afternoon, as the one-time servant taught her erstwhile mistress the art of pleating and folding a sari, the two women shared confidences. Bhagmati had had a vital life, distinct from waiting on *firangi* households. Why had Hannah not sensed that before? Perhaps Rebecca's embracing of the wilderness had started like this: a moment's sharp awareness, *My God, they're alive!* She remembered her mother, suddenly, wearing the beaded belt her lover had given her, showing it to Hannah for admiration. They're humans; they have a richer life than I do.

"You wear the sari well," said Bhagmati. They had giggled, going through the elaborate process, getting it even. If Martha Ruxton could see her now! And Samuel Higginbottham!

Bhagmati had been born with the name of Bindu Bashini. Hannah spun the alliterative name like a ball on the tip of her tongue. Her own mother, she realized suddenly, must have taken a Nipmuc name. A new name for a new incarnation. Rebecca Easton was dead. Hannah Easton Fitch Legge was dying.

Bindu Bashini had been born into a merchant family in faraway Hughli. Hooooghleee. Bhagmati's father had procured taffetas, floretta yarns, raw silks and the finest muslins for the English Chief Factor to ship out from Hughli. Hannah pictured another English factory run by another chief factor on the banks of another wide river sludgy with silt meandering into the Bay of Bengal. She pictured Bindu Bashini's father and brothers as the spitting image of Pedda Timanna, touring the wharf on palanquins.

As a child Bindu had lived in a large mud hut crowded with parents, grandparents, widowed great-aunts, uncles and aunts-in-law, girl cousins, boy cousins and servants. She learned to sew, sing, cook, paint auspicious *alpana* designs on holy days, swim in the hyacinth-choked pond behind the hut, and chant a weekly prayer to Lord Shiva so he might direct a kindly, preferably motherless, husband her way.

"Why motherless?" asked Hannah.

"Fewer beatings."

Then, at age ten, the unspeakable had happened. On her way upriver by barge to Nadia with three widowed aunts and a bachelor cousin for the funeral of a great-grandfather, she and her family had been set upon by river pirates. The cousin and two bargemen had been killed, the women robbed, and Bindu Bashini herself violated and thrown into the river. She'd been meant to drown. A dishonored Hindu girl couldn't go back home. To have been abused was to have brought shame to the family for its failure to protect her.

She had swum against the current. She had scrambled up the muddy, sloping riverbank. She had survived. Mahouts washing an elephant had saved her. The elephant had lifted her from the water. Individual effort thwarted divine fate. She had neither wanted to, nor known how to, drown. So her relatives—all of them decent, affectionate men and women in untested times—had done the disowning in accordance with neighborly pressure and Hindu custom. Only cowards chose shameful life over honorable death.

"And so that's the reason you worship the elephant god?" Hannah asked, remembering the crude drawings of elephant heads on human bodies she'd seen in Bhagmati's sleeping room.

She smiled, but shook her head. "I don't worship elephants," she said.

Bindu, twice a victim, had run from her family, from her

village, from all the familiar taboos and traditions. She'd kept running. She'd found herself a series of servant jobs, starting with buffalo and elephant washing. She'd staved off starvation in a hundred shameful ways. When she was twelve, she found work scrubbing the cooking pots in the house of an English factor in Hughli. Let her proud merchant family share in her shame! The factor's name had been Henry Hedges. It was fate. He treated her like a slave, and then he treated her like a queen. He'd craved her with the urgency of an addiction. And when he'd been moved from Hughli to Kasimbazar, he'd taken Bhagmati—his name for her, for her reborn self—with him, and from Kasimbazar to Dacca, to Madapollam and finally to Fort St. Sebastian.

When a man craves you like that, you feel very powerful, said Bhagmati. Dressed in similar clothes, sharing the same space and the same fate, the distance had vanished between them.

"I wouldn't know," said Hannah.

Would Henry Hedges have moved her to London? Certainly not at the beginning of their long, strange relationship. But toward the end, he was talking about it; he would train her in the English arts, in cooking his strange foods. "Joints," she suddenly giggled, "Hedges-sahib loved joints on Sunday." She might have gone. She trusted absolutely Hedges' ability to keep foreignness at bay, just as she trusted Raja Jadav Singh to keep her safe. But when Hannah had offered to take her to England, she had refused to go. It wasn't religious. She could not conceive of England without Hedges. She preferred to keep his shrine alive, to walk the parapets in his clothes, in her queenly silks, than to abandon him to the Coromandel Coast.

5

H A N N A H G O T a glimpse of Raja Jadav Singh and his *subedar* that evening. She was standing at the only window slit of her tower room when the two men, similar in attire and appearance, with the same mustaches, colorful turbans wrapped in the same manner, pinned in the middle with rubies and pearls, rode up the steep ribbon-narrow trail and over the drawbridge on frisky, short-legged *tattu* horses. They led a small band of wounded cavalry. For besieged men, they seemed absurdly lighthearted. The Lion glanced up in the direction of her tower, and though he couldn't possibly have spied her—she took care to stand far back from the window slit— he let a smile hover on his lips.

Such a gentle-looking face, she thought; the eyes so large and luminous, the smile unforced.

Soon the party of warriors and attendants moved out of her limited focus. The shrieks of aghast wives, the tuneful laments of widows, the jangle of agitated anklets floated up from the courtyard.

Hannah felt she had entered a world whose simplest rules about the saintly and the villainous were unknown to her. She had no way to measure new experiences and nothing in her old life with which to compare them. She needed to hold on to objects, to be able to name and memorize the new.

Even above the shrieking, the obvious suffering, she heard music from the inner palace. That Indian music she sometimes heard on her solitary walks in Black Town. King David, she thought, remembering her Scriptures, was he not the Lion of Judah? Shepherd and king, cruel and kindly, a soldier, a musician. A voluptuary. The general he killed to claim the widow. The bitter old man who lost his rebellious son. Founder of the line of Christ.

But what were the designs of this Lion? *Singh*, she knew, meant "lion," but she'd never taken Indian names literally. The lowliest servants in White Town had been named Rama and Vishnu, and every third person was a Mohammed. Had the Raja plucked her to safety from an angry mob on a raging river out of a royal instinct for chivalry? Or was he just another schemer—like Chief Factors Prynne and Higginbottham, like the unscrupulous Marquis and the self-serving Pedda Timanna, like Gabriel himself, who had tried in their selfish ways to "rescue" her? Was he merely using her, a *firangi* haj-insulter's widow, to taunt his potent enemy, Aurangzeb, the Grand Badshah?

Or could she say, like Bhagmati, that it had not been her fate to die that day? The Raja, like Bindu Bashini's elephant, was simply there, part of a design.

The next morning Raja Jadav Singh visited. Hannah was amazed at how rested he looked in spite of his recent skirmish with the well-armed soldiers of the Nawab. He addressed her in English. To her expressions of gratitude and then her simple question "Why?" he answered, "I was not looking to save you, or anyone. I am not in the habit of pulling bodies out of the water."

His face had the warm tint of almond shells. His mustache

outlined the sumptuous upper curve of his mouth. Hannah couldn't guess how old he was, given the fine-grained luminosity of skin that had been massaged and pampered since birth. He could have been forty-four as easily as twenty-four. He walked, and talked, with a kind of softness that belied the deeds of a warrior; she thought of Gabriel, the Marquis and the men of White Town, whose every adventure was retold, and enlarged on each telling. The Lion's escapades were immortalized in local ballads, sung by every child. He didn't swagger like Gabriel; he didn't preen like Cephus. He invited her to his musical evenings—he played the flute—for what were the pleasures of war without the tranquillity of music?

"Are you comfortable? These quarters are too isolated perhaps—"

"Most comfortable, Your Majesty."

"There are women's rooms, but they are perhaps not suitable."

"Wherever you choose. I am your guest for only a short while, I suppose."

"You may stay here under our protection for as long as you feel comfortable. We do not place limits on our welcome."

"Then how will I know when I am no longer welcome?"

The question seemed to confuse him, the *firangi*'s quest for contracts and assurances. "How does the Raja's favorite war-horse know he is no longer fit to ride? When he is no longer fed the sweetest grass, when he is no longer groomed every day, when his tail and mane are no longer braided . . . when the Raja no longer visits him every day."

"If His Majesty is kind enough to warn me, I shall braid my hair for such visits."

"The successful ruler is the master of the art of surprise," said Raja Jadav Singh. He clapped his hands and a retinue of servants brought a full service of tea and fruits and the sweet milk curd favored along the coast. An enormous bamboo cage holding a small colorful bird was suspended from a hook above her window. Elaborate rugs were unrolled underfoot.

"We pray you will stay with us," he said. "The name of the bird is Horse-Tail"—he smiled—"a miniature peacock, bred only here, specialty of Devgad." So saying, he faced the bird, clapped his hands twice, then spread them in two imaginary fans. The small blue bird raised his straggly tail and suddenly filled the cage with his massive display.

YEARS LATER, in *Memoirs*, she made a brief cryptic reference to what came to pass between the Lion of Devgad and the Brookfield Orphan. "An angel counseled me, a fantasy governed me: bliss descends on the derangers of reason and intellect."

Cynics would say she didn't take any of this seriously, she was slumming in a palace, she expected to die, or be rescued, or to leave. Until then, why not? Or she was suffering post-traumatic shock. Or he was an abusive male, and an absolute despot.

According to the record of Mughal miniature paintings, there was little privacy in the bedchambers of India's *havelis* (mansions) and palaces. Attendants swarm around lovers, advancing aphrodisiacs and fanning peacock-feathered breezes. Legends grow around the gay gossip let slip by one child-attendant, and that child, decades later, relates the tale to an English traveler, who copies it down, half in jest, as though a proper English lady could ever—ever, even in England!—have done what the maid allegedly saw.

For what it's worth: The Lady pushed the Lion of Devgad down on the carpet alive with lion hunters grasping griffins with amber manes. The Lion trembled under her touch at first, and then, as though he too was under a spell, submitted to her slow deliberate caresses.

The *Memoirs* say nothing of Raja Jadav Singh's contemplative brows and panther-quick eyes, nothing of the horror or wonder Hannah may have felt on touching his war-scarred flesh. Only two images of Jadav Singh exist. One is as he appeared at battle's end in the last of the Salem Bibi series of paintings, which I, dutiful asset hunter, tracked down in Salem's Museum of Maritime Trade. The other is a likeness of him etched on a carnelian stone set into a ring of red gold. I own that ring now. On the carnelian, the Raja, caught in three-quarter profile, is a bold, smiling warrior.

OVER THE NEXT few weeks, the Raja sent her odd, occasional gifts. A small songbird in a silver cage. An oval black stone the size of her hand. A copy of Kautilya's treatise, in Sanskrit. A basket of custard apples.

She was becoming like Bhagmati, making a fetish of his gifts, feeling his presence in the tokens he sent.

Before this longing, she had conceived of emptiness as absence, detectable only by the circumference within which it was contained. Now the void became a pleasureful pain, subsuming all the old Salem virtues such as duty and compassion. She wanted the Raja and nothing else; she would sacrifice anything for his touch and the love they made.

What she felt for the Raja was of a different order from what she had felt for Gabriel, or not dared feel for Hubert. Gabriel and Hubert, for all their distinctive eccentricities, were

men cast in one familiar mold, men who thrilled and disappointed within a predictable range. The Raja was an agent of
Providence. He had saved her life, then saved her from the
chilly, unfulfilled life of a governess.

In hours alone that passed alternately like centuries, and
then like instants, she began to believe that the only woman
she'd ever known who could understand these feelings was her
mother. She, too, lifted her gray tunic to the Raja when he
entered, even with Bhagmati in the room. Her life had shrunk
to something so intense, so small, yet so vast, that it wiped
out the possibility of consequence as thoroughly as it erased
all previous histories.

She turned the tower room in Panpur fort into a museum
of indirect tokens. She embroidered samplers with rhymes
Hubert had once recited and with sentiments of which Susannah Fitch would surely have been ashamed.

> *And thou in this shalt find thy monument*
> *When tyrants' crests and tombs of brass are spent.*

or

> *What freezings have I felt, what dark days seen!*
> *What old December's bareness everywhere!*

When she bathed, she tattooed a pink alphabet of guilt
all over her body with the fibrous roots Bhagmati had taught
her to use as cleansing agents. She embroidered elaborate knuckle covers for Jadav Singh to use under his shields: scenes of
Nipmuc warriors scalping amber-maned Puritans; a field of
Massachusetts wildflowers (imagine the consternation of the
first Sotheby's catalog, trying to explain the origin of such
transcontinental adumbration!). She hung shield covers, her

pennants of love, in crowded rows from the ceiling. She fastened a sampler embroidered with snowdrops and crocuses on the window slit so she would not have to look out on the milling confidence, and strange cowardice, of the Nawab's men. By day, she taught the songbird fanciful tunes from the Puritan service, as Rebecca had done with the Nipmuc women. But during the nights she suffered nightmares of war: the Nawab burned the Raja's bright eyes with red-hot irons; the Nawab's elephants trampled the Raja to death.

And then one evening Jadav Singh reappeared as though he had not been away harassing the Nawab's scouts nor stealing the Nawab's swift *turki* horses, and wooed her with sweetmeats and confidences.

To Hannah his life story was as alien as a gypsy's. His birth had been prophesied to his mother after forty years of barrenness. Barrenness was a tragedy for all parents, but a queen's barrenness was a catastrophe for all her subjects. Thrones vacated by the deaths of issueless kings were promptly usurped by Aurangzeb.

After thirty-eight years of barrenness (they had, of course, married as children), his father had taken on a second wife, the very young, very beautiful daughter of a minor Deccani raja. The elderly King became desperately aroused by the child-queen's flat boyish body and lisping monotone of a voice. More than his throne, more than an heir, he craved his child-bride beyond all possibility of fulfillment. He banished his first wife to a small palace built of rose-tinged sandstone, delegated royal tasks to a war-weary general and an abstemious Brahman priest, and locked himself and his child-love inside a specially constructed pleasure suite. The second wife provided him with extreme and unholy pleasures, and eventually a son.

The first wife, however, got her revenge. After forty years

of barrenness, his first queen gave birth to Jadav Singh, whom she had miraculously conceived by lying in her spurned bed with a court painter's likeness of her husband, the King.

"More likely, I think, she lay in bed with the court painter," giggled the Lion, for whom the unthinkable was quite expressible. He did not seem an especially pious man, not by the standards of Salem and the Coromandel, yet he was waging a war against the Great Mughal, a religious purist, on religious principles of his own.

"Then you also have a half brother," Hannah said.

"No longer. I was obliged to kill him," answered the King. He read apposite paragraphs from Kautilya, not bothering to translate, but appearing very moved.

I'VE COME to trust the psychological integrity of oral narratives. The Queen Mother must have brought up the infant-king Jadav Singh with hate in his heart for his father. She had given him as toys jaws-of-death daggers and tiger claws of sharply honed metal. But that hate cannot be expressed openly; it is transferred to the man who banished the father, Hasan Beg, then his son and, finally, Aurangzeb. After he took over his father's old throne, no longer a pretender but as absolute ruler, the old Queen Mother dictated domestic policy. She had the child-bride banished back to the jungle kingdom she'd come from. She ordered the death of the potentially troubling rival. In the ballads that survive about her, she is a multiarmed goddess riding a lion and hurling thunderbolts against the armies of the Grand Mughal.

But this is Psychoanalysis 101, and no one has successfully put Hinduism on the couch. We know that Hannah tried, because for her, the steadfast ferocity of Jadav Singh, his purity

of heart and motive, while still maintaining an outer aspect
of lover, artist, care giver and justice dispenser, were initially
appealing. If he burned with a fire that he carried over from
father to son, and even to the remote figure of Aurangzeb
himself, it must be explained by some compelling vision of
cruelty, one of those moments that call for vengeance even in
the gentlest of hearts.

And when he couldn't answer her questions, when he fell
silent whenever she asked *But what did he do?* she felt his anger
rise, his jaw start working. He would stalk out of her room
and not return for days.

I know that reaction. It is the reaction of Mr. Abraham
when I offered to dry-clean his clothes, the reaction of Venn
when I tell him about some new discovery I've made about
the Coromandel, or Hannah, or even the diamond. In India,
it takes a classic apprentice five years to learn how to sit at
the sitar before he's allowed to play a note. It's not just the
reaction that says *How dare you know?* It's something deeper:
How dare you presume to say you know?

6

JADAV SINGH continued to court her for one *pahar*,
or one quarter of each night. Hannah seems not to have asked
him where he went after she relinquished him. I ask myself
how I'd have felt in Hannah's situation, and a plausible answer

forms itself at once. With Gabriel she had clung to Salem's do's and don'ts. She had pulled and pummeled the familiar rules, hoping they'd help make sense of her own evolution. With Jadav Singh, she'd finally accepted how inappropriate it was in India—how fatal—to cling, as White Towns tenaciously did, to Europe's rules. She was no longer the woman she'd been in Salem or London. The *qsbas* and villages of Roopconda bore no resemblance to the fading, phantom landscapes where she'd lived in Old and New England. Everything was in flux on the Coromandel coastline. The survivor is the one who improvises, not follows, the rules.

What she had left Gabriel for just months before, she would accept from Raja Singh. She was no longer a wife. She was the bibi.

HANNAH AND JADAV SINGH wooed each other in a cupola-roofed balcony overlooking the distant bay. Love made Hannah a selfish guardian of their privacy and isolated the King from the pleas and sorrows of his subjects. For fourteen days and thirteen nights the lovers abandoned themselves to pleasure. Attendants fed them pomegranates, sprinkled them with attar of roses and lit his *huqqa*. Musicians serenaded them with flutes, drums and stringed instruments from the courtyard below. For fourteen days the King mounted his lady without surcease. "Forever regal," he called his instrument; "Unbow'd," she corrected. No innocent posture, no contortion, failed to yield a new delight. Flower vendors in *kuttamarams* tossed fragrant petals to the shore, and the faintest of distant odors now caught her attention, the flapping of birds' wings, the scuttling of mice in distant fields. The moon seemed to burn, and on dark nights, the stars crackled like embers.

"Don't you hear them?" she'd ask. "Can't you smell it?"

"Hush," the King replied, "I'm listening to the fishes swimming."

And while the lovers tossed and twisted in the sweet carnality of their embraces, the drought season deepened in Panpur. The glossy soil, silken with moisture, that had once supported crops enough to feed the thousand villages of Devgad now flaked into dust in tillers' hands. Cattle grazed in tinder-dry meadows, udders dry and bleeding, the sickened falling to buzzards even before they died. Hyenas and foxes and even a man-eating tiger prowled the palace's peripheries and carried off goats and children.

The Nawab Haider Beg sent his most ruthless commander, Morad Farah, a mercenary Moor from the Barbary Coast who'd battled infidels on both sides of the Mediterranean, the Black Sea and up and down the Malabar Coast, to head an invasion force of horsemen, foot soldiers and engineers to erect batteries for light cannons and dig a tunnel under the Raja's moat. Finally, the Nawab had his hard intelligence: Raja Jadav Singh was in the fort at Panpur. No rumor spreads quite so fast as that of sexual abandon. The Raja could have ridden his horse in plain sight under the Nawab's nose, and still his existence would have been in doubt; let him hide behind a curtained cupola with his Salem bibi, and all of Hindustan would know before morning.

Morad Farah's men had closed the river route to the interior and blocked the boat route through the roadway. The Emperor Aurangzeb's battle standard flew over a city of tents. Soldiers leaned their muskets and spears against the beached canoes, awaiting the signal to ford the river and start the attack. The sound of their drunken curses carried cleanly across the water.

Troupes of singers, dancers, whores and eunuchs moved between the camps. Sword sharpeners had set up their grinding wheels. Mahouts had already started to hang armored plates on the General's battle elephant; grooms were rubbing down and readying for battle the noblemen's horses. Grappling hooks, scaling poles and catapults were piled into carts for the assault that could be launched on a moment's notice. And still the Raja did not order a response.

Morad Farah herded up Panpur's cows and goats, seined the streams, and shot the birds nesting in the trees so his men would not complain of niggardly rations. Farmers who resisted were dragged by the hair to the tent of punishment; their feet and hands were severed by hatchet; their wives and daughters assaulted. This was efficient genocide: every dishonored daughter destroyed a father; every helpless father starved his family; every dead son condemned the souls of his parents to eternal return.

ON THE SECOND quarter of the fourteenth night, the limbless trundled into Panpur fort's Hall of Audience. Their wails were louder than the music of flutes and gourds. *Morad Farah has set fire to our huts! Morad Farah has dishonored our women! Morad Farah has rendered me a beggar the rest of my life!*

Jadav Singh stirred uneasily in a bed strewn with blossoms. He sent his musicians away.

Morad Farah has razed three temples! Morad Farah has slaughtered cattle and smeared beef blood on the lips of pious Hindus!

Hannah bound his wrists with the silken *patka* he had worn fourteen days before as a girdle. "Stay, I beg you!" she commanded. "Don't give in to gossip!"

She had not been raised in a world of savagery, not on the scale of India. The vast inequalities, as well as the injustice and superstitions of India, seemed to her unnatural and unbearable. And yet it was here in India that she felt her own passionate nature for the first time, the first hint that a world beyond duty and patience and wifely service was possible, then desirable, then irresistible. In her former life, the possibility of intense pleasure was as remote from her as the likelihood of abject suffering. In old Salem, from her mother's shameful example and under the Fitches' tutelage, she'd thought capitulation to pleasure, outside of convention, was a sin. In New Salem with Gabriel she'd equated being happy with not being unhappy. She had felt no love, not as she now understood it, for Gabriel. For the first time, she pitied him for never having known her, and she even wished him happiness with his bibi. In Panpur fort's scorpion-rife rooms and lizard-infested terraces, she'd come to understand the aggressive satiety of total fulfillment.

And she knew, for the first time, the contradictions of a passionate nature. She wanted to run down to the interior courtyard, where the wounded and the dying and breast-beating parents, wives and husbands were congregated, and throw herself into nursing them all, not eating or sleeping until their flesh and bones were mended, ashamed of her happiness, wishing herself as mutilated as they. The next moment, she could not imagine their survival, their future, nor her possible connection to any of them, and not seeing herself or her lover belonging with them, she would have scourged them from the face of the earth.

The stench of living flesh carried across the courtyard, up the turrets to the balcony. The raped wives and daughters of limbless peasants broke into the zenana, beat Bhagmati and set fire to her Hedges shrine. They wanted to die, but there were no daggers to fall upon. Protective eunuchs, wakened from their sentry duty outside the zenana apartments, blocked the doors and pushed them away.

The world was rotting; there was no honor, no protection. These people were innocents, the troops were innocents, but corruption was everywhere. Peace brought profit to everyone, but peace was a curse word on the Coromandel Coast. She had traveled the world, a witness to unimagined visions, merely to repeat her mother's folly, and to live her mother's life over.

I T   T O O K the apparition of Bhagmati, her face and neck scratched, nose and lips split open, to wake the drowsing Raja. "The villagers have no food," she cried, under the lovers' balcony. "The soldiers will mutiny."

The loyal *subedar*, his near double, had been killed outside the gates, his body thrown to the crocodiles. The Raja sent his most persuasive minister to Higginbottham, requesting English gunners and long-range guns in exchange for rebates on indigo prices, but the Englishman, loyal tool of the Nawab, refused to meet him.

From her pink stone palace in Devgad, two days to the interior, the Queen Mother goaded her son with real or imagined perils: the Emperor had razed Devgad's holiest of temples! The Emperor had erected a mother-of-pearl mosque on the desecrated altar of God Vishnu! *Lion*, the Queen Mother pleaded through the humble mouths of messengers, *cease your slumbering! Return to assert your power.* The messengers were trapped by spies and led in chains to the tent of punishment to have their feet and hands cut off.

A cornered rat, Jadav Singh withdrew to a windowless cell

in the corner of the fort, into a foodless and waterless period of meditation.

7

B E F O R E   D A W N   Jadav Singh had made up his mind to beg for a truce, then slip out of besieged Panpur before the truce was signed. Devgad, fifty miles to the interior, was more defendable and more fully provisioned. From Devgad he would launch the battle of his life against World-Taker Aurangzeb. The decision made him happy, a singing, smiling, flute-playing schoolboy once again.

"*Deception precedes triumph*, says the wise one," quoted the Raja, the wise one being Kautilya. "*Ruses are the strategies of courage*." He swept his arm toward the distant campfires of his enemies. "He believes only in power and showing his power. A fool flexes his muscles. The wise man hides his strengths."

She coped with the Raja's alien concept of heroism. Appear weak before a boastful enemy; hit hard, flee fast. Men like Gabriel and the Marquis, even desk-bound power brokers like Higginbottham and Prynne, savored the flaunting and strutting more than the confrontation itself. And what, the Raja might have asked her, had become of them?

H E   S H E D   the intimate folds of silk gauze and lover's cotton and allowed his attendants, for the first time in a fortnight, to dress him in the robes of state. As his situation was obviously hopeless, he sent a petition for truce in exchange for Panpur fort and fifteen chests of gold, twenty chests of silver and a cash tribute of eight lakhs—eight hundred thousand rupees —to Morad Farah, whose foot soldiers were already crawling like roaches into the tunnel they'd dug under the moat. Others had already beached their landing boats on the Panpur side of the river. The petition was welcomed by the General on behalf of Nawab Haider Beg, and the treaty signing set up for Farah's tent the following day.

Whereupon, the Raja knew, his exit would be barred, and immense suffering would be extracted from his final hours. Haider Beg would watch every minute, then report to his liege lord every delightful turn and twist of hot irons, extractions, crushings, beggings for mercy.

"His Excellency requests the lady accompany you," said Morad Farah.

"My intention precisely," the Raja replied.

SHORTLY AFTER the first quarter that moonless night, Jadav Singh bundled Hannah and Bhagmati into one palanquin, and a servant, disguised in royal jama, turban and jewels as Devgad's Lion King, into another, and set off for distant Devgad at the head of an army of six hundred foot soldiers and three hundred horsemen. If Haider Beg had not been born to greed, the special greed of a provincial nobleman, he would not have been so easily stupefied by the promise of gold, the anticipated delight of inflicting torture. He would have recognized in the abject generosity of a surrounded, defeated adversary a subterfuge worthy of Kautilya himself.

In the valleys, the rain-moist air hung like smoke, condensing on every leaf. Every tree, every slightly cooler surface (and in such heat, even inflamed human flesh was cooler than the air), became its own small rain cloud, squeezing moisture in thick, heavy droplets to the slippery red Devgad clay. Rivers formed at the base of every forest tree, cutting their way through the rutted clay to form rushing torrents behind high grass just out of sight. Hunting parties broke off from the main band and returned minutes later with deer impaled on poles. Banana leaves, inverted, delivered the condensation like long green flagons, songbirds hopped along the paths, unable to gain altitude, and even mosquitoes, landing on her flesh for a bite of blood, found themselves skidding on her skin, unable to lift their sodden feet and drenched wings to get away. She squeezed her sari end; the water hit the ground in hissing droplets. The horses were scraped for leeches, which seemed to rise like locusts from the very grass. She thought: If the earth can melt from heat and humidity, it will today; she could brew her tea by waving a cup in the air and setting it in the sun to boil.

And as soon as she accustomed herself to the hell of a dripping, canopied rain forest, the path rose steeply through bands of cloud into the true coastal premonsoon heat, to a near-desert oven blast that made her long for the restful infirmities of the forest. The salt-stiffened sari flared off her shoulder and wouldn't drape.

Up ahead, the Lion kept up a steady pace, racing forward with his advance scouts, galloping to the rear to make certain of no pursuit. He rode beside her a few miles, dabbing her forehead with scented water.

"What will become of people in the fort?" she asked.

"They will understand. They helped me get away."

Guilt did not enter his makeup, only duty, and his duty was to lead, to defend, to fight.

"The General will not waste his time on them. He is a

general because he kills kings, not eunuchs and women." All of this he announced with a boyish smile. It was as Bhagmati once said: men fight because war makes them young. Even the old Emperor, fifty years on the throne through filicides and fratricides and still roaring with fire.

Then she said something that startled Jadav Singh. "I would rather die, however horribly, than see others killed."

He began to laugh.

And then she added, "Why would one people desecrate another god, if they weren't horribly, desperately afraid?"

She was asking on her own behalf as well as Morad Farah's, or the Emperor's. It was the same fear her own people had exercised, back in the forests of Brookfield.

He sped off, again to the rear where his horsemen had called him. After two more hours, with the sun beginning its flat western trajectory directly in their eyes, it was time to break for the first night. But when they arrived at the small fort that was their goal, the *subedar* welcomed him, then gave the Raja less accommodating news. The Emperor's men, indeed, had entered Panpur fort, suspecting that the Raja had fled, and the soldiers, so restless from inactivity and the promise of glorious battle, had been issued practice rounds of bullets, cannons and burning balls of pitch. Panpur was no more, the outlying villages were burned and corpses lay facedown in the paddy fields. Cows were butchered in front of the priests, then the priests in front of the statues of Lord Vishnu, then soldiers urinated on all the statues—Lord Hanuman, and elephant-headed Ganesh—or washed them in the blood of slaughtered cattle, then they razed the temples.

The villagers who'd survived were making their way to other forts, carrying bundles of rice, pitchers of water, their calves and their children slung across their shoulders.

"Then we must not stay here," the Raja decided. They replenished what meager stocks they could carry and set out again, by the fading sun and then the moon, along the main path to Devgad fort. If Morad Farah was the great general he claimed to be, there would be an ambush along the defile where the paths all narrowed to scale the Deccan escarpment. If he was nothing but Aurangzeb's mercenary butcher, he would linger in the captured villages, devising devilish entertainments and waiting for morning to launch an assault wherever the Raja's army had camped for the night.

So they would not camp. The Raja would run the risk of ambush, but trust to his enemy's baser character. And again he was happy, having calculated his enemy, having raised, in his own mind, the odds of battle. As happy as some Company factor figuring a profit.

8

DAWN WAS streaking the eastern sky behind them, but straight ahead where the path snaked upward into a rocky defile, the sky was a pure, lustrous, nighttime black. If they scaled the defile safely, the road to Devgad, their allied fort, was open, sanctuary was assured.

The Raja raised his sword, addressing his officers: "Today is but another death. Who frightens and who fears is irrelevant. A warrior faces death with cowardice or courage." The words were no longer empty; the morning light revealed that all

along the ridge, Morad Farah's men squatted like birds of
prey.

Jadav Singh lifted his shield, spurred his caparisoned *tattu*,
and uttered a war cry. The Muslim warriors answered from
atop the ridge. Like an upward-flowing river, the hundreds of
Devgad soldiers stormed the escarpment. Thousands of the
Emperor's cavalrymen spilled down the defile, arrows flying,
spears thrust forward. Hannah caught a glimpse of the Raja's
scarlet knuckle cloth. All around her she heard the chants of
Jai Ram! Jai Devgad! Jai Singh!

No sooner had the syllables escaped their lips than they
fell. It was, as the Lion had said, the worst place on the journey
to fight a battle. He had bet against an ambush, and he had
lost; but if, in his strange battle logic, not to fight was some
sort of peculiar dishonor, he had won. Unless any battle, no
matter how one-sided, was preferable to peace. At the top of
the ridge, illuminated in the full flat sunbeams of the eastern
sky, she saw Morad Farah seated in the canopied howdah of
his decorated, battle-clad elephant.

She smelled the blood, vomit and feces of men yielding
to panic, or to death, and heard the enemies' eerie whoops of
hate. Bhagmati tugged at her sari and held out the Raja's
ceremonial dagger. "Use it," she said, "he would want you
to." So remote was Hannah from the meaning of the words
that she at first looked around her for a likely enemy to kill,
but then Bhagmati took a smaller knife of her own and made
a single sharp thrust to her own stomach, stopping just before
slashing herself open.

"This time, death is better," she said.

But Hannah had Tringham's faith. Nothing could happen
to her, not from alien enemies.

"No, you mustn't," said Hannah, and she suddenly seized her servant's arm and threw her down into the tall grass at the edge of the trail, where the bodies of fallen Hindus and Muslims were strewn like rocks at the bottom of a cliff. Hannah lay with her; they did not move.

The battle, what there was of it, consisted of one charge, one volley of response, hand-to-hand combat, heavy losses and the survival of the Muslim General. The winning soldiers scattered immediately, freed for the day to take their pleasures in neighboring villages, to loot them, kill the infidels, rape the women, burn the evidence.

In battle as in chess, positioning and superior numbers lead to the checkmating, the killing, of the King. *King is fallen!* she heard, early in the battle, and after that, the rest was hate and instinct battling on until the immediate lust, or the concept of honor, was placated.

Amid the bodies, Hannah lay across Bhagmati, their saris giving away their religion and putting them both at risk. She lay helpless, afraid to move for what seemed like hours, not flinching when bullets passed all around her and thudded into the ground, or tore into another body. Random or deliberate, she didn't know.

There is a sound associated with battle scenes in that time and place, one of the few sounds in human history that have no analog. It is the sound of the elephant walk, the prerogative of the winning General to survey the scene atop his battle elephant, protected under a silken canopy in his high, up-holstered howdah, which rests upon the elephant's broad, flat back and is cinched around its girth. It is the sound a trained elephant makes as it untangles bodies from protective piles, rolling them over with its pink-tipped, bristly trunk; then,

once the enemy corpses or the still-living bodies are laid out
straight, the sound it makes as it plants a broad front foot
directly on the face of each stretched-out body, grinding the
head into a featureless mash with a calm, almost gentle,
ruthlessness.

It is the sound of skulls caving in, of air expelled, of the
human body treated like coconuts or sugarcane, a sound no
different, really, from any great force exerted against any soft
resistance. And that is the surprise, for the very few who have
ever heard it: the human body is nothing very special, or very
different from any small obstruction. In the eye of Brahma,
Bhagmati used to say, the world is less than a grain of sand,
all human lives less than anything clinging to it. Hannah
remembered the Brookfield stories, the sounds of scalps ripping, like pulling up roots. It pleased her that in these last
minutes of her life, as the elephant made its implacable approach, these were the thoughts the Lord God had planted in
her brain.

She clung tightly to Bhagmati, but there was no resisting
the second insistent shove of the elephant's stiffened trunk,
which toppled her from the mound of her servant's body.
Suddenly, all fears vanished. She would agree to die, but not
in the way of some simple ant, some worm on the ground. If
I lie here it will crush me. And so she sat up, and then she
stood; the only human left standing, the only human with a
face not obliterated. Let the elephant, the soldiers, kill me
now, she thought. But what few survivors who lingered
were too busy looting corpses, dashing from body to body,
pulling off rings and tugging daggers out of the folds of
tunics, to waste a bullet on a woman. Jackals, human jackals.
Humans are beasts, base-driven, venomous, unfeeling. She

deserved this death, Lord knew, the way she'd lived for pleasure amid the sufferings of others, but at least she would not surrender. The General shouted orders, laughing. The beast maneuvered its head, feigned with its trunk, like some monstrous version of swordplay. The elephant's trunk was just a bloated version of a pig's snout, the sort of moist, smooth pink and bristly thing she'd fed as a child. She'd always thought of elephants as wise and slow and gentle beasts, comically jolly like the elephant-headed god, Ganesh, curiously tolerant of abuse and overwork, like the Indian coolies themselves. India seemed determined to teach her the cruel side of every pleasure, the evil behind every innocence.

The General gave a sharp new command, and the elephant raised its trunk and held it curled over her head, like a hammer ready to fall.

"The *firangi* lady," the General shouted. "The English lady."

"Not English," she cried out.

The elephant's trunk descended like a lightning bolt, knocking her to her knees, then curled about her, lifting her straight out, like a wooden log. She'd watched the work elephants do the same, lift the logs, hold them out, then drop them wherever their mahouts ordered. She'd heard stories from Gabriel and all the factors of mass executions in the hinterland—trampling by elephants, Roman circus carnage—where the laws of England or the more palatable trappings of Mughal justice were not observed.

She was conveyed upward, then turned to a sitting position and deposited on the elephant's granite-hard hindquarters. General Morad Farah, a grizzled, fair-skinned Moor with a thick, short beard, gold earrings under his turban, turned in his howdah and asked, "Where is the Raja?"

Far below, Bhagmati took advantage of the moment of inattention and ran, diving into the taller grass.

"You have killed him."

"He is wounded. He will die of his wounds, but that will deprive me of my mission."

"He has suffered enough, then. Even for you."

He laughed again, or at least bared his perfect teeth in a kind of victorious grimace out of which he might dispense the grace of survival or a blood burst of violence.

And so they began the tour of the battleground, the elephant's feet thick with brown blood and with fresher blood from bodies still living when the foot had come down upon them, causing blood to spurt across the elephant's chest, up to the level of its eyes, caking its gold-capped tusk stumps with gore. The beast looked like a victim of the battle rather than its finalizer. It had not rained, but blood, tankards of blood, had churned the ground to mud.

Where are the survivors? she wondered. No victors, no prisoners, just a ghoul here and there completing his rounds of looting. Overhead, buzzards were circling ever lower. That night, the fields of Devgad Defile would teem with hyenas and jackals.

"Now we find your Raja," the General announced, giving the elephant a solid, reverberating whack with the decorated iron *ankus*, the elephant prod with a hawklike talon that could just as easily crush the skull of a man. The beast turned toward the steep ascent. Hannah moved slowly, inching her way from the great flat hipbones along the spine to the slight cavity between the mounds of hips and shoulders, where the canopied

howdah swayed. From the great height, Hannah saw Bhagmati, a white ghost running low through the stalks of grass,
keeping pace.

Ah . . . came the long, satisfied, victory sigh of General
Morad Farah. Raja Jadav Singh lay beside his dead white horse,
attended by a woman in a white sari.

The elephant raised its trunk to brush Bhagmati aside, but
before the General could deliver his order, Hannah thrust the
long dagger she'd hidden in the folds of her sari into the
exposed flesh under Morad Farah's battle tunic, through
the muscle and organs, back across to the spine itself. Even
his scream was cut short, barely an in-suck of breath, barely
the registering of pain and death from an unexpected source.
He lurched straight forward, Hannah pushed, then rolled him
over the precipice of the elephant's brow, still clutching his
heavy metal *ankus*, landing with a metallic thud. Dutifully,
the beast lifted its foot and drove it down upon its master.

And now Bhagmati stood. In the harsh, throaty voice of
a street vendor, a tone and pitch Hannah had never heard from
her servant, she commanded the beast. With immense slow-
ness, it dropped to its rear knees, then its front knees, never
tipping the howdah platform. The women lifted the dead
weight of the unconscious Raja to the platform. He seemed
to be breathing through the deep, ragged wound in his chest.
Hannah put her hand over it and felt a faint tug, the suction
of life. She knew that it must be cleaned and sealed, the blood
loss stopped, but that even an expert surgeon with all the
proper equipment would place more faith in Providence than
in his skills to save a life so far gone.

They climbed back on the beast, and again it rose and,
with Bhagmati's guiding, made its way up the path to which

the Raja had been leading them, up to the ridge where the General's troops had waited in ambush but were now scattered in roving bands of looters, to the open plains of Devgad and the fort beyond.

9

H A N N A H, her red sari stained even redder, arrived in Devgad on the blood-encrusted, stolen elephant of the enemy General, bearing the wounded body of her warrior-lover.

The Queen Mother met the horses in the outermost courtyard of the complex. She seemed hardly a queen, a bent brown stick of a woman in a dingy white sari wrapped for mobility rather than grace. Her head was carelessly shaved, her eyes bleached gray by age, her lips browned by chewing tobacco. Her skin smelled of despair and sleeplessness.

"Carry him to my palace!" she commanded in a harsh, croupy voice. Burly servants lifted their wounded Raja from the blood-soaked floor of the howdah. Hannah walked between them, hand still cupped over the Raja's breast. They laid him out on a litter. The Queen Mother lowered herself on her haunches and swabbed the Raja's forehead.

"Take that away," she ordered, meaning the white woman's hand, which had already polluted her son's caste, but Hannah refused, with a minimum of respect, in order to demonstrate her seriousness. To lift her hand would tear away the clotting that had already begun. The Queen Mother spoke the language of her western regions, unknown to Hannah, only roughly translatable by Bhagmati. Toothless, ancient, spirit dominated, perhaps demented, she communicated one idea: Hannah had brought bad luck. The Raja had left the fort healthy and ready for battle, he met the *firangi* and a spear had found his heart.

"Mataji," Bhagmati began, "she has plucked him from the fields of the dead. She killed the General of the Grand Mughal. She has avenged this wounding."

"She is a better raja than my son? The witch has weakened him? Now she even kills his enemies?" The old Queen spat a brown jet at Hannah's feet. "Look at him. He is useless. He cannot fight."

Behind her, her attendants formed a sullen semicircle. They swished the air with their ivory-handled flyswatters and peacock-feather fans. Litter bearers lifted the inert Raja shoulder-high, to the high-pitched lamentations of the women, who formed a corridor for his passage across the inner courtyard.

"Let him die in peace," his mother cried. "This woman has taken his manhood. He has become a woman, so let him die in a woman's palace."

Hannah pushed through the cordon of attendants, then shouted back at her servant and the old Queen. "Tell her, Bhagmati, tell her I know magic. Tell her I can save him."

She found her lover laid out as though already dead on a deathbed of hemp hammock and bamboo legs on the terrace of the Queen Mother's palace. At least there was light. She cut away the blood-drenched undergarments, exposing a wound to his chest that flashed bone, pooled blood, and smelled already of death. Women tried to wash the wounds, but Hannah stopped them. Soak up the blood, she said, tearing strips off their saris, bring me only women who sew, bring me only the girls with thin fingers. Bhagmati used her sharp, querulous voice, and the women ran from the terrace to do her bidding. Out over the plains of Devgad, the skies were black with buzzards.

Those women, directed by the old Queen, would have decorated his wound, painted it, scented it, and prepared the fires to receive him. They would have lit lamps, called in the priests. The idea of cutting deeper, of pulling away the shards of bone, of connecting the blood vessels with the finest silk against his distant moans and the rattling in his chest, of keeping small bowls inverted over other wounds, were signs to them of *firangi* arrogance. Her white, casteless hands had touched him, touched his blood, her hands that had touched beef; even if she brought him back from Yama's grip, what sort of half-human monster would he be?

The old woman stood over the bed, wailing, "He is a hawk. There is no more harm you can do!"

"Get her out of here!" Hannah commanded. His dagger, the sharpest, finest steel in all of India, became the extension of her fingers. She cut away the dying tissue, scooped out flecks of dirt, sutured the gelatinous tangle of muscle and nerves.

Women remembered old cures, cobwebs; roots to stanch the bleeding; leaves, which squeezed, slowed the heart rate, others that brought relief from pain. There would be delirium, for which crushed barks were known. The smaller girls were especially helpful, tying knots with the finest silk thread, even where they couldn't see. The fastest and surest among them would grow up to tell this tale; nothing is ever lost. (Thank you, Venn.) They watched as Hannah kneaded together flaps of flesh as though she were sealing bread dough, and finally stitched together the outer flap. He looked intact.

The Queen Mother returned, informed of the miracle. She touched her hand to her son's forehead. "May you take back your soul and fight the Grand Mughal," she blessed him.

Eight servants hoisted their king and his deathbed high above their heads and, singing songs of praise to Vishnu and ballads of hate for Aurangzeb, they portered him out of the *firangi* witch's gaze.

They sang the old song: *"The Lion will lead us into battle again!"*

The old Queen stood her ground. Hannah, her hands, arms and sari nearly a solid coat of blood, would not be permitted to exercise her spells.

"I have restored your son. Now there will be no more carnage!" She did not save him to send him back into battle. Bhagmati translated: *no more blood.* She saved him in order to have him totally to herself.

Hannah saw the source of the war in the implacable hate of the fierce old woman. She saw that her native New World forgetfulness would be forever in conflict with Old World blood-memory. There was no great unutterable crime, no great analog to a lifetime's single-minded dedication that had set Aurangzeb and Jadav Singh on their course—to believe in that had been naive. She had demanded something big to justify the insanity of a man so good and wise, and so she had overlooked something small. He was a king. They were kings. It was their duty to fight.

She thought of their nights in Panpur under the cupola,

behind the gauzy curtains, when the Raja had been as devoted to love, and to her, as he now was to death. He'd read to her from the poets, he'd sung to her and played his music, he'd called in drummers who throbbed all night outside the curtains, and he'd read to her from the book he called, with a smile, the Gita, the Song of God, the Hindu Bible. He was a warrior, born to lead men into battle. There was no other calling for him. As Krishna had said to his prize bowman, Arjuna: *"There is no greater good for a warrior than to fight in a righteous war."*

With serene fingers the Queen Mother folded a bloodied shred of her son's battle vest. The blood of her son did not sadden her. She said, "A mother's duty is to place the needs of her son above her fears. A wife's duty is to walk through fire to please her husband. A king's duty is to sacrifice himself for his subjects."

When Bhagmati finished translating, she added: "You see why I prayed for a motherless husband?"

"I am neither wife nor queen," Hannah retorted. A bibi had the right, the duty, to live for love. Gabriel's black bibi had seized happiness for Gabriel and for herself; a bibi had the power to laugh in the face of a *firangi* wife.

She slept beside him on the terrace floor, changing the bandages, applying the cooling ointments, administering the barks and herbs. Five days later, the Raja awoke, spoke briefly, and fell back asleep. Ten days after the operation he awoke for good and discovered his right arm hung limp and could not be moved. Had he been stronger, he would have found his dagger and killed himself with a single blow of his weak left arm.

His grief set the palace to weeping. The helplessness of

the King turned the whole palace barren. The old Queen called for the expulsion of the witch who had done the only thing worse than murdering him. She had dishonored him, made him unable to function, the way old Hasan Beg had taken a broom, and then a shoe, to her husband when he had refused to leave his palace. The old Shia King had been properly beheaded. Her husband had been laughed at and forced, ignominiously, to take his own life.

So now Hannah knew. The war of the broom. The war of the shoe.

She had him where she wanted him, on a bed, unable to move, ready at last to listen. She confessed her love for him, her wish to marry him in the eyes of whatever gods he proposed. The condition of his arm in no way disqualified him. It might even make him listen.

"What good am I to my people—a king who cannot raise his arm in battle? When a tiger grows old, the younger ones must drive him out," he said. "I must die."

"Leave this," she said. "Come home with me."

"Leave?" It was an obscene idea, to alter one's fate, to abandon one's duty. The Gita said the Spirit is not an old garment, changed at will. Only when life is over does the duty, the garment, change. All he said was, "Land of Higginbottham."

"England is not my home. My home is America."

"America, England. Fort St. George, Pondicherry." He sighed. "Same."

"My father was your age when he left England and came to America. He was a clerk, and he became a farmer. My stepfather was a farmer in the woods, and he became a carpenter in the city. My husband was a factor, and he became a pirate.

I was once a respectable married English lady and look at me now—a bibi in a sari. We can all change."

And she thought, *My mother, my mother.* I must see my mother.

"What change do you propose for a one-armed king?"

"He is going to become a one-armed father."

He stared out at the high blue sky, with just its normal allotment of circling buzzards. "My mother had a premonition. She said you cast a spell—"

"I am with child for the usual reasons."

The Raja slowly sat up at the side of the bed. Then he stood, plucked the sleeve of his right arm, lifted the dead weight inside and let it flop. She reached for him, but he sidestepped her.

"A very long time ago it now seems, when I was still a young man, you asked me how you would know when you were no longer welcome. I said when you were no longer fed the sweetest grass—"

"I remember," she said.

He gathered himself up into the semblance of a raja, striking a pose with his left arm out. "The women's rooms are attached to my mother's palace. You . . . and your child will always have a place. As I promised. You will not need a personal servant, but she is a loyal worker, and there is a place for her as well."

She did not see him again until the night of the fearful final panel in the Salem Bibi series.

I HAD NO elephant for the climb to Devgad fort; I made do with a pair of Easy Spirit walking shoes.

What remains of the palace complex sits on a two-hundred-foot-high hillock. *Deccani Hill Fort, Devgad,* says the guide-book. Vandals and colonials have gouged the jewels from mosaic work; Victorian Englishmen whitewashed the murals, then plastered them over. Squatters have taken over this fort, and Aurangzeb's forts as well.

The hillock's sides are revetted with stones and bricks so that the fort appears massive, impregnable. In Hannah's days the palace buildings were plastered a spectacular white and decorated with tiles the color of emeralds, sapphires and topaz. On the walls of Jadav Singh's palace, tile lions prowled chartreuse forests, peacocks danced in amethyst rain, crocodiles bobbed in lapis lakes. Secret passages connected Hannah's palace to the Queen Mother's, to the Vishnu Temple, to a subterranean hideout lined with treasure chests. Even the courtyard where palace servants slept was longer and wider than the houses of Salem aristocrats.

The local equivalents of Mr. Abraham gather around me, offering their expert services. In their retelling, the great Raja Jadav Singh of Devgad was Peter the Great of India, the most advanced, most sensitive, most intelligent leader of his time. The Gandhi-Nehru-Reagan (they've spotted me for an American) of the seventeenth century.

"Please," I say. Some concepts don't translate.

"And one more informations, madam," one man confides. "His rani was an American woman! A Salem witch—true! She had magical powers, killed whole armies, operated on everyone, transplanted body parts before Christiaan Barnard. True, true!"

"What happened to this Salem witch?" I ask.

"She went over to the Great Mughal," one answers. A second, more scholarly: "The Great Mughal installed her in his harem. She was called Farah the Fair and is buried in Aurangabad." Another shouts, "Rubbish! She was a spy! Mata Hari before Mata Hari. She killed the Hindu god!"

"Then all the books are wrong?" I ask. Most books take a racy interest in a white divorcée, more rumor than fact, who consorted with a Hindu noble. They call her an adventuress of obscure origins, a pirate's wife who comes off less well than the socially prominent Sarah Bradley, widow of the hanged pirate William Kidd. *Tales from the Coromandel*, it's called, and I've done some borrowing from it here. Higginbottham's Guy Fawkes debacle, for example. The impaling of Two-Headed Ravanna, the Denosing of Thomas Tringham. A book of casual cruelties.

"She was after the diamond only." This gets my interest.

"What diamond?"

"Most perfect diamond ever."

"Bigger than Koh-i-Noor."

Casually, I ask: "And what do you think happened to this so-called perfect diamond?"

A loud chorus breaks out—England, America, Japan, Paris. This is a convention that Bugs Kilken has not yet polled.

"I think," says the articulate young man I've already picked as a guide, "that the Salem Bibi came to Devgad to steal the Emperor's Tear. The war was fought over a diamond and the demands of an American lady."

10

VENN SAYS, I know what you want me to do: time-travel. Not just to October 29, 1989, but back three hundred years. He and Jay Basu and all the other strategists at MIT are looking for an information formula, an Einsteinian theory that will organize facts, the billions of facts that swarm around us like microbes, like pond scum, into some sort of pattern. He wants facts to grow like a crystal garden, he wants to create a supersaturated medium, a data plasma, in which just a sprinkling of data cues on top will precipitate a forest down below.

Yes, I say, that'll do.

What's in it for me? he asks.

How about the most perfect diamond in the world?

THE NIGHT that Hannah was consigned to the zenana, the women's rooms, as a wife but no more than a wife, she had a vision. The life inside her compelled it; she would offer her life, if necessary, to end the war. Only a person outside the pale of the two civilizations could do it. Only a woman, a pregnant woman, a pregnant white woman, had the confidence or audacity to try it.

She remembered Tringham's nose, and the Raja's reaction to the poor boy's astonishment. Even the little people think they are gods. Only a person who thought she was God Almighty could have struck out through the jungles of India at night, heading back into Roopconda and the battle tent of the Great Mughal.

That night Hannah dressed herself with care in the dusty regal garments abandoned by the Deccani child-widow when she had been driven out of her prison-palace by the old Queen. Bhagmati tried to dissuade her with stories balladeers told all over Hindustan of the Emperor as father-killer, brother-killer, son-disinheritor, brutal converter of infidels and dedicated desecrator of temples and churches. And when she failed to dissuade, Bhagmati, reluctant guide and stout protector of the foolhardy foreigner, heaved aside the decorative panel in a wall that hid the opening to the secret passage out of the fortified hillock.

For a day and a night the two missionaries followed the debris of war lust through banana groves filled with frightened monkeys and ruined temples crawling with rats, over streams white with the bellies of floating fish and across villages of looted granaries and torched huts, until, on the morning of the second day, they came to the northern periphery of Jadav Singh's kingdom, and there found Emperor Aurangzeb's slaves leveling the lush and swampy plain into the foundations of a new fort, mosque and palace. And out as far as the eye could see, the forest was burning faster than woodsmen could cut or elephants could haul. With typical efficiency, the Emperor was building another city, perhaps to celebrate his victory over Devgad. Thousands of men and women carrying bowls of excavated mud trailed into the infinity of forest and grasses, miles away. All of the Coromandel factories, Devgad and Panpur palaces and their outlying fields and villages could be dropped inside this clearing. Only the elephants were of the

proper scale; men looked too puny, their efforts almost laugh-
able. Only the elephants looked capable of building the vision.
For years afterward Hannah mesmerized children with her
stories of the Emperor's field guns, swivel guns, brass guns in
gaudy horse-drawn carriages; of siege trains and carts loaded
with cannonballs weighing up to one hundred and twelve
pounds and with gunpowder packed to stay dry in dewy or
monsoon weather; of matchlocks together with their forked
rest-pieces of heavy wood carried on the backs of anxious men
with singed eyelashes and beards; of spears to hurl with great
precision from afar, and of maces and sabers for fighting the
enemy hand to hand when victory was near. In Hannah's
stories, the Imperial Army was made up of the curious or the
conquered from all four corners of the universe and from Hindustan's every kingdom and *suba*: Sunnis and Shias, Hindu
Rajputs and Christians, Jews and Armenians, Turks, Moors,
Afghans and Uzbeks, Chinese, Burmese, fuse and form for the
pious Aurangzeb, what he described to Hannah as "the bat-
tering ram of Allah."

HANNAH CAME to negotiate and was instead taken
hostage by the Emperor. His spies had alerted him the moment
she and Bhagmati had entered the secret passage in the child-
queen's palace in Devgad.

She flounced into the war camp with Bhagmati, demanding
and expecting to get an audience with the Emperor at once
so that she could free the two warrior-kings from their self-
destructive obsession. Instead, the camp commander seized
and bound her and hauled her off to the huge tent that housed
the haram. There a Tatar slave woman with thick, tattooed
arms stripped and scrutinized her for concealed weapons, then

handed her over to two Kashmiri slave women who scrubbed and depilated her, hennaed her hair and palms, rubbed rose oil between her breasts and reddened her lips with carmine. The Kashmiri slaves handed her over to three Rajput women who fastened a tight *angya* as a bodice around her breasts, slipped a *pishwaz* over her head that hung like a knee-length dress of the sheerest muslin, squeezed her legs into brocaded *izar* trousers that fitted as snugly as stockings, stuck jewels in her ears and nose, hung more jewels around her neck, ankles, wrists and hair parting, pushed rings up her fingers and toes, then discharged her to eunuchs who escorted her to the Great Mughal.

She had expected grandeur and a display of opulence. The very old man before her, still sharp featured and commanding, fairer than most Indians she had seen, with a long white beard, sat on a gilt throne in need of paint. She noted his fingers, the knuckles grotesquely large, the fingers splayed, unable to flex. The garish rings would have to be cut from his fingers.

She'd known, of course, that he was more than eighty, that he was older than America, older than the Massachusetts Bay Colony, more experienced in conquering and acquiring than anyone but the kings of Spain, France and England. All the same, from the gossip of terrorized villagers in Panpur and Devgad she'd imagined not the frail ascetic before her, but a warrior as virile as Morad Farah, a nobleman as debauched as the Nawab, a demon uglier and wilier than Ravanna. His face was lean and hard. Dignity and self-discipline and probably creeping joint disease had stiffened his spine. His *qaba* was cut from a coarse, cheap cloth she could not imagine Jadav Singh wearing. His only jewelry, apart from the rings, was a spinel-ruby pendant; an emerald secured an aigrette to his turban. He was as somber in manner as any Puritan of the same great age.

In this tent of informal audiences, he had allowed himself just one stark symbol of power. A mobile fit for an emperor who had seized all other empires contained in the universe, a globe of gold cupped in the cradle of a perfect golden replica of Aurangzeb's hands, was suspended from the roof of the tent and came to rest just over the throne. Each ridge of fingernail, each wrinkle around an aged man's knuckles, were etched with accuracy by the master goldsmith in the imperial atelier. On the sides of the gold sphere, a lion nuzzled a lamb. Embedded on the top of his gold universe, like the polestar, was a single diamond, the largest, most beautiful she had ever seen or imagined.

So he was more than a conqueror and acquisitor. He had instructed his master goldsmith to merge the metaphoric with the literal. She had come to speak logically, reasonably—politically—to a race of omniscient dreamers. How much easier it would be if she could have dehumanized him as the old Queen did, as the Raja did. To them, he was Ravanna, the demon-king of Lanka, in Muslim disguise.

He registered her presence with a kind of detached alarm, then turned to his attendant for an explanation. They spoke in Persian, obviously about the conditions of her apprehension, perhaps about her connection to the Raja, maybe even her killing of Morad Farah. The Emperor stared at her more closely with each new disclosure, then swiveled his whole body to address short questions to the attendant.

When he spoke, his voice was raspy. She felt the eunuchs reach for her again.

"His Imperial Highness will not order your execution," the translator announced.

The Emperor spoke again.

"You will be given instructions. You will find it most convenient to be obedient."

She began by loosening the cinch of her trousers and *angya*, then by tearing off her jewels, one set for every word she spoke, and flinging them at the Emperor's feet.

"You despot! You tyrant!" she screamed. "You may have made me your prisoner, but I am not your plaything!" The look, first of rage, then of confusion, as the veiled translator conveyed her words, seemed to inflate, then compress, His Imperial Majesty. He raised a gnarled hand and recited a few words with the rhythm of verse.

Hannah's head was whacked into a low bow and her arms jerked into the Mughal court's ritual obeisance. She staggered and would have fallen on the carpet if a veiled attendant had not glided out of line and steadied her. When she regained her balance, she stared—with all the insolence she could summon—at the man who had discarded the only rules of fair play she knew and had guiltlessly imprisoned her.

"I am with child."

The translator did not bother to render her words. Instead, he said, "His Imperial Highness says we are neither prisoners nor playthings. We are all servants of Allah, fulfilling His commands."

She heard footfalls behind her, turned, and saw Bhagmati being led by two attendants, pushed to the edge of the throne, then roughly bent, as Hannah had been, in the ritual courtesy.

"It will not go so easily for the idolater," said the translator. "The troops will do with her as they wish."

"We are here on a mission, then we shall leave. If you detain us, or dishonor us, we shall die."

The Emperor spoke. Bhagmati translated. "His Imperial Majesty says we all must die. Allah is merciful."

He gestured for Bhagmati to come closer and spoke to her in a low voice, then gestured her back. She said to Hannah, translating: "His Majesty has heard that I hear and speak for you. So His Majesty will not cut out my tongue or cut off your ears."

The Emperor and the translator chuckled.

"His Majesty has heard you corrected the rough manners of Commander Morad Farah."

"Morad Farah . . . very . . . expensive . . . man," said the Emperor, in clear English.

"And who hears for you in Devgad Palace?" asked Hannah. "Why must you destroy the Raja?"

The Emperor answered only obliquely, and then again through his translator. Statements to him were always posed as questions, for a statement in his presence implied arrogance. Earnest questions were never asked, for they implied uncertainty.

"A skillful ruler trusts no friend, no family member. Trust only the hunting tiger or the vengeful enemy. The survivor is he who distrusts his own shadow. He destroys himself who does not submit."

She hated the Emperor for his self-righteous terrors that forced him to see her not as a person on a mission but as a pawn in his endless game of *shatranj*. To him, she was just another case of brandy, or a cannon, that an ambitious factor like Cephus Prynne might barter for a land grant or new concession. Her only value to him was her bibi power to lure the Raja, as Ravanna had lured Sita, outside the white circle of his hill-fort's safety.

"Look around you!" Hannah shouted. "There is no golden world. It's a dream, all a dream!"

The Emperor nodded his head at the eunuch to indicate the audience was over. The eunuch escorted Hannah and Bhag-mati into a tent of their own, luxurious with silk canopies, hangings and floor spreads, in the haram section of the war camp. Then he settled down to sleep outside.

ALL THE NEXT DAY, defying the rules of modesty that decreed the veil and head covering, Hannah roamed the tent city of the haram, accepting an old woman's offer of a tour of the grounds. There would be a city, and a fort, and several mosques, and perhaps even a burial vault, but before all of that, there would be a glorious battle. The Mughal's vast army was prepared for the kill.

All day, contingents of spear throwers and lance bearers marched across the battlefield. Cavalrymen with their shields out, lances low, pounding forward on armored horses, staged mock assaults. Engineers directed the digging of trenches and burying of mines all around the revetted hill. Horses in teams of two and three pulled gun carriages into place behind newly erected battlements. Slaves packed powder horns and counted primers. Metal grinders sharpened the blades of swords, scimitars and saddle axes. Servants polished the steel of arm guards, breastplates and helmets. Smithies hammered smooth the skirmish-dented shields.

Oh, the murderers' vanity!

Hannah, knowing the condition of the Raja's armaments, wanted to call off his mission of suicide, wanted only a chance to speak. The trajectories of hate and love would intersect on this field. And she, the would-be peacemaker, had made herself Aurangzeb's bait, had allowed herself to be staked like a goat to lure the tiger from his lair.

That night the Emperor sent again for Hannah and her servant. He sat, as he had the night before, under the gold mobile of the world grasped tight in his rigid gold hands, but this time he sat on a cushion no bigger than the one assigned to Hannah herself. As he spoke, he forced his fingers to grasp a needle and to embroider a simple prayer cap. The tent was empty of his vast retinue of slaves and servants. The attendants were slumped half-asleep, guarding the entrance to the tent.

For minutes the Emperor did not look at or address his guest. He sewed. Bhagmati fanned her mistress, more against flies than the evening's trapped heat. Only when the needle fell out of his misshapen fingers did he break his silence.

"Your night was comfortable?"

She merely nodded. Bhagmati made the proper affirmations. The interpreter rendered all speech in the flattest of monotones.

"You are wrong to think that you have been wronged. As woman serves man, man serves the will of God. You have placed yourself where no woman has a right to be. I have decided to be merciful and return you to your people."

"Even the Great Mughal cannot do that."

"The *angrezi* are your people. Do not think I am unaware of the name of Captain Legge. You are the prostitute of infidels and idolaters, and you reject the offer of my protection."

All of this was said without rancor, not as a taunt, but as a kind of incontrovertible preamble. The tone of voice hinted at a fondness for paradox, that this lowest of outcasts should even be sitting before him, polluting his tent on the eve of battle.

This was the moment, if she was ever to have one, when the gods that controlled the universe had conspired to put her Christian-Hindu-Muslim self, her American-English-Indian self, her orphaned, abandoned, widowed, pregnant self, her *firangi* and bibi self, into a single message, delivered to the most powerful man those separate worlds had ever known. She stood.

"It is you, Great Mughal, Your Majesty, if you forgive a mere woman's speech, a prostitute's speech, who calls the condition of servitude protection. It is you, Noble Badshah, who confuses a cruel and vindictive nature with a generous spirit. I speak as one who has lost everything, who owns nothing, and who desires nothing for herself.

"I have come late in my life to the feeling of love. Love for a man, love for a place, love for a people. They are not Devgad people or Roopconda people, not Hindu people or Muslim people, not Sunni or Shia, priests or untouchables, servants or kings. If all is equal in the eye of Brahma as the Hindus say, if Allah is all-seeing and all-merciful as you say, then who has committed atrocities on the children, the women, the old people? Who has poisoned the hearts of men?"

"The blame belongs with the rat of Devgad" came the response.

"The blame lies with anyone who confuses protection with power."

"No idolater can thwart the Lashkar-i-Islam."

"I agree. Your army is most formidable. Your enemy is weak." She waited for his satisfied agreement. Then she cried out, from her heart, "Oh, Great Emperor, build your city, build your mosques and your palace, but stop this war before it destroys the world! You speak of mercy, but where is the quality of your mercy?"

"Mercy before Allah, not mercy before men. Allah judges men, and the Emperor is but a man who must also be judged. The duty of the Emperor is to bring the infidel before the throne of judgment. There is no escaping the judgment of Allah."

"Duty! Duty, judgment! I have heard enough of duty. And of judgment. You cloak your lust for vengeance and for gold and diamonds in the noble words of duty and judgment and protection and sacrifice. But it is the weakest and the poorest and the most innocent who suffer, who sacrifice, whose every minute of every day is obedience to duty—"

The Emperor slapped the floor. He stood. He reached slowly above him and lifted the diamond off the top of the world. He held it in front of him, the pale candlelight reflecting off a thousand facets as he spoke.

"I do not fight for treasure and glory in this life. This diamond is the tear I shed as I discharge my duty. That is why it is called the Emperor's Tear. The dutiful and the innocent, if they are pure and if they submit, will be judged by the all-seeing, all-merciful Allah. The sum of their lives will be weighed in the scales of judgment."

He restored the diamond to the crown of the world, the seat of the universe.

11

H O W   C O M F O R T I N G a world that can be divided into halves. The Dar-ul-harb and Dar-ul-islam. Infidels and believers. She had come from softer versions of the Emperor's world, of her lover's world, of the factors' world, that retained many of the attitudes of light and dark, fallen and saved, caste and outcaste, but failed to act on them quite so decisively. And so life had robbed her of easy consolations.

The only certainty had been her vision—a very clear vision, stronger than a wish or a dream—of peace. She'd trusted in her *firangi* status, and while it had gained her a hearing and allowed her to keep her ears, tongue and head ("How I was trembling!" Bhagmati told her in their tent that last night. "No man, no matter how powerful, may speak to the Grand Badshah like that!"), her message had failed.

The Emperor had sent attendants with chests of jewels. "For the Tigress who bested my General" came the message. She returned them, without regret. "For your white skin, for the luster of your spirit, for the one-in-a-lakh, I give you these pearls. I call you Precious-as-Pearl."

She sent them back, too, with her gratitude. To accept would be to acknowledge his attempt to influence her.

This time, the return of the necklace of pearls was rejected, and they were re-presented with the indication that returned gifts were received as serious insults. Dutifully, she wore the necklace, acknowledging even to herself that no queen of England had ever seen its equal.

When the necklace had been satisfactorily adjusted, the attendant read the Emperor's proclamation. *"When the battle horns are sounded, His Imperial Majesty wishes you to view with him the destruction of the rat-worshiping idolater."* The invitation was forcefully delivered, her head was covered, her face veiled, and she was escorted by guards in polished armor to view the train of elephants dragging travois of cut stone and platform logs, and a hundred of the finest stonemasons of Agra and Aurangabad, who were to lay the foundations of a new city with walls and parapets around the Emperor's battle tent.

In one rainy season, Hannah Legge had gone from woolen-clad English married woman on the Coromandel Coast to pregnant sari-wearing bibi of a raja; a murderer, a widow, a peacemaker turned prisoner of the most powerful man in India. Her only friend was her former servant, perhaps the only friend she'd ever had apart from the innocent days with Hester Manning, and the language they communicated in was more Bhagmati's than hers.

She wasn't Hannah anymore; she was Mukta, Bhagmati's word for "pearl." And she gave Bhagmati a new name: Hester, after the friend she had lost. The friend who had indirectly brought her to the Coromandel Coast.

The Emperor watched from his palanquin.

"The pearls are indeed most rare and perfect. I wear them out of respect," she said.

"*Angrezi* eat the flesh of the shellfish, that is what I hear."

"Yes, we do."

"It is unclean. You may wear the pearls, but I ask you never to eat unclean food again."

Against all of her instincts, she bowed her head. The

Emperor was a builder of cities, a designer of human lives, a converter to Islam of everything in his path.

"Your Majesty, it is not too late. I beg you to reconsider—"

"The rat and his mice have already left their burrow."

"Let me meet with him. Let me carry a message. I will tell him of your strength—"

He raised his hand and immediately her arm was seized by one of the attendants.

"Word has been sent," he said. Then he smiled. "Word of my serious illness. Word of the panic of my troops. Word of our helplessness." He raised his frail arm, opened his trembling hand as far as his fingers could unfurl, and took in the vista of elephants, the thousands of laborers, the soldiers still busy polishing and sharpening their steel. "Look, Precious-as-Pearl, do you see the panic?"

He was still laughing as she was led away.

T H E Y   W E R E   S T I L L the Emperor's guests, or his special hostages; the officers who passed their tent on the way to the tents of the haram women were told not only to stay away, but to keep their voices down and their language respectable. But they knew their survival was provisional. They knew that even the exaggerated respect was a possible future bargaining point, raising their desirableness. After the coming battle, which could only end in total defeat for the Raja, the Emperor would be generous with his rewards, harsh with his judgments. In the lust of executions that would follow, who would speak for two women from the Raja's own fort, for the prostitute carrying his child, and her faithful servant?

She knew precisely the route the Raja would take; he would

leave at night, march through the day, and be ready to strike in the final quarter of the night. He was out there now in the moonless night, camped in the forest beyond the ring of the Emperor's clearing.

She left the sweltering tent, just to fix the bright stars in her head. She had failed in her mission; this was the final night of the life she had known. She prayed for the first time in years, for the strength of survival.

The night was crammed with noises, the snuffling of horses, the lowing of cattle, the distant trumpeting of elephants, coughs, songs, drums and laughter from the haram tents. Every creature in the world was taking its pleasure tonight.

Thou, silent form, dost tease us out of thought
As doth eternity: Cold Pastoral!

JOHN KEATS
"Ode on a Grecian Urn"

PART FOUR

IT HAS TAKEN ME a year and a half to assemble these notes, to make my travels, take my pictures, attend the auctions. Yes, I bought *The Apocalypse*, or *The Unravish'd Bride*, that terrible tableau of Jadav Singh's suicidal attack on the fort of Aurangzeb, at a small auction of "colonial memorabilia" in Bangkok. With its steep forty-thousand-dollar estimated price, it practically shouted Bugs's name. Venn bought it for me at half the price, an act of South Indian patriotism, he said, and Bugs never guessed a thing.

I've always seen it as a painting about a woman misplaced in time. The man who'd titled it for the museum appreciated its carnage.

Historians take note: the Devgad battle was Aurangzeb's last great victory. The flea on the Coromandel Coast, the English concession, proved to be carrying a kind of plague. He died of a thousand small wounds, an emptied treasury from fighting Sikhs on the northwest, Marathas on the east, the freebooters and sharp traders of the various European chartered companies on the southern coasts, and his own infirmities. He died at eighty-nine, seven years after finding and losing the Pearl-of-His-Crown, having alienated all competent heirs. He carried the soul of the Mughal Empire with him to his grave; what lingered was the vacuum that invited the British in.

One year in the life of Venn Iyer and his colleague Jay Basu and X-2989—given their hours, their brilliance, their funding, the speed of computers—is of course vastly more impressive than a single book. Three months ago, as a paid subject, I put on the designer headgear and the electronic gloves and walked in virtual reality for ten seconds on a Boston street, sat in a classroom at UCLA, and spent ten seconds with a Century 21 agent in Kansas City. I don't mean I watched them—I was with them; they responded to me. Those crowds on the Boston street parted to let me pass. I reached out and touched a faucet, touched the sleeve of a student beside me, and felt them both. When I walked up the stairs, I got winded. Venn says I talked and the various monitoring devices showed I was physically reacting to virtual space, not to the lab.

And frankly, I was disappointed; X-2989 is one of the discoveries more exciting in principle than in application. Of course I couldn't say it, and I had long ago understood the baseline importance of pure tedium. The theory worked. The technology is as cumbersome as those room-sized mainframe card-sorting computers of forty years ago, but Americans are nearly as good as Japanese at applied technology; they'll miniaturize it, pump up its power, and twenty years from now little girls in Burma will be working on assembly lines turning out time-space laser disks. Venn and Jay will pocket their awards, MIT will prosper on the patent and maybe buy out Harvard, and the rest belongs to the heirs of the Coromandel factors, the franchisers and marketers jockeying for market share.

They had assembled a past with its own integrity. From raw, programmed data, they had created images; the images had their own brief identity. (The individual programs began fading as the data were used up. It's an eerie feeling, watching faces and buildings slowly dissolve, lose their color and texture, lose their edges and dimension, and revert to gray.) It's a primitive technology with infinite applications. It solves man's

oldest or second-oldest preoccupation, to master time, which
seems even harder than mastering space.

But this wasn't another 3-D movie house, and we weren't
kids with our special glasses, jumping back whenever fists and
spears burst from the screen. I retrieved thirty seconds from
lives I've never lived—but which now I have. But why did I
intercept a lady in her yellow jacket demonstrating faucets in
a Kansas City bathroom?

W H E N I L O O K at all my notes, the five hundred books
consulted, the endless paintings, engravings, trade records,
journals, the travel and the documentary picture taking, and
stack them up in my study, they look impressive. And from
them I have reconstructed a life through three continents and
thirty years. And when I look at the raw data Venn's program
has ingested to create ten seconds from just three years ago,
with no character, no narrative, I think, who am I fooling?

He talks about the bare sets of old movies, the generic
"New York Street" and "Frontier Main Street," even old television series, the telltale sparsity of convincing clutter (even
"Hill Street Blues," his touchstone of sufficient data, will look
austere and artificial in a decade, he says), and he sees it as a
kind of informational senility, a loss of image diversity. I talk
about asset hunting, the fact that data are not neutral. There
are assets and debits. There are hot leads and dead ends. To
treat all information as data and to process it in the same way
is to guarantee an endless parade of faucets in Kansas City.

He's still looking for his crystal garden. The data plasma
that will generate a fully interactive world. He guesses that
the rules that govern information are subject to formulas;
anything that has ever happened can be reproduced without

all the tedious inputting of raw statistics. The process is merely the next step beyond the most powerful computer ever imagined, for now we are talking about the recapturing of past reality, not just the retrieval of information. Everything that has ever happened is still out there, somewhere, like light from distant stars.

I have seen it. I have seen the crystal, the biggest, most perfect crystal in the world. I have held it.

L A S T W E E K , on a Sunday night when even Jay Basu might be home (he's a fan of "Murder, She Wrote"), we went down to the lab, through the elaborate security. Imagine if the program fell into commercial hands before MIT patents it! I have a "subject's clearance." The first thing I saw was *The Unravish'd Bride* hanging on the wall above Venn's desk, not that he has ever learned to sit at one.

"I think what I have may interest you, Beigh. This is my present to you."

He has absorbed my manuscript and all the documents, the travelogues and computerized East India records, the lavishly illustrated *namas*, or chronicles, of the emperors of the Mughal dynasty. He is a thorough researcher; all this is to be expected, even on his own time. Literary prose, as he calls my book, poses certain hierarchical problems for a computer, or for his program, but he thinks, just thinks, he may have found a way of rendering even my words into images. And the diamond is the clue: the fact that it is the biggest and most perfect crystal in the world may just be an accident, a kind of informational pun, but it gave him an idea.

"Would you like to find the Emperor's Tear?" he asked.

It's necessary that I undergo the search; the program is

interactive, and when Venn tried it, all he got was a postcard view of modern Madras. The program will give you what you most care about; your mind is searching through the program though you don't realize it—it is interacting with my thousand-answer questionnaire—until it finds a place it wants to jump in.

While he did his adjusting, I took down Hannah's— Pearl's—picture from the wall. The blond woman in a sari, the garish Mughal jewels, the diamond fused into the cupped hands of a proud potentate, the destruction, the fiery sky, the wounded, dying Jadav Singh. Venn slipped the helmet, the goggles, the special gloves on me.

"HANNAH!" I scream against the cannons and flying bullets. I can barely breathe from the sulfur clouds, my eyes burn, and I reach out to hold her, my hand closes on her shoulder and she turns, my hand is brown, with a tinkling gold bangle. She is a beautiful woman, more Pre-Raphaelite than I had imagined, with crinkly golden hair. I try to pull her my way, but she shakes her head, "No, no, Hester—don't you see?" and now I do, though clouds of smoke are rolling in and the light is still faint, and a fine, misty rain is falling. What I see is the old man standing with his back to the battle, facing the inner courtyard where the small figure of the bent warrior is slumped, his face bloody, and the old man is holding the diamond aloft, turning its facets to capture the light of a hundred fires.

He turns—I know that face from a hundred portraits of Aurangzeb, or 'Alamgir, the World-Holder'—a look of demented satisfaction on his face. Victory is his, vengeance and retribution and an open road to unlimited plunder and mass conversion, and suddenly his mouth opens wide, he tries to scream but the battle sounds are too loud, his attendants are all focused on the wave of Devgad warriors shooting at the fort from kneeling positions in the plowed-up field.

Now we are running along the parapet; I squeeze past the rows of sharpshooters, bumping them, they curse me as I pass, and suddenly I feel her warm hand and hear her command, "Hester, take it," and a heavy warm glasslike object is in my hand, and we are flying down the deep stone stairs set so far apart that descent is a kind of leaping into a darkened void, each landing jars my knees and my ankles, but I am fast and strong, I have never run like this, breathless now, pulling Hannah behind me, and we are out into the field in the middle of a firefight, fair game for either side.

I scream with agony from the hot white flaming explosion in my shoulder that has spun me around and dropped me to the cool, wet soil. Hannah is on her knees, crying, Hester, Hester, Bhagmati, pray, pray, we must get back. . . . I try to hold the diamond out, but it is slippery with my blood.

"Mukta!" I scream, the pain blacking me out, and now a second bullet fired down on me from the parapet rakes my leg, puncturing the fleshy portion of my calf, and I think almost with satisfaction, Well, that settles it, no more running for me.

"Go, I command you," but I can't raise my head, and my voice is like a metal file rasping through my shoulder, astonishing pain, my words are pain, my breathing is pain, but I am like a dreamer aware of her dream even as she can't escape it. I feel in the folds of my sari for the knife I know I have, and it is there for me.

Hannah, my Pearl, is no longer visible. Light is spreading but it is not the light of dawn; it is the light of extinguishment. . . . I plunge the knife deep in my belly, watch with satisfaction, and now with the mastery of my pain, the blood bubble from my beautiful brown flesh. More, I think, and plunge the knife deeper, plunge it as Hannah had into the back of Morad Farah, and make a burrow inside me. I feel the organs, feel the flesh, the bowels of history, and with my dying breath I plunge the diamond into the deepest part of me.

V E N N   S A Y S   he was about to pull me out of it, the screaming, running, writhing, my tears, my adrenaline and heart rate and endorphins all indicated a near-death experience; even the plunge in my blood pressure and pulse was consistent with mortal trauma. He understood me—apparently I was shouting partially in his language, which, of course, I don't know.

My shoulder still throbbed, and it continues to ache at night, and sometimes I feel in my gut that I really am incubating an enormous diamond.

"I know where the diamond is," I said, for suddenly the name Hester Hedges in the graveyard of Fort St. Sebastian makes perfectly good sense. She was given a Christian burial, maybe out of respect to the wishes of Henry Hedges, in which case only Hannah would have known, or could have arranged it. Or Hannah had named her a Christian, to be buried and not cremated, in order to preserve her body as a carrying case. The litter bearers would have gathered the dead Hindus off the field the next day and burned them in a mass funeral pyre. Jadav Singh was borne back to Devgad for the proper public grieving and ceremony, and the new Mughal administrator moved into the palace, cleansed it of what he called idolatry, and ruled it in the name of the Great Badshah for about thirty years, when it fell into British hands.

If Hannah had carried the gem back to the coast, and then

to America, it would have turned up by now. It's not here; it's in India. I think the world's most perfect diamond lies in the remains of Bhagmati, "Hester Hedges," just under the feet of Mr. Abraham, under the hooves of goats and cows.

AS THE FOCUS NARROWS, the facts grow surer. We have the shipping and housing records, we have the letters and journals and the *Memoirs*, and of course we have *The Scarlet Letter*. Who can blame Nathaniel Hawthorne for shying away from the real story of the brave Salem mother and her illegitimate daughter? But they lived in Salem until 1720, when Rebecca Easton died: Rebecca and her five half-Nipmuc children; her daughter Hannah Easton, now called Pearl, and the proof of *her* "Indian" lover, the quick, black-haired and black-eyed girl called Pearl Singh. Hannah/Pearl stayed on in Salem until her death in 1750 at the age of eighty. Pearl Singh, born in 1701 somewhere in the South Atlantic on the long voyage home, saw in her old age the birth of this country, an event she had spent a lifetime advocating, and suffering for.

Hannah/Pearl returned to Salem with the infant and immediately began the search for her mother. She found her in a workhouse for the mad and indigent in Providence Plantations, speaking some tribal gibberish and insisting on wearing her outmoded woolens with the shameful *I* boldly sewn in red to her sleeve. It meant "Indian lover," though there was no sign, apart from the progeny, of the Indian's existence. She claimed he'd been killed raiding chicken coops to feed his children. And her daughter had a badge as well, her black-eyed, black-haired, lively daughter, named Pearl Singh. The town gossips named them White Pearl and Black Pearl.

Salem children were warned about the small house jammed with brass and copper items, called by many the House of Enchantment, meaning the place of ultimate debauchery. They were warned of ingesting the attitudes of such a house, along with the strong food and drink, where all the inhabitants, particularly the younger generation, carried the double taint of voluptuaries' blood, where seditious sentiments were openly aired. "We are Americans to freedom born!" White Pearl and Black Pearl were heard to mutter, the latter even in school.

Respectable people expressing such attitudes would have gone immediately to jail. But the women had for so long indulged a liberty of eccentric dissent that their certification of certain extreme positions was considered advantageous to the maintenance of social order.

White Pearl eked out a living as a nurse, veterinarian, even, on rare occasion, doctor. Responsible citizens avoided her services, but she did enjoy a clientele of divers men and women who came from curiosity and stayed for the wealth of her storytelling, the pungency of her opinions. A more refined age in a more sophisticated city might have called it a salon.

JOSEPH HATHORNE, a boy of ten, "My doleful young Joseph," White Pearl called him in her letters, son of the witchcraft judge, John Hathorne, was only nine years old when Pearl returned with her baby and her mother, and he seemed to have found in her company, doing odd jobs, running errands, a corrective to the orthodoxy of his household. He even went to sea, driven from the taint of Salem, drawn by the stories of the China and India trade that White Pearl related as she sewed. His great-grandson, Nathaniel Hawthorne, was born in Salem in 1804.

And so all of this had happened a century before the writer's birth, a century and a half before he wrote his morbid introspection into guilt and repression that many call our greatest work. Preach! Write! Act! He wrote against the fading of the light, the dying of the old program, the distant memory of a shameful, heroic time. Time, O Time! Time to tincture the lurid colors, time for the local understudies to learn their foreign lines, time only to touch and briefly bring alive the first letter of an alphabet of hope and of horror stretching out, and back to the uttermost shores.

A Note on the Type

The text of this book is set in a digitized version of Garamond No. 3. It is not a true copy of any of the designs of Claude Garamond (1480–1561), but an adaptation of his types, which set the European standard for two centuries. It probably owes as much to the designs of Jean Jannon, a Protestant printer working in Sedan in the early seventeenth century, who had worked with Garamond's romans earlier, in Paris, and who was denied their use because of the Catholic censorship. Jannon's matrices came into the possession of the Imprimerie Nationale, where they were thought to be by Garamond himself, and so described when the Imprimerie revived the type in 1900. This particular version is based on an adaptation by Morris Fuller Benton.

Composed by PennSet,
Bloomsburg, Pennsylvania
Typography and binding design by
Iris Weinstein